PRAISE FOR THE AUCTION BLOCK MYSTERIES

RECEIVED

MAR   2017

By

Death & the Brewmaster's Widow

"There are fewer auctions in this second series entry, but readers won't mind as the twisty, Hitchcock-style plot unfolds."—*Booklist*

"Lively."—*Publishers Weekly*

Death & the Redheaded Woman

"[A] winning debut."—*Publishers Weekly*

"Fresh and enjoyable ... a well-told story with appealing characters."—*Mystery Scene*

"The witty sarcastic banter between the lead characters was charming and endearing."—*RT Book Reviews*

"Ross's debut features a likable pair of sleuths, some local Missouri history, and a nice little mystery."—*Kirkus Reviews*

NO LONGER PROPERTY OF
SEATTLE PUBLIC LIBRARY

D0192099

DEATH

& the Gravedigger's Angel

ALSO BY LORETTA ROSS

Death & the Redheaded Woman
Death & the Brewmaster's Widow

LORETTA ROSS

DEATH

& the Gravedigger's Angel

An
Auction Block
MYSTERY

MIDNIGHT INK
WOODBURY, MINNESOTA

Death & the Gravedigger's Angel © 2017 by Loretta Ross. All rights reserved. No part of this book may be used or reproduced in any manner whatsoever, including Internet usage, without written permission from Midnight Ink, except in the case of brief quotations embodied in critical articles and reviews.

First Edition
First Printing, 2017

Book design and format by Donna Burch-Brown
Cover design by Lisa Novak
Cover illustration by Tim Zeltner/i2i Art Inc

Midnight Ink, an imprint of Llewellyn Worldwide Ltd.

This is a work of fiction. Names, characters, places, and incidents are either the product of the author's imagination or are used fictitiously, and any resemblance to actual persons living or dead, business establishments, events, or locales is entirely coincidental.

Library of Congress Cataloging-in-Publication Data

Names: Ross, Loretta, author.
Title: Death & the gravedigger's angel / Loretta Ross.
Other titles: Death and the gravedigger's angel
Description: First Edition. | Woodbury, Minnesota : Midnight Ink, [2017] |
  Series: An auction block mystery ; 3
Identifiers: LCCN 2016039127 (print) | LCCN 2016045345 (ebook) | ISBN
  9780738750415 | ISBN 9780738751566
Subjects: LCSH: Auctioneers—Fiction. | Private investigators—Fiction. |
  Murder—Investigation—Fiction. | GSAFD: Mystery fiction.
Classification: LCC PS3618.O8466 D426 2017 (print) | LCC PS3618.O8466
  (ebook) | DDC 813/.6—dc23
LC record available at https://lccn.loc.gov/2016039127

Midnight Ink
Llewellyn Worldwide Ltd.
2143 Wooddale Drive
Woodbury, MN 55125-2989
www.midnightinkbooks.com

Printed in the United States of America

Dedicated to the memory of my nephew,
Christopher VanHoozen,
and his lovely wife, Cindy VanHoozen
CV2 4EVER
Please watch for motorcycles.

ACKNOWLEDGMENTS

No book gets written without the contributions of various people along the way and this book is no exception to that rule. I'd like to thank, as always, my family and friends for their continued support and encouragement in my literary endeavors. Also, I'd like to thank them for never reporting me to the FBI when I randomly say things like "you know, I just figured out the best way to kill someone with a plastic spork…"

I'd like to thank the various experts who have gifted me with their advice. Chief among these is, once again, Deputy Jeramiah Sullivan of the Henry County, Missouri, Sheriff's Department. He's been extremely generous with his time and expertise.

I'd like to thank my editors, Terri Bischoff and Sandy Sullivan (no relation to Jeramiah, as far as I know), for the work they've put in on this book, the design team and cover artist, for making it look so beautiful, and everyone at Midnight Ink.

I'd like to thank Janet Reid, the finest agent a writer could hope for. In addition to what she does for her clients, Janet spends a lot of time dispensing helpful advice for struggling young writers. If anyone reading this is starting out on a writing career, you should definitely look up her blog.

I'd like to thank the 2015 Kansas City Royals, who, while I was writing this, were busy winning our first World Championship in thirty years. You made for a wonderful distraction, fellas!

And, finally, I'd like to thank the readers who have come back to this series. You all mean more to me than you'll ever know.

Loretta Ross

21 November, 2016

ONE

"He was dead, but that wasn't the creepy part."

Ahead of them, an early morning mist blanketed dense woods. It was barely dawn and sunlight slanted through the trees at an acute angle. Golden rays of light fell across late-summer foliage like a glittering illustration in an old children's book, or a photo on a motivational poster.

"I don't want to know the creepy part!"

"I want to know the creepy part," Randy Bogart said.

His brother, Death, paused to help Wren Morgan navigate a slippery patch of fallen leaves. The path they were on led to the haunted Hadleigh House, a nineteenth-century plantation and local legend. Wren had been dying to get inside since she learned that Keystone and Sons, the family-owned auction company she worked for, had contracted to sell the contents. As an auctioneer, part of Wren's job included appraising and cataloguing the items to be sold. They hadn't been able to start work on the Hadleigh House, though, because the place was being treated as a crime scene after hikers found a dead body. An elderly man, who had yet to be identified, had gotten drunk and ridden a stolen horse down this path. In the dark, he'd ridden full tilt into an overhanging branch and been killed.

Earlier that morning, Death had run into Duncan Reynolds, the chief of police in their tiny town of East Bledsoe Ferry, during his coffee-and-donut run. Ever since Death had begun his new career as a private investigator and part-time bounty hunter, the chief had become a close friend and mentor. At Randy's urging, Death shared the latest gossip now.

Apparently, the old man's death was causing even more of a sensation than one would expect because of the legends already surrounding the path. It was known as the Vengeance Trail, and the story was that during the Civil War a soldier (Confederate or Union, the accounts varied) had killed an old man and stolen his horse. That night, as he was riding on the Vengeance Trail, the horse had bolted, taking revenge for his master's death by dashing the murderer against an overhanging limb and killing him.

"Okay, so, you know the dead man was wearing a Civil War cavalry uniform, right?" Death began.

"Like the ghost story."

"Like the ghost story. Right. Well, the state crime lab came back with a report on the uniform. You ready for this?"

His companions stopped and watched him expectantly.

"The uniform was saturated with formaldehyde and traces of … how do I put this delicately? A substance known as 'body liquor.' It's the result of human decomposition. They think the dead guy got the uniform he was wearing off a recently embalmed corpse."

"Oh! Gross!" Wren moaned. "That is so gross!"

"Wow!" Randy said. "That's cool! Where exactly did he get killed, do you know?"

"Somewhere right along here, I think, where the climb gets steep."

Wren covered her face. "I don't want to see the dead guy!"

Death laughed. "There is no dead guy!"

"But there was one." She hung back, hiding behind the muscular bulk of her ex-Marine boyfriend and trying to peek around him without actually seeing anything.

"There was, yes," he told her patiently. "But that was, like, three days ago. The police have been here and they took him away."

"But what if they missed bits?"

He half turned to peer down at her, his right eyebrow cocked up in amusement. "Missed bits? Really?"

"It could happen."

"No, sweetheart. I promise. It couldn't. The police are very thorough when it comes to dead guys. They always make sure to get all the bits."

"What if they were invisible bits?"

"Like dead guy cooties?"

She glowered at him. "You say that like it isn't a thing."

"They even took the branch he brained himself on," Randy said.

He'd ranged a little ahead of them and shinnied up a tree. He sat, now, astride a branch, and indicated the fresh-cut marks where another branch had been removed.

"Get down from there before you fall and break your neck," Death scolded. He glanced at Wren. "You know, when we were little and we went to the zoo, my brother always used to get switched with a baby monkey. To this day I'm not sure which one we ended up with."

"Ha, ha." Randy dangled full-length from the branch and dropped the few inches to the ground. Both brothers were tall and muscular, but where Death was burly and built like a tank, Randy was long and lean. He turned his attention to Wren and spoke kindly. "There really isn't anything to be afraid of. I've been around lots of dead people and they almost never do anything creepy." Randy was a firefighter and a nationally accredited paramedic. "Except for that one guy whose head fell off, but that's another story. My point is, there's nothing to be scared of here and now. It was just some old man who got drunk and had a stupid accident. Tragic, but not dangerous at all."

"That's easy for you to say," Wren replied sourly. "The last time some guy did something stupid and got himself killed I wound up getting kidnapped, your brother got beat up, and the guys who did it cut off my hair!" She ran a hand over her still-short cap of red hair, lamenting the braid that had taken her years to grow out.

"She does have a point," Death agreed reluctantly. "But"—he turned his attention back to her—"you wanted to get started on the Hadleigh House. Unless you've got a helicopter in your pocket, we're going to have to suck it up and go up the path to get there. Here. Close your eyes and take my hand."

She did, taking his hand in both of hers and allowing him to lead her past the deadly spot on the trail. His heartbeat under her fingers was strong and not racing, and his breathing had evened out. Before they'd stopped to talk he had been gasping, with an alarming wheeze deep in his chest.

Death Bogart didn't look it and didn't like to admit it, but he had returned from the war a damaged man. A combat injury had left him with a severely compromised lung capacity and symptoms of PTSD that he denied suffering from.

"Look," Randy said from slightly ahead of them. "There are stone steps set right into the hillside. The dead guy had to jump his horse down them. You can still see where they landed because the horse's hooves gouged out divots in the path."

"Randy," Death growled. "Ix-nay on the ead-day uy-gay!"

4

"Right. Because I totally don't speak pig Latin," Wren said drily.

Death ignored her, stooping to examine the steps. "This is worked stone. This path must have been heavily used at one point." Now it was overgrown with moss.

"It probably was. You'd never know it now, but from the mid-1800s to the Second World War there was a whole little community out here. There was a one-room schoolhouse, a flour mill, a smithy, and a general store back that way"—Wren pointed back the way they'd come—"and a church and a bunch of houses up beyond the old boundaries of the plantation, that way." She gestured ahead. "The church cemetery is still in use, in fact, though the church was abandoned decades ago. A lot of people who've never even lived around here get brought back and buried in old family plots."

"You know, I'm kind of surprised to see a plantation this far north," Death said.

"There aren't many," Wren agreed, "but some of the earliest settlers came to Missouri from Virginia and Georgia and they built the same kinds of houses and outbuildings they were used to down there. The land is good here, but the climate isn't right for cotton or tobacco. There was never a land rush, but a few of the big old houses remain. Where there were settlers, especially wealthy settlers, little towns grew up."

"Is there anything out here now?" Randy asked. "The whole area looks pretty desolate to me."

"Well, it's not a city," Wren said with a wry smile. "There are still a fair number of houses, scattered well apart, back in among the trees. The cemetery, as I said, is still in use. And there's a camp for wounded veterans, Warriors' Rest, in the northeast corner of the old plantation." She and Randy exchanged a meaningful look behind

Death's back. "They keep horses, and it's centered around the old stables."

"That must be where the..." Randy paused and cleared his throat. "The ead-day uy-gay stole his orse-hay."

"You think?"

Death just shook his head and went before them, up the steps and between two enormous lilac bushes at the head of the trail. Wren followed. As she came up behind him, he stepped aside so that she could appreciate the view.

They were standing at the front gate, the Hadleigh House rising from the overgrown garden like it was, itself, a specter from the past.

———

The wrought-iron fence that enclosed the front yard had been white once. Now the paint was yellowed and speckled with rust. The gate hung crooked from a single hinge. A bolt hole remained where the latch had been, but it was long gone now. A loop of wire held the gate fast to the gate post.

Off to the left, deep-worn ruts marked the upper end of the long driveway, untraveled for so long that saplings grew between the tracks. The ruts led through another, wider metal gate and made a circle through the side yard, passing under a carport. That entrance to the house was blocked now; the roof of the carport had fallen and a small tree grew beside the doorstop.

They had left Wren's pickup at the bottom of the drive, but had had to take the old path through the woods. An ancient bridge had once carried the driveway across a deep gully with a creek running through it, but it had long since tumbled into the water.

In late summer, almost fall now, the long grass in the front yard of the Hadleigh House was dark green tinged with brown and gold.

It was a big, rectangular block of a building with a dozen windows on the front side alone and a front door covered in flaking black paint. Low steps led up to a broad verandah. Six massive columns topped with carved Corinthian capitols supported the porch roof two stories above. A pair of tall, straight oak trees flanked the entryway.

The hill fell away behind the house, so that the house and its attendant trees stood framed against a clear blue sky. It looked, Wren thought, like a ship sailing on the crest of the world.

Death unhooked the small gate, lifted the trailing corner, and pushed. It opened with a dismal creak and they went into the yard. An uneven path, paved with red bricks, led to the steps. Wren could see the green blades of irises, their flowers long gone, massing along the fence line. There was a concrete goldfish pond, filled now with dirt and debris, a broken birdbath, and a trellis covered in sweet-pea vines. Once this had been a well-manicured garden, but now the black-eyed Susans scattered among the weeds and the roses growing in such proliferation along the iron fence were wild.

"So how does this happen?" Randy asked. "A place like this go up for auction, I mean."

"Usually," Wren said, "somebody dies."

At the foot of the steps Death put out a hand to stop her and went ahead, testing the boards to make sure they were sturdy enough to hold his weight.

"That makes a lot of sense," Wren said, frowning at him. "Using the heaviest of us to see if the porch will collapse."

"I'm a Marine," he said, bouncing a little to see if it would hold. "Marines always go first."

"You know what 'Marine' stands for?" Randy asked conversationally. "Muscles Are Required, Intelligence Not Essential."

"I'll kick your ass for that later," Death told his brother, almost absent-mindedly.

"Whatever, Jarhead."

Wren followed Death up onto the porch, Randy trailing behind her. The door sat in the center of the facade, with everything else balanced around it. It had a single light. A rural scene was etched into the glass.

"So somebody died," Randy persisted. "I'm assuming you mean someone other than the dead guy on the path?"

"Key?" Death asked.

Wren handed over the key ring Sam Keystone had given her and continued her conversation with Randy. "Some man out in California, a descendant of the family that built it. He's owned it all his life, from what I hear, and never even set foot in the state. When he passed away, this was only a small part of his estate. I guess his heirs weren't interested in it either. We're supposed to clear out the contents and then they're going to sell the house and land separately. It's just the house and a few fields and the woods out front now. A lot of the old plantation was sold off years ago."

Death was wrestling with the key in the rusted old lock. "Yeah, Randy. You need a house, right?"

Due to a strange set of circumstances, the two brothers had spent the past year each thinking the other was dead. Now that they were reunited, Randy had moved to East Bledsoe Ferry to be close to Death. Right now he was camping on the sofa in Death's tiny combination office/studio apartment.

"I think this is just a bit more house than I'm looking for. You gonna get that, Scooter? If you need someone more talented to take over, you can just give those keys to me."

"These old locks can be temperamental." Wren reached past Death to grip the key. She adjusted it slightly and the knob turned easily under her hand.

"Smartass," Death muttered.

The door swung open and the three of them stood on the threshold, peering into the dark interior.

"So," Randy said, "where does somebody find a corpse in a Civil War uniform?"

"You had to ask that now," Wren sighed.

———

"So, we know he got the horse from the veterans' camp," Death reasoned. "The chief said they found it spooked outside the fence the next morning." He pointed to the left. "That's off that way. He must have ridden between the fence and the tree line. I can't see a drunk on a strange horse managing to jump that gate."

"How does a drunk even stay on a horse?"

"Beats me. How does anybody stay on a horse?"

They had made a quick search of the mansion without finding any corpses, embalmed or otherwise. Thick dust lay everywhere, undisturbed for decades, and Wren had decided that, while the old house did feel haunted, it didn't feel sinister. Leaving her happily ensconced among the antiques, the Bogart brothers had returned to the head of the trail to explore the mystery of the dead stranger more thoroughly.

"You realize the police must have been over this ground already?" Randy asked.

"You'd rather go help my girlfriend catalogue knickknacks and dishware?"

"I was just making conversation."

They pushed along between the fence and the foliage, noting broken branches and finding the occasional hoof mark in the softer earth along the tree line. There was a path, overgrown but hard-beaten, along the outside of the fence. The brothers circled the house, waded through hip-deep weeds on the long slope behind it, and found themselves in an overgrown apple orchard. Many of the trees were dead—tall, black skeletons dropping branches into the mould to decay. A scattering of young trees grew among them, volunteers sprung up from windfall apples. Several were large enough to have produced fruit of their own and Death and Randy went from tree to tree, tasting what they found.

"What the hell kind of apples were they growing in this orchard anyway?" Randy demanded after half a dozen trees yielded nothing but small, hard, bitter fruit.

"Doesn't matter," Death said. "Apples don't grow true from seed. Don't even ask me how I know that. But these are kind of the apple equivalent of mutts. You plant an apple and it's anybody's guess what kind of tree it's going to produce. Here, try this one. It's not too bad." He tossed his little brother a small, dusky-pink apple and pocketed a couple more for later, and they wandered on through the orchard and out the other side.

Through a stand of pines and over a ridge they came to another fence. This one was chest-high, shiny, and new. A small herd of horses grazed on the other side. A big, light gray stallion watched them warily.

"Oh, look! A pale horse! We found your ride."

"Funny," Death said. "Hey, you remember that time we saw the Clydesdales?"

City boys, the Bogart brothers had little experience with horses. About the only time they'd ever been in the presence of the big animals had been at a parade once, when they'd been close enough to touch the famous team as it pulled the beer wagon past.

"See if he'll let you pet him," Randy urged.

"Why don't you see if he'll let you pet him?"

"You're the one with a pocket full of apples."

"Oh, right."

Death took one of the apples from his pocket and held it out, trying to look friendly and non-threatening.

Watching him, eyes wide and nostrils flared, the horse edged closer. He got within reach and stretched his neck out, obviously trying to reach the fruit without getting too close. He took the apple from Death's palm, but shied away when Death tried to rub a hand down his nose.

"I was just trying to pet you," Death said.

"Something I can help you fellas with?"

At the sound of a new voice, the brothers turned. A strange man had come out of the trees to their right and he stood now, watching them suspiciously. His feet were firmly planted and his muscular arms crossed over his chest. He wore jeans and a tank top and his exposed arms and upper chest were covered with tattoos.

"We were just trying to pet your horse," Randy said.

The man scowled at them. "That horse has been messed with enough by strangers."

"Is he the one that was stolen by the dead guy?"

The stranger's eyes narrowed. "That's a matter for the police. This is no place to come snooping around trying to satisfy your curiosity."

Death stepped between the two men, holding up his hands placatingly. As he did so, his T-shirt sleeve slipped up, revealing his own tattoo. The other man's eyes fell on it and his face and body language softened.

"Jarhead?"

"Big dumb Jarhead," Randy clarified helpfully.

"Ex-Marine, yeah," Death said. "Don't mind my brother."

"Kurt Robinson. Army artillery, retired. This, well, the pasture and what's beyond is a camp for wounded vets. Warriors' Rest. I'm the caretaker."

"I've heard of it," Death acknowledged, moving forward to shake Robinson's hand. "I'm Death Bogart and this is my little brother, Randy."

"The private eye. I've heard of you. Were you looking for us?"

"No, we weren't looking," Death said.

"But since you found us," Randy cut in, ignoring the dirty look his brother was giving him, "I'd just like to say that I'm a paramedic. I'll give you my cell phone number. If you guys ever need my kind of help, just let me know. No charge."

Robinson's demeanor warmed even more. "Thank you. I appreciate it. Any kind of help we can get, we're glad to have. Listen, I'm sorry if I snarled at you about the horse. It's just that the big guy's been pretty freaked ever since that jerk stole him and got himself killed. He won't even go back in his stall. We've had to fix him a makeshift stable in an old tool shed."

"Yeah, I'm not surprised," Death said. "I don't know a lot about horses, but isn't it kind of surprising that the dead guy was even able to get on him? From what I've heard, horses have a pretty keen sense of smell, and that guy must have stunk to high heaven."

The formaldehyde and body liquor were not common knowledge, so Death didn't elaborate. Even without them, the dead guy had to have smelled like a distillery.

"Well, Sugar was confined in a narrow stall, so he didn't have anywhere to get away. The guy just had to open the gate, then climb the rails and jump on his back before he could get out."

"His name's Sugar?"

The big horse had edged back over, reassured by Robinson's familiar presence, and was gazing pointedly at the pocket Death still had a couple of apples in.

"Because he's such a sweetheart," Robinson said.

"Can I give him another apple?"

"Let me see it."

Death showed him the apple and Robinson nodded. "Go ahead. I just wanted to make sure it wasn't green. Green apples will give a horse terrible stomach pains."

Death held it out to the horse.

"Not like that," Robinson said. "Hold it flat on your palm. Otherwise he might bite you accidentally."

Death did as he was told and, almost delicately, the big stallion took the apple from his palm.

"So, what kind of things do you do around here?" Randy asked, again ignoring Death's glare.

"Whatever we can to help whoever needs it."

Sugar moved close, stretched his long neck over the fence, and rubbed his cheek against Death's.

"He wants you to pet him."

Death obliged, and Robinson nodded at the horse as he continued his conversation with Randy.

"Sometimes it helps someone who's traumatized just to be around someone who understands." He sighed. "Sometimes, nothing at all is enough." He looked hard at Death. "I appreciate your brother offering his help, but it seems to me that you're the one whose help we really need right now. I don't know how much we'd be able to pay you …"

Death waved away the concern. "Don't worry about that," he said. "Brothers-in-arms. If you really need help, I'll be glad to do what I can. What is it that you need my help for?"

"I need for you to prove that my best friend is insane."

TWO

WREN LOVED CLASSIC ROCK music. She had probably eight hundred songs stored on her phone—everything from the Everly Brothers and Chubby Checker to '80s hair bands and U2. But there was no electricity to the Hadleigh House at the moment and thus no way to recharge her phone. She needed to keep from running the battery down in case the boys needed to call her for something.

That was why she'd turned it off in the middle of the first song and tucked it back inside her pocket. She was being practical. Thinking ahead. It wasn't at all because the bright notes echoed oddly in the silence, or because it felt like the music might disturb something that was best not wakened.

She'd reassured Death that she didn't think the house was creepy, and it wasn't. But it did have a feel to it. She looked out the etched glass window in the front door and could picture what the lawn must have looked like in its heyday. In the side yard, to the south, there was a sagging summer house overgrown with vines and a grape arbor. In the back, a single clothesline still stretched between two uprights that had been designed to hold four or six lines.

Beyond the back fence, and visible from the second-floor rear windows, were a row of slave quarters crumbling into rubble, a reminder that the house had seen dark days as well as sunny ones.

Hadleigh House was filled with the possessions of its former owners, everything from rare antiques to rubbish. It was a small miracle that it had never been burgled, but its remote location and the ruined bridge across the driveway had protected it. As far as Wren knew, no one had lived there during her lifetime.

The place seemed like it was caught in a bubble, existing outside the normal, twenty-first century world. Wren felt as if the people who'd lived there were there still, just out of sight around a corner or in another room. As if she might walk through the wrong door, not paying attention, and step into the 1920s or the 1800s even.

She was on the second floor at the north end, in a room she'd found filled with a jumble of furniture, decaying cardboard boxes, and old trunks. It was stuffy in the room, so she slid the locking lever on one of the windows over and pushed it up. The wood frame was swollen with humidity and squealed going up, and it stayed open without anything to brace it. Wren brushed her hands against her jeans to knock the dust off, donned a pair of vinyl gloves to protect anything valuable she might find, and turned her attention to the nearest container.

It was an old metal footlocker, painted dark brown and latched but not locked. The hinges were stiff with rust, but she put her back into it and the lid came up in her hands.

The first thing she saw, right on top, was a gas mask. At a guess, she'd say it was from World War One, but it could be from the second World War too. She took a couple of pictures of it from different angles, to help with her research, and set it aside. Below the mask was an assortment of old clothes, men's clothes, in styles rang-ing from the 1920s to the 1950s. At the very bottom of the trunk was a drawing pad, filled with pen-and-ink sketches.

The pages were brittle, the ink beginning to fade, but the artwork was exquisite. Leafing through it, turning the pages ever so gently, Wren realized the drawings were of the same scene, with the same group of people, over and over and over again.

She moved closer to the light from the open window and studied one of the drawings. There was a well in a courtyard, with a ruined house in the background. A group of exhausted, bedraggled soldiers gathered around it. From the uniforms, the way their shirts bloused out above their belts and the puttees wrapped around their lower legs, Wren placed them in World War One. One man sat leaning against a bombed-out vehicle. Another lay on the ground with a bandage over his eyes.

In the center of the group stood a young woman, as ragged and as bedraggled as they were. Her dress was ripped, her hair in tangles around her shoulders. She had dark shadows under her eyes, and a dirty bandage was wrapped around her left hand and wrist. A bucket sat a her feet, and she was offering the soldiers water from a ladle.

Wren turned the pages. Although every picture was the same scene, some were from different angles, and some had the composition slightly different. Many of them were only portions of the larger picture, this bit or that rendered in careful detail.

"It's ... " Without thinking, Wren spoke aloud. "It's a study for a larger work, I think. And the artwork is amazing. I wonder who drew it, and if they ever finished the main painting or whatever it was." She looked through the pad, front-to-back and then back-to-front, but there was no writing in it at all.

Setting it carefully to one side, she dove back into the chest in hopes of finding something to identify the artist. "Who were you?" she whispered.

From a great distance, someone answered.

Wren sat up, shocked, and listened. After a moment, the voice came again, and then a second time. It was a conversation, clear enough to be definitely there but too soft for her to understand the words.

She rose and went to the window and had to laugh at herself.

Death and Randy were returning from the direction of the veterans' camp, talking quietly between themselves as they approached over the field.

"Death took a new case, pro bono," Randy said.

"Won't make any money that way son," Sam Keystone said.

Half a dozen members of the Keystone family had arrived just after the Bogart brothers returned. They were planning to start building some sort of bridge across the gully, so that people could at least walk up the road to the auction, and then help Wren start sorting out the estate. But at the moment they were all sitting on the front porch, drinking coffee out of thermoses and gossiping about the dead guy.

"I can afford to donate some time to a good cause. And, honestly, I don't know that I can do anything for them anyway," Death said.

"Who's 'them' and what do they want you to do?" asked Sam's brother, Roy. Sam and Roy, the original sons in Keystone and Sons, were sixty-two-year-old twins who dressed and acted so different that someone who didn't know them would never guess they were identical. Sam wore a dark suit with a hat and a string tie, no matter the weather, whereas Roy always dressed in overalls and a flannel shirt.

"Kurt Robinson and some of the guys over at the vet's camp," Death said. "Any of you ever heard anything about a guy named Anthony Dozier?"

The Keystones all had.

"Sure, it's been all over the news," Sam's son Liam said. "Lot of folks think he should get a medal instead of a murder charge."

"Well, I've never heard of him," Wren said. "Who is he and who did he kill?"

"Army vet," one of the Keystone grandsons piped up. "Came back from Afghanistan really messed up, they said. Spent time in a psych ward."

"He was a medic," Death told them. "He and his unit got pinned down in a village that was caught in the crossfire between us and them. Dozen soldiers, a lot of civilians. He was the only medic and there weren't very many survivors. They said he held it together until it was all over and then he just lost it. Nightmares, prolonged flashbacks, panic attacks, depression, a couple of suicide attempts. He's been out of the hospital, living with family, for about eighteen months now."

"So what happened?"

"Have you ever heard of a group called 'the Church of the Army of Christ'?"

"CAC for short," Sam offered.

Wren frowned and thought about it. "It seems to me I might have seen the name somewhere. Posts on Facebook, maybe? If I did, I skimmed over them. Who are they?"

"A hate group masquerading as a church," Sam said with an uncharacteristic amount of heat in his voice. While most of the Keystones were at least casual churchgoers, none of them took it as seriously as

Sam and his wife Doris. "They claim that it's a Christian's duty to convert or eradicate everyone who isn't Christian."

"Hate thy neighbor?" Wren observed ironically.

"It was founded by a man named Tyler Jones, and most of the members are part of his extended family. They're against anyone who isn't Christian, including atheists and agnostics, but their main target at the moment is Muslims. And here just recently they've taken a page out of another group's book and started protesting at funerals."

Death, sitting beside Wren, slipped his hand into hers and squeezed, as if to reassure himself that she was still there. "Dozier married a Muslim woman," he said. "One of the other survivors of that firefight in Afghanistan. Ten days ago she was killed in a car accident. The CAC showed up at her funeral and Dozier confronted Jones and threatened to kill him."

"Oh God," Wren said. She leaned her head on Death's shoulder.

"There was a reception after the funeral. Kurt said that Dozier was supposed to come out to the veterans' camp after it was over, but he never showed up. They searched everywhere for him, reported him as an endangered missing person, nothing. Then, the next morning, a cop stopped Dozier up in the city. Dozier claimed to think he was back in Afghanistan—he told the cop he had a wounded soldier in his car and was trying to find the base hospital.

"He was covered in blood, and Tyler Jones' twenty-three-year-old son was in the backseat. The guy was wrapped up in makeshift bandages and very dead. He'd been stabbed repeatedly."

"Naturally," Randy said, "the defense is claiming temporary insanity. But the prosecuting attorney is going for murder in the first degree. He thinks it was premeditated and that Dozier intended all along to use insanity as a defense. If he succeeds, Dozier is looking at life in prison at best. He could even get the death penalty."

"Kurt's terrified for him, grasping at straws," Death said. "He wants me to help prove in court that Dozier's insane."

———

"What is this and where do I put it?"

Wren looked up from her notes to find Robin Keystone, one of the grandsons, standing in the doorway. The contraption he was cradling consisted of two rollers set in a frame, with a crank that caused them to turn toward each other.

"It's a manual wringer, for doing laundry by hand," she said. "Where did you find it?"

"On a corner of the back porch. I knew it was a wringer, but where's the rest of the washing machine?"

"That wasn't part of a washing machine," she told him. "People used to wash clothes by hand, with a washboard. They'd have the wash water and the rinse water in big metal tubs. This thing clamped on the edge of the tubs. You'd wring the soap out before you put them in the rinse, then wring that water out before you hung them up to dry."

"Sounds like a pain in the butt. Where do you want it?"

"We're putting the non-furniture antiques in the parlor for now," she said, pointing. "Gadgets on the right, clothes on the left."

Robin lugged it into the other room, his voice drifting out behind him. "This is gonna be a huge sale."

"Yeah. It'll probably take two days to sell it all."

"Did you see the car?"

"No, there's a car?"

"Yeah, in one of the outbuildings, under a tarp. An Impala, from the sixties. I'm not sure what year. Needs a bit of work, but it looks like it's in really good shape." He came back out of the parlor and leaned on the doorframe. "You know, I'm gonna be sixteen in a couple of months."

Wren shot him an amused look from under her lashes. "You don't say?"

Heavy footsteps crossing the porch interrupted their conversation and Wren glanced toward the open door, hoping to see Death. He and Randy were helping Roy and a couple of the sons with the bridge, and Wren was worried that he'd overdo it.

Instead of her boyfriend, she found a deputy sheriff in the doorway.

"Hey, Orly! What brings you out this way?"

Orly Jackson had been a couple of years ahead of Wren in school. He was a short, balding man with a round face and a generally cheerful demeanor. At the moment he was scowling slightly, but she couldn't tell if he was genuinely annoyed or putting on a show.

"Just the woman I was looking for," he said.

"Me?"

"No, him. Yes, you."

"What did you need me for?"

He came inside and helped himself to a seat on a dust-cloth-covered settle. "I'm still trying to identify that dead horse thief." He paused and cast Wren a slanted look. "You heard about the dead horse thief?"

Wren just looked at him. "This is East Bledsoe Ferry. I heard that Buddy Zimmer fell off his porch and I heard that Melanie Vansant was late to Sunday school. You really think I'm not gonna hear about a dead horse thief?"

"Whatever." He took a 3x5 photograph and an evidence bag with a square of paper inside from his breast pocket and looked at them for a moment. Then he held out the picture. "Recognize him?"

Wren shied away. "You want me to look at a picture of a dead guy? Really?"

"Yeah. It's not gory. He just looks like he's sleeping, I promise. C'mon. Look at it!"

Reluctantly, Wren took the picture he handed her and peeked at it. It was an old man, from the neck up. He lay on his back with his eyes closed. His face had an unnatural pallor. The wrinkles around his mouth and eyes looked like they had been molded in clay. His eyes were dark and sunken and his lips were blue.

She shuddered. "He doesn't look like he's sleeping. He looks like he's dead."

"Well, he is."

She gave Orly a withering look, but he just raised his eyebrows and shrugged.

"Can I see?" Robin asked, coming over to look. "Oh, wow. He does look dead. Cool!"

"I suppose we can be thankful there're no brains showing." Wren sighed.

"He didn't hit his head that hard," Orly said. "It wasn't the head trauma that killed him."

"No?"

"No. The branch just knocked him out and made him fall off the horse. He actually died from alcohol intoxication. He drank himself to death."

Wren tried to hand the picture back. "That's too bad."

"Yeah." Orly held up a hand, refusing to take the photo. "But who is he? Or who was he? Look at it and tell me if you know him."

Wren looked at the picture again. "No, he doesn't look familiar."

"Are you sure about that?"

"Yeah. I mean, he looks a little familiar. Like someone you've seen in the grocery store, maybe? Or maybe he just looks like someone on TV. I don't know. But I know I don't know him. You act like you think I should."

"Well, yeah."

"But why?"

"Because," Orly said, holding up the evidence bag, "he had a note in his pocket. It has your name on it, and I'm pretty sure that this is your handwriting."

THREE

THAT SAME MORNING, ROY's wife Leona was presiding over an auction at a small, two-bedroom, one-story brick ranch-style home on a treeless lot. They were selling the contents first, with the house itself set to go on the block at one p.m. Some of the younger Keystone sons and grandsons were with her, handling the set-up and calling while Leona kept an eye on things from the cash tent. It was a beautiful late summer day, and although she'd had them set up the tent for shade, she'd rolled up the sides to let the breeze through.

The sale had just gotten under way when Sam and Roy returned with Wren, the Bogart brothers, and Deputy Jackson. Leona glanced up from her crossword puzzle and looked at her husband.

"I don't even want to know what you did to get brought home by the cops at this hour of the day."

"You malign me," Roy said with mock indignation.

"I know you."

"Well, missy, it just so happens you're wrong this time. It's not me that's got the cops involved. Wren is a person of interest in a murder investigation!"

Orly rolled his eyes. "She's not a person of interest, she's just helping us with our investigation. And it's not a murder investigation, it's just an accidental death investigation."

"Bah!" Roy waved one hand dismissively, pulled over a folding chair and helped himself to a seat. "Semantics."

"Leona," Wren said, "look at this! It was in the pocket of the dead man's Confederate cavalry uniform!"

Orly Jackson handed over a note in a clear plastic evidence bag. It was stiff and stained with some dark liquid but still legible. They gathered to read it over Leona's shoulder:

Will of J. K., ex. 5/27/1923 in St. Clair Co., mentions. SAS db-CW at NARA confirms Andrews wounded at 1st b. of Booneville. Repaired bullet hole in left shoulder matches recorded wound. Ext. CW insig. is correct—some pins and patches appear to have been added later, e.g. removed WWII-era P.H. and returned to fam.

"Wren wrote this," Jackson said. "Look, I'm just trying to identify the guy. Wren says that Keystone and Sons must have sold the uniform he was wearing, but she couldn't tell me when, or who bought it. Roy and Sam said you keep all the business records."

"He made me look at the picture of the dead guy," Wren put in, sounding aggrieved. "I didn't recognize him. And you don't even want to know what that stain is!"

"But what does this note mean?" Jackson persisted.

"May I?" Death asked, taking the paper from Leona and studying it. "Wren was trying to authenticate that this was an actual Civil War uniform. She made these rough notes and tucked them into the pocket, and then forgot to take them out again. Right?"

"Yes!" Wren said. "I wrote that the uniform was worn by a Civil War cavalryman named Andrews, apparently. I checked the Soldiers and Sailors database-Civil War at NARA—that's the National Archives and Records Administration—and confirmed that he served, and that he was wounded at the First Battle of Booneville. There was probably a family story about him that I was authenticating. I was also able to confirm that his wounds matched damage visible on the uniform, and that the Civil War era insignia present was correct for his rank and unit. There were also some patches and pins that had been added later, and I noted that I removed a World War Two–era Purple Heart and returned it to the family."

"Wouldn't they have taken it off if they wanted to keep it?" Jackson asked.

"It doesn't matter. It's illegal to buy or sell a Purple Heart. And it's disrespectful. And we don't do it."

"I see. But the point is, you sold the uniform that my dead guy was wearing?"

"We must have."

"So can you look in your records for me and find out who bought it?"

Leona gave him a withering look. "You know, it's really not that simple."

"Why not?"

"Young man, we sell thousands of items every week. Keystone and Sons has been in business since the 1960s and Wren has been with us since she was in high school. In fact"—Leona peered at the note again—"given the teddy bears on her notepaper and the fact that this is written in metallic purple ink, I'm going to say it probably dates from when she was in college."

"But you keep records."

"Business records, yes, but only for six years and not for every item sold."

Orly sighed. "Well, can you at least look at the man's picture and tell me if you've seen him at auctions before? Because it seems to me that there's a good chance he's the one you sold the uniform to."

"But then how did it get on a dead guy?" Death said.

Leona gave him an odd look. "I'd imagine he put it on before he fell off the horse."

"Yeah, I don't mean that dead guy."

"That stain on the paper?" Wren said. "The uniform is soaked in formaldehyde and, um, icky dead body stuff."

"That's the technical term," Randy Bogart said.

"Okay," Leona said. "That's disgusting."

"We figure the old man must have taken it from a corpse," Jackson explained. "We searched the nearby cemetery, but there's no sign anyone's been digging into any of the graves. Also, we talked to the guy who operates the back hoe and checked with the cemetery board. There's no record of anyone being buried there within the last six months. Here." He held out the photograph. "This is the dead man. It's okay. He just looks like he's sleeping."

Leona took the picture and peered at it. "He doesn't look like he's sleeping. He looks like he's dead."

"Made you look. Do you know him?"

"No."

"There's no reason we *would* know him," Wren said, exasperated. "I keep telling you, if the dead guy stole the uniform off the body of a previously dead guy, then the previously dead guy is the one who's most likely the one who bought the uniform at our auction. He's the one we'd know. The buried dead guy, not the drunk dead guy."

"Unless they were relatives or best friends or something and the drunk dead guy bought the uniform for his brother, or whatever, but then his brother decided to be buried in it. Or something," Jackson countered.

"Maybe the first dead guy stole the uniform from the drunk dead guy and the drunk dead guy was just stealing it back. Then he'd have been the one who bought it and you might know him after all," Randy suggested facetiously.

"Maybe they bought it together and had one of those things where the last one standing was supposed to inherit it but then the first dead guy cheated the drunk dead guy. That'd work too," Death offered.

Wren glowered at them. "Guys. You're not helping."

"This is the only lead I have," Orly said. "There must be something you can do to help me identify him! You know, he could have family somewhere that doesn't even know he's dead!"

"Listen," Death said, "an authentic Civil War uniform is something you'd put in the auction listing in the paper, right?"

"Yeah, absolutely," Wren agreed.

"Okay, and based on your stationery choices, we figure this happened about, what? Four to eight years ago?"

"Yeah."

"Right. And the paper keeps a copy of every edition they've put out. So"—Death looked to Jackson—"if you go back through the papers and read all the auction notices, you might be able to figure out where and when the uniform was sold. You also know that the uniform was worn by a Confederate Cavalry officer named Andrews who was wounded at the First Battle of Booneville. And in 1923, it was mentioned in a will that was executed at St. Clair County on May 27th. Look for someone with the initials J. K., and you might be able to identify the family that the uniform originally belonged to."

"How would that help?" Orly asked.

"Maybe the drunk dead guy was a member of the family that sold the uniform," Death reasoned. "Maybe he thought he was going to inherit it, but then it got sold out from under him, so when he found out the buyer was buried in it, he decided to steal it back. I mean, think about it. He had to be pretty attached to that thing to take it off a dead body and *put it on!*"

The deputy sighed and his shoulders slumped. "Yeah, okay. I guess that's a starting point. Thanks for your help. If any of you think of anything else, let me know?"

They said goodbye and watched him walk away.

When Jackson was out of earshot, Wren gave Death a puzzled look. "You really think that looking for J. K. from 1923 will help identify the person who bought the uniform, or the person who apparently stole it from a dead body?"

Death shrugged. "Not so far as I can see. But at least I made him go away."

Susan Leopold was a small woman in her mid-fifties with sharp, dark features. She wore a dark red skirt suit with spiked heels, and a large metal clasp held her hair up in a knot on the top of her head. She walked down the hallway at a brisk pace, her heels clacking on the pale gray institutional linoleum, and even with his long legs, Death found it a challenge to keep up with her.

When Robinson had introduced them, Death had only planned to ask her a few questions to help him start his investigation into the Anthony Dozier case. She was a woman who made things happen, though, and within two hours he was following her through the high-security wing of the state mental hospital in Fulton, on his way to interview Dozier in person.

This part of the facility was locked down. They'd had to produce photo IDs and go through a metal detector to gain access. The individual rooms had locks on them, and there were uniformed guards among the medical staff.

Apart from that, the place resembled a college dormitory more than the stereotypical insane asylum one might see on television. There was no evidence of padded cells or straitjackets and, when they passed a common area, the people milling around were supervised but unrestrained.

"Do you know anything about the law, Mr. Bogart?" Leopold asked as they followed a guard down a side corridor.

"Not a lot," he admitted. "My grandmother was a DA in St. Louis in the seventies."

"And what did you learn from that?"

"Don't argue with Grandma."

The guard stopped in front of a door and knocked, then used a key card to unlock it. He turned the latch and opened it just a little.

"Anthony? You have visitors." He motioned for Death and Leopold to go on through. "I'll be out here. Just knock when you're ready to leave."

Death didn't know what he was expecting on the other side of the door, but it wasn't the slight, pale man who sat at a card table in his room playing Solitaire. He was slender and fair-complected, with light blue eyes and hair so blond it was almost white. The window shade, a solid sheet of fabric with no strings attached to it, was pulled all the way down and, even indoors, Dozier wore a floppy fisherman's hat.

31

Given the man's coloring, Death suspected he'd learned the hard way to avoid the sun. He'd probably spent his whole tour in Afghanistan trying to avoid a sunburn.

"Anthony," Leopold said, her voice softening, "this is Mr. Bogart. He's a private investigator who's going to be helping me with your case. I need for you to tell him what happened. Can you do that?"

Dozier was staring at Death with a fixed intensity that made him feel uncomfortable.

"What's wrong with your breathing?" Dozier demanded.

"What?"

"Your breathing. It's wrong. Too shallow and labored."

"Nothing." Death shifted a little and gave the other man a small smile. "Really. Nothing. I'm fine."

Dozier continued to stare at him, eyes narrowed.

"I've just chased your attorney halfway across Missouri," Death joked. "I might be a little out of breath from that."

"You're a Jarhead," the man replied. "That shouldn't be anything. *What's wrong with your breathing?*"

Death sighed and took a seat on the twin bed. The bed and table were bolted to the floor and the chair was made of lightweight, molded plastic. The only decoration in the room was an unframed photograph taped to the wall. In it, Dozier stood next to a smiling woman in a long dress and hijab, who was holding a bouquet.

His late wife, of course. This was his wedding picture

"I was wounded in action," Death admitted. "I have a compromised lung capacity. But I'm fine. I deal with it."

"Can I—" Dozier moved nervously, feinting toward Death and almost hyperventilating himself now. "I know it's intrusive. I need—I'm sorry. Can I—can I take your pulse?"

Death offered the other man his left wrist, tilting his head and watching him, considering. As his fingers circled Death's wrist and found his pulse point, Dozier's tension eased a little.

"Good," he said. "Strong. A bit fast, but strong."

He let Death's hand drop and reached, almost absent-mindedly, for Leopold's. She gave him her wrist without a word, as if she were expecting this, and met Death's eyes over Dozier's head.

She knew he does this. She could have warned me. Probably testing me or something. Lovely.

"This is what you did, isn't it?" Death asked, comprehension dawning. "When you were under attack, with all those wounded and you were the only medic. You went from person to person, checking their vitals to be sure they were still alive."

Dozier nodded, concentrating on her pulse. "They kept dying on me." His voice was nearly a whisper. "You know, people think OCD means cleaning stuff." He rose and paced the room nervously, stopping beside the window with his back against the wall and peeking out around the blind like he was expecting bullets to greet him. Reassured that they were not under fire, he drifted back over and took his seat at the card table. Death allowed him to take his wrist again.

"Anthony," he said, "I need you to tell me what happened the night of the funeral."

The corner of Dozier's mouth turned up in a wry, bitter smile. "Obviously not what I remember," he said.

"But what you remember is all we have to go on. Tell me anyway."

The man shrugged his thin shoulders. "It was dark out. I remember heading for the veterans' camp outside of East Bledsoe Ferry. I'd wanted to be by myself for a bit, but Kurt was afraid I'd kill myself, so I promised him I'd come to the camp in a couple of hours. And I kind of remember driving around, thinking about things. Remembering. And then … "

"And then?" Death prompted.

Dozier sighed. "You won't believe me."

"Tell me anyway."

He tugged on the bottom of his T-shirt, worrying the fabric, and bit his lower lip. "And then I saw my wife," he said finally.

"You … I'm sorry. What?"

"Zahra. My wife. I saw her ghost. She was standing off to the right, among the trees, looking at me."

"He was hallucinating," Leopold whispered helpfully.

Death shushed her. "Tell me about that," he said to Dozier. "Did you stop? Did she say anything or do anything?"

"Of course I stopped. It was my wife. I wanted to see her and hold her and tell her I love her. I wanted to tell her I was sorry."

"What are you sorry for?"

Anthony Dozier looked down. Tears ran down his face and dripped on the playing cards.

"I promised her family I'd protect her."

"So, you stopped. Was she still there? Did she say anything or do anything?"

"No, she didn't move at all, or speak, or anything. She just looked at me. She was perfectly white, pale like the moonlight, in a long robe and a hijab. I remember her eyes, over her veil. And I got out of the car, but I stumbled in the dark and fell in the ditch and there was a wounded soldier there, bleeding out."

"Okay, and then what?"

"And then … and then I couldn't see her anymore, but I had wounded I had to take care of. He'd taken a load of shrapnel and I didn't have any gear with me. So I bandaged him up as best I could and put him in the jeep, but I couldn't find my way back to the base hospital. And none of the roads were right. So I drove and I drove for a long, long time. And I kept stopping to check his pulse and his breathing. They got worse and worse and then they stopped and I knew it was too late, but I finally found an MP to ask for directions. But I wasn't in Afghanistan at all. I was in Kansas City and they told me I'd killed him."

"Obviously he wasn't in his right mind," Leopold said as she unlocked her car in the parking lot. "I'm sure the psychiatrists are going to agree, but the DA is being a hard-ass, so anything at all you can do to help make our case for temporary insanity will help. What do you think?"

"I think you're all nuts," Death said. He folded his arms on the roof of her car and met her startled, hostile gaze. "There is no way in hell that man killed anybody."

"What are you talking about?" she said. "Of course he did. The CAC protested at his wife's funeral. Anthony confronted Jones and threatened him at the funeral."

"Anthony confronted Jones Sr. at the funeral, right? But the victim was his son, August Jones. In the heat of the moment, anyone can say anything. Dozier's not a killer." Death slapped his hand down on the car roof, opened the door, and got in.

He waited for Leopold to join him before continuing. "Does Dozier have any injuries that Jones might have made trying to defend himself? August was a big guy and Anthony's not. Did they find a murder weapon on him or in his car?"

"No, they didn't. Listen, Anthony Dozier is a likeable man and I understand that you don't want to see him as a killer, but we need to face facts. He murdered August Jones in a fit of blind rage and grief and the best thing we can do to help him is to prove that he wasn't in his right mind at the time."

"What we need to do," Death countered, "is find the murder scene."

Leopold started her car and put it in gear. "And there I'm not going to disagree with you," she said. "If we find a murder scene—apart from the back seat of Dozier's car—maybe we can get the case moved. Right now it's being tried in Kansas City. If we can prove that Jones was attacked somewhere else, I'll have something to argue. A different jurisdiction means a different DA. Maybe we'll get one who's more receptive to hearing our side of things."

"Right," Death said, leaning back. Susan Leopold drove a little compact and with his seat upright Death's head brushed the roof liner. "And also, we can figure out who really killed August Jones."

FOUR

"I'M NOT SAYING THAT I never want to see you again. I'm just saying that we've only even known each other for a few months. I think we should slow down a bit. That's all."

Madeline Braun, who had been Madeline Bogart before an ill-considered divorce, shifted uncomfortably in the booth at the coffee shop and tried to put a little space between herself and Eric Far-rington. It didn't work. He had his arm around her waist and she was firmly squished against the wall.

It was ridiculous.

Manipulating men was Madeline's forte. She'd been doing it since she was in middle school. Pick them up, string them along for as long as they were useful, then drop them like a hot rock. But Eric, a small-statured jail guard who was commonly considered the most obnoxious human being in the central United States, clung to her like gum on the bottom of her best stilettos.

She'd only taken up with him because he was handy and she was trying to make her ex-husband jealous.

And—speak of the devil—there he was! Death Bogart himself, sitting across the tiny coffee shop with his new girlfriend, Wren Morgan, of whom Madeline was absolutely, positively not jealous.

Wren was a plain-Jane, girl-next-door type with an average build and a horrible wardrobe. Today she was dressed in an old T-shirt with a faded cartoon on the front. She'd paired it with shorts and sneakers, and her red hair was a wild cloud around her head. Her waist was larger than Madeline's and her bosom was smaller and she had freckles she didn't even try to hide.

She hadn't even bothered to put on lipstick.

She and Death were sitting on opposite sides of their own table, each engrossed in their own electronic device. As Madeline watched, Wren reached out blindly and Death, almost absent-mindedly, slid the sugar into her hand.

Death always had been a gentleman. He was as kind as he was strong and when he was Madeline's husband he'd treated her like a princess and never taken her for granted.

"So what exactly are you saying here, Sugar Boobies?" Eric asked, only half paying attention to her as he leaned in close and took a selfie of them together.

Madeline gritted her teeth. "I'm saying that I want for us to have a more open relationship. I think we should start seeing other people."

Eric lit up. "Really?"

Madeline blinked, surprised by his reaction. "Yes. Really."

"Awesome!" He looked across the coffee shop and called out, "Hey, Wren! You hear that? My Maddy-booby wants to have a threesome! Are you in?"

"Wants to—? What? I never said—!"

Wren pointed at Eric without bothering to look up. "You come within ten feet of me, Farrington, and I'll stab you to death with my spoon."

"Aw, baby," he said, "you know you want to!"

Madeline growled to herself. Everyone in the shop was watching them now. This was a small town. She was going to be a laughing-stock.

Because he'd always been an easy target for her, she turned on Death. "Really, Death? Eric's hitting on your girlfriend and you're not going to do anything?"

"Of course I'm going to do something," Death said. The condiment bar was behind his seat and he reached one long arm back, snagged a plastic-wrapped utensil, and tossed it on the table in front of Wren. "Here, honey. Here's a clean spoon for when you've finished."

Eric finally released Madeline and slid out of the booth. "Don't worry, baby," he said, "she'll come around. Meantime, I know this chick out at the biker bar who'll do anything, and I mean anything! I'll call her and see if she's busy tonight. It'll probably depend on whether or not her rash has cleared up."

He planted a big, wet, sloppy kiss right on Madeline's mouth and sauntered away. She shuddered and reached for a napkin, certain she couldn't possibly be any more humiliated.

Eric stopped at the door and shouted out to the early-morning crowd. "You all hear that? I'm getting me double nookie tonight!"

He pushed out of the building, the jangling door chime competing with a wave of laughter, and Madeline dropped her head. When she looked up again, Wren Morgan was regarding her with amusement, but not without sympathy.

"I suppose you think this is funny," Madeline spat.

"A little, yeah. Okay, a lot. But listen. It's sweet that you're trying to let him down gently, but I've known Eric Farrington all my life. He doesn't do subtle. You're going to have to be a lot more direct if you want to get rid of him."

Madeline considered, for a moment, whether she should be insulted or amused that Wren thought she would take relationship advice from a woman of her caliber.

"What would you suggest?" she asked finally, a sharp edge to her voice.

"Treat him like a cockroach. Hit him with a shoe and put him out on the curb on trash day."

"Trash guy isn't going to pick up Farrington," Death said. "They're not licensed for toxic waste."

"This is a valid point."

"I don't necessarily want to get rid of him," Madeline explained condescendingly.

Wren stared at her, shocked. "What?"

"He's not a bad person. He can be fun. I mean to say, he has his good points."

"He takes her places and buys her things," Death explained, voice dry.

"Okay, fine. He takes me places and buys me things. So? Don't you take Wren places and buy her things?"

"Well," Death considered, "we drove Wren's truck this morning, so technically, she brought me to the coffee shop."

"But you did buy me a new jar of mustard last night," Wren reminded him.

"It seemed only fair, since my brother drank yours."

"Yeah. I really thought you were joking when you dared him to do that."

"I can get Randy to do anything."

Wren looked slantwise at Madeline, a speculative look in her eye. "Can you get him to kiss Madeline?"

"Okay, maybe not that."

Madeline scowled at them. "So it's true, then? Your brother's back from the dead?"

Death grinned and it was like the old Death, the boy she'd fallen in love with before he got weighed down by war and grief.

"He is indeed."

"I'm surprised you didn't stay in St. Louis to help him recover from his ordeal." Madeline knew that Wren had a job here in East Bledsoe Ferry. Surely, if they spent a little time apart, Death would realize Wren was just a fling.

"Oh," Death beamed, even larger, "haven't you heard? Randy closed up his house in the city and moved down here. He's staying at my apartment right now, but eventually we're going to find him a house. He's got a job with the medevac helicopters and he's joined the volunteer fire department."

"He's out on a call now," Wren added. "Brush fire out by Racket, somewhere. I'm sure you'll be seeing him around though."

"Oh." Madeline forced a smile that she knew didn't reach her eyes. "Lovely."

"I know, right?" Wren grinned a big, full grin. "Must be karma!"

———

When Madeline had huffed and stomped her way out of the coffee shop, Wren looked up. Death glanced up at the same time and their eyes met, both amused.

"That's the thing about a small town," Wren said. "You never know who you're going to run into."

"I know, right? It's like dinner theater, only at breakfast. It's breakfast theater."

"I wonder how she'll get out of Eric's threesome."

Death snorted. "I wonder if she really wants to." He caught Wren's raised eyebrow. "What? It's not like she was choosy about who she slept with when we were married. Hey! Maybe I can get her to let me babysit tonight. I haven't introduced Benji to his Uncle Randy yet."

Benji was Madeline's son, a charming little boy hugging the line between infant and toddler. He had been conceived while Death was serving in Afghanistan. Even though he wasn't Death's child, Death adored him. Benji returned the affection and had even upset his mother by saying the word "Deese" before "Mama."

Death leaned over the table and read Wren's phone upside down. "What are you so lost in this morning?"

"I found a 1930s book about Rives County history at the University of Missouri's online library, in their Missouriana collection. There's a list of boys from here who fought in World War One and I'm trying to figure out if one of them lived in the Hadleigh House."

"Why's that?"

"I found an artist's sketchbook full of what looks like studies for a larger work. There's no name on it, but the men in the picture are in World War One uniforms. Here, I took some pictures."

She pulled up the photos and handed him the phone. He scrolled through them slowly.

"Someone was seriously talented," he agreed.

He stopped at one particular drawing, a close-up of a woman's head and shoulders. Her long hair was blowing across her face and she had her left hand up, trying to hold it out of her eyes. She was not a classical beauty, but her face had character. The unknown artist had captured, with his pencil, a depth of sorrow and compassion in her eyes and a kind of gentle strength.

Death frowned. "I know I've seen this woman somewhere before."

"What? Where?"

"I don't know." He thought about it. "It wasn't this angle, exactly, but it was this pose, with her hand up by her face. She was holding something in her other hand, I think."

"Yes! A ladle. Look at some of the other sketches. She had a bucket of water at her feet and she was offering the soldiers drinks from a ladle."

"How do you know it's water?" Death joked, scrolling back through the photos. "If the soldiers are drinking it, it's more likely to be booze."

One corner of Wren's mouth turned down. "They're grouped around a well," she said drily.

"Okay. Point." He handed her phone back. "Sorry. I know I've seen her, but I can't place where."

"This looks to me like a study for a painting. Could you have seen that painting somewhere? Did you go into any parts of the Hadleigh House that I haven't been in yet?"

"I might have seen the painting. I've barely been in the house, though, so it would have had to be somewhere else. Hey! Maybe it's a famous painting and I saw it in a book or a museum or something. If you found the sketches for a famous painting, that would really be something, wouldn't it?"

"Yeah! That would be amazing! I'll ask Doris. She's our art expert. If it's a well-known painting, she'll recognize it for sure."

FIVE

THE BEDROOM WINDOW CAME up with a long, rusty creak, the swollen wooden frame stiff in its sill. Wren had already raised the window on the north wall. Opening the one on the east gave the room a cross breeze. The east windows opened above the roof of the kitchen ell. Squirrels played in the oak trees that loomed over the old slate shingles and a loose section of guttering squeaked rhythmically in the breeze.

Looking out across the back of the property, she could see the camp for wounded veterans off to her left. The abandoned church was out of sight behind a grove of trees, only its steeple showing, but the graveyard spread across the opposite hillside, tombstones and monuments shining in the sun.

Most of the trees were still a dark, summer green, but a few of the maples had begun to blaze into orange and russet. There were stands of scarlet sumac along the fence rows and autumn lay gold on the long grass. It occurred to Wren that the scene she was seeing would have changed very little, autumn to autumn, in the last hundred years.

She was in the room across from where she'd found the drawing pad two days earlier. There was no closet—old houses rarely had them because in the 1800s closets were taxed—and the antique wardrobe that served the same purpose would bring a good price at auction. The clothing she'd cleared out of it had been unremarkable: men's dark work pants and white cotton button-down shirts, a black suit that was probably from the '30s or '40s, and two pairs of shoes. One pair was dress shoes, barely worn, with rounded toes and a polish that remained under the layer of dust. The other pair was sturdy and serviceable, well-worn but also well cared for. They would sell the clothing as a lot, and it would bring very little. It was possible that no one would bid on it at all. If they didn't, Wren would buy it for a dollar or two and donate it to the local thrift shops.

A small dresser stood next to the window, another nice antique. The drawers were filled with undergarments and she put them aside to be disposed of. It reminded her of the afternoon earlier in the summer when she'd been doing this same thing with Randy's belongings. At the time, when they'd thought he was dead, she had taken on the heartbreaking task of getting rid of his clothes to spare Death having to do it.

Fortunately, they'd found him before she'd taken the majority of his things to Goodwill. She remembered, with wry amusement, the embarrassment of admitting to Randy that she'd thrown away all his underwear.

On the top of the dresser was a lamp, an old wind-up alarm clock that still kept time when she set it, and a pair of horn-rimmed spectacles with dust-coated lenses. There was also a brown pill bottle and she picked it up eagerly, but it had been sitting in the sun and the name had long since faded from the label.

The sound of a door opening reached her and she froze, tilting her head and holding her breath. She half expected her mysterious dead artist to come in demanding to know what she was doing with his things.

"Yoo hoo! Wren! I know you're in here!"

She relaxed and called back, "I'm up here, Doris! Hang on. I'm coming down."

She hurried down the hall and stopped at the top of the grand staircase. Sam's wife, wearing a flowered dress and a white sun hat and carrying a takeout bag from a local sub shop, waited in the formal entryway. Wren gave her a cheerful wave and slid down the curving bannister to join her.

"That looks like fun," the older lady said. "I'll have to come back and try it when I'm not dressed up." She held up the takeout bag. "I thought we could have lunch together. Sam said you found some artwork you wanted to show me. Besides, I've always wanted to see the inside of this place."

"Lunch sounds great. Let's eat in the dining room. What I found is an artist's sketch pad with a study for a painting, I think. I'll show you while we eat."

The big table in the dining room was stacked with books and glassware, but Wren was able to push it together enough to clear off a corner. Doris set out the sandwiches and chips and a stack of napkins while Wren fetched cans of soda from the cooler she'd brought with her. Because she was always conscious of protecting the antiques she worked with, she also took two cheap cork coasters from a mesh bag tied to the cooler handles.

Before she sat down, Wren ran back into the parlor and got the sketch pad. Doris set her sandwich aside to take the pad and flipped carefully through it.

"Oh, my," she said. "This is just gorgeous."

"Does it look like anything you've seen before?"

"The whole of it, no," Doris said thoughtfully. "But this—" She indicated the central figure, moving her finger as if she were tapping the drawing but taking care not to touch the paper. "I know I've seen this woman before."

"Really? Where?"

Doris sighed, closed the drawing pad, and set it aside. "I haven't the faintest idea."

They dug into their sandwiches. While they ate, the older woman looked around, taking in the furnishings and architecture.

"I've always wondered what it looked like in here."

"Yes." Wren nodded. "You said that before."

"You know I grew up in this neighborhood?"

"No, I never knew that."

"My father's farm is off that way." She tipped her head, pointing her chin back toward the southwest. "My oldest brother lives there now."

"Is that Billy? The one with all the daughters?"

"Indeed." She laughed. "He's jealous of me because he wanted a son and I'm jealous of him because I always wanted a girl." She took another bite of her sandwich and patted her mouth daintily with the corner of her napkin. "We used to walk right along that path outside the fence on our way to church when I was a child."

"The Dead Guy Path?"

"Well, we never called it that, of course, but yes. We called it the Vengeance Trail and had great fun scaring ourselves with ghost stories. Especially if we were walking it in the dark, if there was an evening program at church for example. Or in the gloom of winter, when the sun came up late and night came early. And then, of course, we'd have to walk past 'the gravedigger's house'!"

"The gravedigger's house?"

"That's what we called this place. There was an old man who lived here all alone. He always wore a black suit to church on Sunday and he rarely spoke to anyone. Everyone referred to him as the gravedigger. I don't know if he was, really, or if it was just us kids being morbid. Because he lived so close to the cemetery, you see?"

"I wonder if he could have been my artist. I don't suppose you remember his name?"

Doris sighed and shook her head. "Honestly, I don't know if I ever even knew his name."

"Would it be in the church records, maybe? I wonder what happened to them when the church was deserted? And how did it get deserted, anyway?"

"Sam and I left after we got married and moved into town."

"I figured that."

"Well, it wasn't just that, exactly. We were married in that church, you know? And we honestly never thought of leaving. For the first couple of years of our marriage, we drove out here every Sunday."

"What happened?"

"We switched to Northside Baptist after my cousin, Chloe, married the pastor."

"Your cousin's married to the pastor at Northside Baptist? I didn't know that."

"No, dear. My cousin married the pastor here."

"Oh." Wren frowned down at the tabletop. "I don't understand."

"Chloe is, how shall I put this? A difficult woman. She was always difficult, even as a child. When the rest of us were in Sunday school singing 'Jesus Loves Me,' Chloe was singing 'Jesus Loves Me Best.' She marries the pastor and all of a sudden, in her mind, she's the lady of the manor and we're all her vassals."

"Ah. I think I see."

"The last time I came to church here was for a work day, to get things ready for the church bazaar. It was supposed to be a committee meeting, but instead Chloe was handing out assignments. 'You're going to do that and you're going to do this and I'm going to give everyone a list of exactly what I expect them to bring to the bake sale.' Well, several of us took exception to her attitude. She just laughed, real condescending, and said, 'A flock has to do what its shepherd says. My husband is the shepherd of this flock, so obviously that makes me the queen bee.' I said, 'Yes dear. And I think we all know just exactly what that B stands for!' And I left, and the next Sunday Sam and I started looking for a new church."

"So is that what happened, then?" Wren asked. "Cousin Chloe drove everybody away and the church had to close?"

"Well, she certainly didn't help matters any. Sam and I weren't the only ones who left because of her, and it was a small congregation to begin with. In the late seventies or early eighties a big storm came through and damaged the roof. When they started looking at it, they found a lot of wood rot and other structural problems and they simply couldn't come up with the funds to fix it. I'll admit, it makes me sad seeing it standing there in disrepair. I spent a lot of happy hours there as a girl."

"I'm sorry."

"Oh, sweetie. It's okay. Things have to change. Time does march on. It always has and always will."

"Do you have any idea what became of the church records when it closed?"

"No, I don't. Chloe might know. I hate to have to contact her, but I suppose since it's for a good cause, I could bite the bullet and call the old bee."

They finished their meal in a pensive silence. Wren was fighting a yawn and thinking she needed more caffeine when Doris spoke again, suddenly.

"He died, you know."

"Hmm? What?"

"The gravedigger. The man we called the gravedigger. He died, you know."

"Yeah, I kind of figured he must have."

"No, what I mean is, I remember when he died. It was while I was in grade school. The whole church turned out for his funeral. If we walked over to the churchyard, I bet I could find approximately where he's buried. If we look for a grave of an old man with no close family who died in the mid-sixties, maybe we could find his name that way."

"Doris! That's a great idea!"

"Well, come on then! Let's go right now!"

At the side of the dining room, a French door opened onto a cobbled terrace. Wren glanced out and noted a few dark clouds rolling in from the west.

"It looks like it might rain," she said. "Let me run up and close the windows first just in case."

They tidied up quickly, stuffing their trash back into the bag the sandwiches had come in, and then Wren ran up the stairs and down the hall to the room where she'd been working. The window in the north wall was stubborn and she had to wrestle it down. The east window went down easily and she stood for a moment, her hands still on the top of the windowsill, looking out across the countryside.

Off in the distance she could see a gray Jeep driving up the driveway to the vets' camp. It stopped outside the main cluster of buildings and a pair of familiar figures climbed out.

Wren smiled to herself. She and Doris would pass by there on their way to the cemetery. Maybe they could collect some help in their search. In any case, they were going to see Death and Randy shortly.

Death always brightened her day.

———

Warriors' Rest was nestled in a slight dip between the hill with the Hadleigh house and the hill with the old church. A tidy office building stood at the head of the driveway. Death could see half a dozen tiny, rustic cabins scattered back in among the trees, and trails leading off into the underbrush suggested that there were more out of sight. He parked his Jeep between a sedan and a motorcycle on the gravel parking area, slid out from behind the wheel, and stood looking around.

Randy got out on his own side, yawned hugely, and stretched his long arms up toward the blue sky.

"You wouldn't be tired if you hadn't stayed up half the night texting your girlfriend," Death teased.

"She's not my girlfriend," Randy said. "She's just a girl. Who's a friend."

"Sure she is."

"Mind your own beeswax."

"I love the way you've matured so well."

A high-pitched, inhuman scream interrupted their witty repartee.

"Was that a horse?" Randy asked.

"There." Death pointed. "It came from that old barn."

The barn sat away from the office and cabins, inside a pasture ringed with the same shoulder-high fencing they'd run into in the woods the day they'd met Kurt Robinson. Death and Randy made a dash for the structure as another terrified whinny split the air.

Randy outpaced his brother easily, to Death's dismay, but Death caught up as he was wrestling with the heavy board that secured the barn doors. He slid it aside and pulled the doors open and the two men stood for a second, blinking into the darkness and waiting for their eyes to adjust.

The main section of the barn was maybe nine feet in height, with a wide corridor separating a series of work and storage rooms on the left from the half dozen or so stalls that lined the right-hand wall. Sugar, the big gray horse that Death had fed apples to, was in the corridor facing them, fighting against a thin, scrawny man who was trying to force him into one of the stalls. The horse reared back, hooves flailing at the air. His nostrils were flared and he rolled his eyes in terror.

The man, just a silhouette standing with his back to them, cursed at the horse and slapped it in the nose, hard. Death recognized the voice.

"Blount? What the hell are you doing here and what do you think you're doing to that horse?"

"You know this guy?" Randy asked.

"Oh yeah," Death said grimly. "I've picked him up a couple of times when he's jumped bail." In addition to his work as a private eye, Death Bogart was a part-time bounty hunter.

"Well, I ain't jumped bail this time," Blount said, still fighting the horse. "I'm right where I'm supposed to be and what I'm doing is none of your damned business, so just get the hell out and leave me alone."

Death hadn't heard anyone else come in, so he jumped slightly when an angry female voice came from behind him.

"Hey! Weasel! What the hell are you doing with that horse?"

At the sound of the woman's voice, Blount cringed, loosened his hold on the reins, and turned, shoulders hunched and chin thrust out defiantly. "I'm putting him back in his damned stall where he belongs."

"Who told you to do that?"

"Nobody told me. I'm taking the initiative."

A young woman pushed her way between Death and Randy and stormed forward to confront the petty criminal. "You don't get 'initiative'! You do what I tell you to and nothing else, do you understand?"

He muttered petulantly under his breath.

"What was that?"

"Yes! I said yes, okay?"

The horse was edging back, pulling at the extent of its lead and clearly anxious to escape the barn. Death, who knew fear and anxiety a little too well himself, made so bold as to tug the reins loose and lead the horse to the other end of the barn, where another open door led into a fenced paddock. Once outside, Sugar stopped in the middle of the yard, his flanks heaving. He was trembling. Death ran a hand down the animal's neck, marveling at the sleek feel and the underlying muscles, and Sugar moved close and draped his head over Death's shoulder.

The other three followed them out. Blount and the woman were still arguing.

"Well, I'm the one that has to go lugging feed and water out to him and there ain't no sense in it. And it's one more place that I gotta shovel horse crap out of. Make him go back in his stall where he belongs, and if he won't then you oughta just shoot him. Damned old bastard's crazy anyway. Always fighting me all the time!"

"He's not crazy. He just doesn't like you because you're an ass. Now get the hell out of here and don't let me catch you messing with him again."

Blount stomped off across the paddock and Death studied the woman while she watched him go. She was just a little bit taller than Wren, fit and muscular, with dark brown skin and a head full of short, tight curls. She wore shorts and a tank top and a bright prosthetic that took the place of her missing lower left leg.

"There's a reason Sugar doesn't like that guy," she said, turning around. She saw Death hugging the big stallion and smiled. "He likes you, though."

"He's nice," Death said. "I've never been this close to a horse before." He hooked a thumb toward Blount's retreating back. "What's he even doing here?"

"Community service," she said drily. "Lucky us." She studied Death, tipped her head. "So, what can we do for you, Jarhead?"

"Death Bogart. This is my brother Randy. We were looking for Kurt Robinson."

"That's my husband. He's not here right now. He had to run into town. I'm Nichelle, by the way."

"Like the lady from *Star Trek*?"

"Yes, I was named after her."

Death gave the horse a final pat and turned to offer her his hand. She shook hands with him and with Randy, and then took Sugar's halter off and opened a gate to release him into a pasture.

"So what branch of the service were you in?" Death asked.

"Corps of Engineers. You're the detective, aren't you? Are you here about Tony? Have you seen him? Is he doing okay? I mean, as okay as he can be. You know?"

"Yeah. I think he's doing as well as can be expected. You know him pretty well?"

"He's my husband's best friend. He and Zahra and Kurt and I had a double wedding. Tony's family."

"What do you think of all this?"

"I think it's crazy." She turned and led the way back to the barn. Again they had to stop and let their eyes adjust from the bright sunlight. "I can't believe he killed someone. I guess a part of me doesn't believe it. I would have said that I was more likely to fly into a homicidal rage than Tony was."

The first five stalls they passed each held a horse facing the wall, tails swishing idly as the humans walked past. At the far end of the barn, next to the door that Death and Randy had first entered by, the last stall stood open and empty.

Randy stopped beside it. "Is this the stall that Sugar was in when the dead guy stole him?"

"Yeah, and now he won't go back in. Absolutely panics if you try to make him. Poor guy must have been really traumatized."

Death stepped inside the small enclosure and looked around with interest. "This seems like pretty small quarters for such a big horse."

"Yeah, we don't normally keep them in the stalls. We just bring them in to feed them and groom them. They were only in that night because there was a severe thunderstorm in the forecast."

"Do storms bother horses?" Randy asked.

"Not so much, but they bother Kurt. Reminds him of being under fire. He feels like he needs to protect everyone and everything around him."

Randy gave her a sad half smile and stepped a little closer. Death ignored them both and studied the stall.

The barn was sturdy but the wood it was built from belied its age. It was old oak, dried by the years so that the sap had sunk away and the grain stood out in ridges like a topographical map. The stall itself was about five feet wide and eight feet long, not counting the manger against the wall. Since it was in the corner, it was darker than the rest of the room. Broad, thick planks separated it from the next stall over.

A contraption of leather straps and silvery bits hung from a wooden peg on the wall, and a shelf above the manger held an assortment of arcane tools and an empty beer can.

"Could you put one of the other horses in this stall and give Sugar theirs?" Randy asked.

"We tried that," Nichelle said. "None of them will come near it without putting up a fight. Look at Dolly, in the next stall. See? She's staying as far from this corner as she can." She rubbed her upper arms as if she were cold. "To be honest, I'm not too crazy about this stall myself. I can't quite put my finger on it, but something about it just gives me the heebie jeebies."

As she spoke, the hair rose on the back of Death's neck. Randy made a strangled sound and pointed, and Death turned around.

On the shelf above the manger, the empty beer can was moving of its own accord.

Death stepped closer and leaned in to look. The can jittered and bounced in fits and starts, dancing toward the edge of the shelf. There were no wires and nothing he could see to account for the phenomenon. Besides the beer can, the shelf held a device that looked like a large ice pick, a silvery metal doodad he didn't recognize, a circular comb with metal teeth and a heavy wooden handle, and an old horseshoe.

Nothing was moving but the can. It skipped to the edge and toppled over, bounced once, and lay rocking in the dust.

"What would make it do that?" Randy asked.

"Wasp in the can?" Death suggested. "It could have been attracted to the residue in the bottom."

"Great. I'm allergic to bee stings. Maybe we should go outside now," Nichelle suggested with just the faintest quaver in her voice.

Death backed out of the stall and swung it closed. The three of them strolled back out of the old barn in the carefully casual manner of people who did not run unless there was a damned good reason.

"My girlfriend is afraid of bees," Death said, "but she won't kill them because they're important for the environment. So if she sees one, she tiptoes and tries to stay out of its line of sight, on the theory that if it can't see her it won't sting her."

"And speak of the devil," Randy exclaimed.

Death followed his brother's gaze. Up and to the southwest, the Hadleigh House sat half-hidden behind the trees, silhouetted against a bank of dark clouds that hadn't yet reached the skies above the valley. Two figures were making their way down the slope. Death recognized Doris Keystone but he had eyes only for Wren, who was smiling at him as she waded through waist-high wildflowers with the sun in her hair.

SIX

"Fennel … Griffith … Arnold … Zelling …"

Nichelle had sent them off down a bridle path that skirted the corner of the pasture and led them to the edge of the cemetery. They'd climbed over a short, sagging fence and hopped across a narrow stream that ran through a gully at the back of the burial ground. A row of tombs lined the hillside above the creek, looking like macabre little houses with iron doors and windows protected by wrought-iron grills.

Randy was reading the names on the tombs as they passed.

"Those things give me the creeps," Wren said. "What if you looked in one of the windows and something looked back?"

"Just think of them as hobbit holes," Randy suggested.

"Oh, yay. Dead hobbits. That's okay. I didn't want to sleep tonight anyway."

"So, if those are hobbit holes," Death said with a sly look at his brother, "would that make this creek the Brandywine?"

Death and Randy's mother had been a literature professor. Randy's real name was Baranduin, from Tolkien. It was the Elvish name of the Brandywine river.

"You hush," Randy said.

"And again with the snappy comeback!"

Randy blew his brother a raspberry and strode ahead. "There's a staircase here leading up to the rest of the cemetery." He leaned down to examine it. "Um, it looks like the steps are made out of old tombstones?"

"They are," Doris said. "When the lake came in, there were several cemeteries that had to be emptied and the bodies relocated. Of course, with a lot of the really old graves, there was nothing left of the bodies. If the stones were legible, they put them in other cemeteries, but there were a bunch left over. It seemed callous to throw them away, so someone came up with the bright idea of using them for landscaping. I'm not sure myself that it was a right and respectful solution, but that's what was done nonetheless."

If the slope had been less steep, Wren would have climbed it instead of the stairs. As it was, she contented herself with whispering "sorry" on each step. There were a dozen steps and she knew, by the way Death was grinning at her when they got to the top, that he'd heard.

"Now just let me think," Doris said. She turned around, putting the abandoned church behind her as she got her bearings. "As I recall, it was in the spring. It was the first funeral I'd ever been to, you know. I was only allowed to attend because I was in the choir and we sang for the service."

"What did you sing?" Wren asked, interested.

"Oh, heavens! I haven't any idea. 'Amazing Grace,' probably. I remember standing with the choir against a bank of lilacs in bloom."

They looked around. There was an abundance of lilacs.

"It was over this way, I think," Doris said, and led the way off to her left. They were coming up on the northern edge of the burial ground, which was bordered by a deep, overgrown ditch that separated the cemetery from a narrow gravel road. "This is the older part, but I think there was a family plot here where we buried him."

The stones in this part of the cemetery were mostly white, dulled with age, and not at all uniform and shiny like the stones in the newer sections. Here and there a wrought-iron fence or a barrier of low landscaping stones separated a group of graves from the others. Larger stones and obelisks were engraved with family names.

In the northeast corner, a life-sized angel, balanced on one bare foot on a pedestal, looked away from them, off across the road. She was positioned to face the rising sun, her wings furled against her back. Her left hand was up by her face, and in her outstretched right hand she held a ladle.

Wren felt chills run up and down her spine.

The angel stood in a plot of land that was set off by waist-high square plinths at the corners, each engraved with the letter *H*. Wren circled around to where she could see the statue from the front. Doris and the Bogart brothers followed her.

"Of course!" Doris breathed. "That's where I've seen her before!"

"It wasn't a painting—it was a study for a sculpture," Wren said. "The girl with the ladle is the angel he carved for his grave."

———

"I still want to know who she was. She must have been someone important to him. And if he was only going to carve a statue, why did he draw out the entire scene in his sketch pad?"

Wren and Death were back at Hadleigh House. Doris had returned to town, and Randy was out in one of the sheds with Robin Keystone, looking at the classic car the teenager had discovered. Wren was sitting at the dining room table, packing dishes and books into sturdy boxes to make it easier to carry them into the yard when the day of the auction arrived.

"Did you check to see if he's on your list of World War One vets?" Death asked, lounging in an old recliner by the window.

"I didn't have to. I remember seeing him on it," Wren replied. The gravedigger's name was Aramis Defoe. "He must have been a Hadleigh on his mother's side."

"Then that explains who the angel was. She was a woman who gave him water when he was tired and wounded."

"But he must have been in love with her. I mean, he carved her image as the angel for his grave."

"They were in a war together. When you're under fire with someone, being afraid together and working together to try to survive, that can forge a powerful bond."

"Oh." Wren studied the table's dusty surface, fingering it like a piano, and asked in a carefully casual tone, "So, did you ever have an experience like that with anyone?"

Death studied her profile with a slight smile. "Well, there was this one woman."

"Oh?"

"Yeah. I was at her house this one time, working on a project with her. I hardly even knew her at the time. But then some guy came up and started shooting at us. And then I got kidnapped and she came for me, and then she got kidnapped and I went for her. And then she helped me find my brother ... "

Wren turned then and looked at him, and her eyes were shining in the shadowed room. Death thought of Anthony Dozier and how he'd found his own angel, Zahra. He'd saved her and she'd saved him. And he'd married her and brought her safely out of the war zone and then lost her anyway.

He rose and went to Wren, pulled her up, and wrapped her in his arms. She returned the embrace. They clung together, and he let himself be reassured by the rise and fall of her breathing and the feel of her heartbeat against his chest.

And then Randy strolled back in.

"Death and Wren-nie! Sittin' in a tree! K-I-S-S-I-N-G!"

Death released his girlfriend and stepped back, blinking the moisture from his own eyes. "I wonder what he's going to be when he grows up?"

"Do you think he is going to grow up?"

"It could happen."

"Ha ha," Randy said. "You're hilarious. I guess you're not interested in what we found out back then?"

"Not another 'legless lizard,' I hope?" Death caught Wren's puzzled look. "When he was about six he caught a garter snake that he thought was a legless lizard. He smuggled it home and tried to keep it for a pet, but it got loose. Mom was less than happy when she found it."

"Yeah." Randy gave his brother a suspicious glare. "I'd still like to know how it got in her underwear drawer."

"It was a snake! It slithered!"

"The drawer was closed."

"It crawled in from the back. I keep telling you. It wasn't me! I swear."

"Sure you do."

"I'm sorry," Wren said, "but are you two really arguing about something that happened twenty years ago?"

The brothers looked at one another and then back at her, questioningly.

"Yeah."

"Yeah."

"Okay then ... " She sighed and went back to her packing.

"So you found something?" Death prompted.

"Oh, yeah. We found your sculptor's workshop. It's in one of the old sheds out back. Blocks of stone, broken and partly finished statues, chisels, hammers. That isn't the creepy part, though."

"There had to be a creepy part," Wren lamented. "Why does there always have to be a creepy part?"

"What's the creepy part?"

"Tombstones."

"Tombstones?"

"Yeah. Seems old Aramis liked to make tombstones. There are about a dozen in there, all blank. Well, not blank. They have birds and animals and religious images. Just no names or dates on any of them."

"That's not so creepy," Death countered. "He was a stonemason. He made funerary monuments."

After finding his tombstone, with his name and death date, they'd been able to locate Aramis' obituary. He'd been remembered as a talented stonemason and a dedicated member of his church, but the space usually devoted to surviving loved ones was achingly empty.

"What about the other statues?" Wren asked. "The broken and partly finished ones?"

"What about them?"

"Were any of them the angel? Or the soldiers from the drawing?"

"I don't think so, but I don't think you can really tell. None of them were finished enough that you could see any details. Does it matter?"

"I suppose not. It's just…"

"She's curious," Death said with a grin. "She's just curious. Truth to be told, I'm curious myself."

"Oh?"

"Yeah. You know how Doris recognized the girl in the drawing, but she didn't know where she'd seen her before?"

"Until she saw the statue." Wren nodded. "Then she remembered. She'd seen her in the cemetery."

"Right. Well, as I said, I'm absolutely positive that I've seen the girl in the picture before too, but this was the first time I've ever been in that cemetery."

"You could probably see her from the road, driving by," Randy said.

"I couldn't have. I'm not real familiar with this part of the county. I'd never even been out here until we came out with Wren to look at this house, and I've never driven down that road. But I've seen that woman. I just don't know where."

———

"October 4th, 2011! The Hawkins estate! 211 East Wilson Street!"

Deputy Jackson stood in the middle of Wren's living room with his hands on his hips and beamed at them. Randy carefully closed the door behind him and tiptoed around the officer, deliberately giving him a wide berth as he returned to his place on the floor. It was a little after seven p.m. that same evening. Madeline had feigned offense, but ultimately she'd taken Death up on his offer to babysit.

The two brothers were sitting in the middle of Wren's throw rug playing trucks with Benji.

Wren was curled up in an armchair with a sack of clothes she'd gotten at a yard sale and a book bag full of craft supplies, turning odd socks into sock puppets. She looked up at Jackson with interest. "Is this some kind of Kabuki theater or something?"

Death shot her an amused grin. "Kabuki theater?"

She shrugged. "Well, I've heard of Kabuki theater but I don't know what it actually is. So I thought maybe it was walking into a room full of people and shouting out random things with no explanation."

Jackson shook his head and glared at them.

"October 4th, 2011!" he said again. "211 East Wilson Street! The Hawkins estate!"

"Maybe we should call someone with a butterfly net," Randy suggested.

"Actually, I think Wren has one," Death told him. "It's out on the back porch."

"I got it at an auction," she agreed. "But I don't know when or where."

"Maybe it was October 4th, 2011, at 211 East Wilson Street."

Orly plopped onto the couch uninvited and waved his hand at them, disgusted. "I found the auction where you sold the uniform that the dead man was wearing."

"Yeah," Death said. "We figured that was what you were talking about."

"So why the comedy routine?"

"You're just so cute when you're angry," Wren grinned.

Death peered at her suspiciously. "Cute how?"

"Cute like a snarly puppy. Not at all cute like a sexy Marine." She and Death beamed at each other and Randy started softly chanting the "sitting in a tree" song to himself again.

"Will you clowns be serious?" Jackson exclaimed. "I'm trying to identify a dead man here."

"Yes, we know that," Wren said patiently. "We just don't know what you expect us to do. Leona already told you, we don't keep records going back that far."

"Well, then, what am I supposed to do with this information? You—" He turned on Death, who was busy helping Benji build a mountain out of throw pillows. "You're the one who suggested I track down the auction where it was sold. I've spent hours looking through old newspapers to find this. Now that I have it, how does it help me?"

Death scooted back against the sofa and pulled Benji into his lap, giving himself time to think. He didn't really want to admit to the deputy that he'd only suggested that line of investigation to get rid of him.

"Now you need to find out who bought a Civil War uniform at that time."

"Which is why I'm here asking you. Or, rather, asking Wren."

"But Wren doesn't know and neither do the Keystones. So you need to look somewhere else."

"I don't have anywhere else to look!"

"Where would you look?" Wren asked Death, interested. "If you were actually working this case and not just being pestered to do it for free?"

He grinned up at her. "I'd ask myself what I would have done if I'd been the one who bought it. Think about it. You're a Civil War collector and you just bought an authentic, actually-worn-by-a-Civil-War-soldier uniform. What's the first thing you're going to do?"

"Brag about it," Randy said.

Wren's voice overlapped his. "Authenticate it."

"You already authenticated it," Randy objected.

"But he would want to double check, make sure I knew what I was doing and not just making stuff up to get him to bid on it. Actually"—she turned to Jackson—"you know where I'd show that picture? I'd take it up to NARA."

"NARA ... that was ... ?"

"The National Archives and Records Administration. There's a branch up in Kansas City. And that uniform wouldn't have gone cheap. Whoever bought it spent some serious cash on it. And if he was that big a history buff, there's a good chance he spent a lot of time doing research. Some of the librarians might know who he is. Also, a lot of history buffs are into genealogy. You know? Tracing down which of their ancestors served in what regiment on which side and all? The largest genealogy research facility in America is up in Independence."

"Of course," Death cautioned, "being the largest in America means it's going to be a busy place. But there's still a chance that someone might know who he is. Was. Especially if he acted eccentric."

"Huh." Jackson considered their advice, then turned to Randy. "Brag about it where?"

"Online. Where else? Check social media sites. Especially look for places where Civil War fanatics hang out."

"You know, the dead guy had to have gotten that uniform from the church cemetery," Death said. "Nothing else makes sense."

"I know it seems that way, but I searched that cemetery myself. And I talked to the cemetery board and the gravedigger. There have only been a half dozen funerals there in the last year, and four of them were women. I tracked down the families of the two men and both of them were buried in ordinary clothes."

"Did you check on the women?" Wren asked. "A woman could have been buried in a Confederate cavalry uniform too."

He sighed. "I didn't track them down, no. But I did look at their graves and none of them showed any signs of being tampered with."

"Maybe it was an old grave. It would be marginally less icky to take a uniform off a skeleton and put it on than it would to take a uniform off of a decomposing corpse and put it on."

Jackson was shaking his head. "The forensic labs say no. If the fabric had been buried more than a month or so it would have started to decay."

"How did the dead guy get to the cemetery anyway?" Wren asked. "That's what I wonder. It's not like he could take a bus. He could have walked, I suppose, but it would have been a really long walk for a really old man. So either he left his car somewhere or else someone drove him out there."

"That's a good point," Jackson admitted. "Hey! Didn't I hear one of the Keystone kids talking about finding a car out in one of the outbuildings?"

"An old Impala," Randy said. "But that's not the one you're looking for. It's been there for years."

"Besides," Death put in, "the bridge over the creek was gone and there were saplings growing in the Hadleigh House driveway. He'd have had no way to get a car up there."

Randy looked around at the other three adults and lowered his voice like he was telling a ghost story around a campfire.

"Maybe," he said, "maybe he didn't steal the uniform from the body of a dead man. Maybe … he was the dead man!"

"Okay," Jackson said. "I know an idiotic theory when I hear it being born. I'm probably going to regret this, but go on. What you got?"

"Maaaybee," Randy said, "the uniform that Wren authenticated belonged to the actual Civil War soldier who was killed by his horse on the Vengeance Trail. When the current dead guy died and was buried in it, the ghost of the original dead guy raised him from beyond the grave so they could steal a horse and recreate the original dead guy's final ride."

SEVEN

"Sir, what's your business here?"

"What's yours?" Death countered.

The gravel parking area at Warriors' Rest was jammed with police vehicles. In addition to the Rives County Sheriff's Department, there were cars from East Bledsoe Ferry and from the Highway Patrol. There were also vehicles from Kansas City, almost a hundred miles away, which told Death that this had something to do with Anthony Dozier.

"Death? What brings you out here?"

"You know this guy?" the state trooper asked.

East Bledsoe Ferry chief of police Duncan Reynolds came over from the direction of the office building. He was stocky and solid, an older man, his black hair and eyebrows grizzled with silver. "Yeah, I know him. He's a friend."

Waving the younger officer away, Reynolds led Death back toward Death's Jeep.

"Aren't you a little out of your jurisdiction?" Death asked him.

"It's all hands on deck for a murder investigation." Reynolds waved his hand around, indicating the wide variety of police cars present. "I didn't know you were involved with this place," he said when they were alone. "Is it helping you any?"

Since returning from Afghanistan, Death had struggled with the aftermath. The euphoria of finding Randy alive had driven down the depression he'd been fighting, but he was still aware of its presence, lurking like a dark, tentacled monster under the surface of a sunny pond. Under certain circumstances stress could trigger frighteningly realistic flashbacks. He still tended towards hyper-vigilance and still sometimes imagined armed insurgents in glimpses out of the corner of his eye.

He was afraid to sleep in the same room with Wren after she'd tried to awaken him from a nightmare and he'd nearly broken her neck.

Reynolds was one of the few people Death had spoken frankly with about his problems. The older man reminded Death of his own grandfather. He was stolid and down-to-earth, listening without passing judgment and offering advice without condescending.

Death shook his head and waved away his friend's concerns.

"It's not like that," he said. "Kurt Robinson has asked me to help investigate the murder charges against Anthony Dozier."

"Ah." Reynolds nodded and glanced toward the office building.

Death followed his gaze. Through the window he could see the massive bulk of the Rives County sheriff, Casey "Salvy" Salvadore. Salvy was listening and nodding to someone. The big man looked unusually grave.

"Robinson called you?" Reynolds asked.

"No, Wren did. She's working up in the old Hadleigh House and she saw all the brouhaha from an upstairs window."

"Oh." Reynolds turned and waved at the distant plantation house and Death fired off a quick, jaunty salute in that direction himself.

"So," Death said, "search warrant?"

"Yep. KC brought it down and we're helping to execute it." Reynolds looked off to his right and Death saw an older officer standing beside one of the Kansas City police vehicles with a map spread out across the hood and a radio up to his mouth. A much smaller and, unfortunately, more familiar figure hovered right next to him.

"Farrington's out here? I thought he was just a jail guard."

"He is. The detective from the city force was rude to me, so I assigned Farrington to be his personal liaison."

"Wow. That's harsh."

"Never mess with a small-town cop. We know crazy people and we're not afraid to use them."

Death laughed and Reynolds leaned back against the Jeep's bumper, scrubbed one hand through his hair, and tipped his face up to the sky.

"The insanity plea isn't going to fly," he said reluctantly.

Death leaned against the car beside him and shoved his hands in his pockets. "You don't think?"

"I know you probably haven't been following the news too closely, what with the goings on with your brother and all. What have they told you about this case?"

Death shrugged. "Dozier's wife was killed in a car accident. The CAC protested at her funeral and Anthony clashed with some of them. The next day he was found in KC with the victim's dead body in his back seat. He thought he was back in the war zone."

"He *claims* he thought he was back in the war zone," Reynolds countered. "But there are a few things that don't add up. I'm guessing Robinson didn't brief you on the inconsistencies?"

"So enlighten me."

"Okay, well, first of all, when the CAC protested at Zahra Dozier's funeral, the victim wasn't with them. He hadn't been seen in public with the group in almost eight months, and during the interim he'd dyed his hair and grown a heavy beard. Dozier's confrontation at the funeral was with Tyler Jones, the victim's father. Even without the facial hair, there was very little resemblance between the two men, so how did Dozier know who August Jones even was?"

"Maybe August Jones confronted him separately?"

"Maybe. There's a bit more to it than that, though."

"Oh?"

"There's a very good chance that Dozier did know August Jones personally, though he may not have known who he was. We know for a fact that they'd met at least once."

Death tipped his head toward the police chief and raised one eyebrow.

"The reason August Jones hadn't been seen with the church lately," Reynolds said, "was because he was 'undercover.' Tyler Jones had sent his son to infiltrate a mosque up in the city, to do an expose on their 'ungodly depravity and dissolution.' His words, not mine."

"That's why August dyed his hair and grew a beard? He was trying to pass himself off as a Muslim?"

"No, he wasn't quite that stupid. The hair and beard were to conceal his identity, but he introduced himself as a journalist who was doing a story on religion in America. He'd been attending worship and interviewing the members for months."

"And I'm guessing Zahra Dozier was one of those members?"

"Yeah." Reynolds sighed. "I'm afraid so."

He took a moment to study the activity at the camp. Officers were going from building to building like a swarm of tan-clad bumblebees, returning to the senior officer's vehicle from time to time with bagged evidence of one sort or another.

"Look, the CAC are horrible people, and I'm not saying August didn't do something to push a grieving husband too far. But the insanity defense just doesn't hold water under the circumstances. I'm sorry to shoot down your theory."

"Oh, you're not shooting down my theory," Death said easily. "You're shooting down the defense attorney's theory. I already told her she was crazy."

Reynolds leaned away and looked up at Death, eyebrows raised. "Really?"

"Have you met Anthony Dozier?"

"No, have you?"

"Yeah, and there's no way in hell that man killed anyone."

Death waited for Reynolds to shoot him down, like everyone else involved in the case had, but the chief of police knew him better than most.

"So what do you reckon happened then?"

"Just what Dozier said happened. He found the victim beside the road and it triggered a flashback. He mistook the knife wounds for shrapnel, bandaged him up as best he could, and went looking for an army base."

Reynolds nodded a little, looking off to one side and pinching his lower lip.

"You're not calling me crazy. So far everyone else I've said this to has called me crazy."

"You're not crazy. And you're a pretty good judge of character. If you don't think Dozier killed anyone, I'm at least willing to entertain the idea. But do you think that Dozier could still be faking the flashback?"

"Why?"

"To cover for the real killer. There's a reason we're out here searching this property."

"What is it?"

"August Jones had a cell phone that he habitually used to record conversations. It wasn't registered under his name, so it took a while for the officer in charge of the investigation to find out about it. The battery is apparently dead now, but before it died they were able to ping the location."

"And?"

"And that cell phone is, or was, somewhere on this property."

"If I were you, I'd be taking a closer look at this guy," Eric Farrington said, giving Death a slantwise, suspicious leer.

"Why's that?" The Kansas City detective was named Stottlemeyer. He was a tall, clean-cut man in his mid-thirties with dark hair, strong Roman features, and a muscle jumping at the corner of his left eye. Death wondered if he'd always had that particular tic or if it was the result of having Eric Farrington follow him around for three hours.

"He's nuts. He's got that post-war trauma crap. You know, he pointed a gun at me. Right at my head. He's not stable at all."

"Really?" Stottlemeyer looked more closely at Death, reevaluating him as a possible suspect perhaps.

"He disarmed you after you pointed a gun at him," Reynolds corrected Farrington. "Besides, he was in St. Louis the night Jones was killed."

"You got any witnesses to support that?" Stottlemeyer asked Death.

Death shrugged. "The fire department and the police department and a bunch of television and newspaper reporters."

"There was an incident," Reynolds said shortly. "Google it. You finding anything out here?"

"Not so far. We're impounding the Robinsons' cell phones and electronics. The afternoon before the murder, someone called Jones from an unregistered cell phone. We haven't been able to trace the phone itself, but the call originated from a cell phone tower less than five miles from here. And the last time we pinged Jones' phone before the battery died, it showed up somewhere in those woods." He pointed past the stable and pasture, to the woods that separated the camp from Hadleigh House.

"But you haven't found it?"

"Not yet. We have dogs on the way."

Even as he spoke, a vehicle drove up. A middle-aged man and a teenage girl got out and opened the back door to release a pair of long-nosed bloodhounds. The man turned to meet them as they walked up and offered his hand to Stottlemeyer.

"I got a call that you needed a couple of extra noses on the job?"

Death squatted in front of the dogs. "They do have noses, all right! Is it okay if I pet them?"

"Yes, certainly. That's Sherlock on your left and Mycroft on the right."

"Tell them *your* name, Dad," the girl urged, grinning.

The dog handler rolled his eyes. "Hi. I'm John Watson."

Death looked up at him, eyebrows raised. "Really?"

"What? It's not that unusual a name, you know. This brat is my daughter, Penny, by the way."

"I appreciate your coming on such short notice," Stottlemeyer said.

"You didn't just bring in a K-9 unit?" Death asked.

"We're looking for the site of Jones' murder," Stottlemeyer said. "A corpse will always leave behind traces. Blood and bodily fluids. These are special dogs, trained specifically to search for humans or human remains."

"They are indeed," the handler agreed. "And bloodhounds have the most sensitive noses in the animal kingdom. They can detect a body in a running stream or buried under ten feet of concrete. Though I should warn you that the boys are still pretty young and not entirely trained yet. They're excellent at finding things, just not so good at differentiating between different sorts of targets. Shouldn't be a problem, though, as long as you haven't had any extra dead bodies lying around recently,."

Death and Reynolds exchanged a look.

"That could be a problem, actually."

———

"No, they did great," Reynolds was saying as they walked back toward Warriors' Rest. The two young bloodhounds led the way, pulling at their leashes and sniffing the underbrush eagerly. The chief walked behind them with Watson and his daughter, while Stottlemeyer, still trailed by Eric Farrington, stomped along in their wake.

Death was waiting for them beside his Jeep. Watson looked glum, his daughter looked creeped out, and Stottlemeyer looked like he'd been sucking on lemons.

"Let me guess," Death said. "They found where the dead guy fell off his horse?"

"Went right to it," Reynolds agreed. "We tried taking them through the woods, but they just kept going back there."

"That wasn't part of our search warrant," Farrington piped up, as if Death had challenged them. "But once the dogs alerted on the woods, we had probable cause to enter the property."

Death ignored him. "Considering what the dead guy was wearing, there must be enough residue there for it to stink to high heaven for these guys. Don't tell Wren I said that, though."

"Wren?" Stottlemeyer asked.

"My girlfriend."

"The redhead who waved at us from the house up there," Reynolds added.

"She live there? Have we talked to her?"

"She works for an auction company," Death explained. "They're getting the house ready for a sale. I don't like to remind her of the dead guy on the path. Wren gets creeped out by dead guys."

"I can think of at least one guy who'd be less creepy if he were dead," Penny muttered with a dark look at Eric.

"And there my Wren would agree with you," Death said with a grin.

"We're going to find that phone," Stottlemeyer said. "I've been holding off on sending searchers into the woods because I didn't want to confuse things for the dogs, but that'll be the next step. We'll set up a grid pattern. We're not going to stop until we have something."

A state trooper came out the near door of the stable and immediately both young bloodhounds set to baying. Stottlemeyer perked up and nodded at Watson to let the dogs proceed.

Death and Chief Reynolds exchanged a look and tagged along after them.

The stables were empty—the horses had all been turned out into the pasture. The dogs stopped and alerted at the entrance to the first stall.

"This looks promising," Stottlemeyer said.

"Do you want to tell him or shall I?" Death asked.

"Tell me what?"

Reynolds sighed. "You know the dead guy on the path? The one who fell off a horse? Well, this is the stall that he stole the horse out of."

"Well, God damn!"

Watson leaned down to pet his hounds and let them pull him into the stable. They were fixated on an object on the floor.

A can.

A beer can.

"What do you bet my dead guy is the one who left that there?" Reynolds asked.

"You know what?" Farrington broke in excitedly. "I bet if we took that can in, we could get his fingerprints off it and run them to find out who he was."

The chief gave him a weary side glance.

"We have his fingerprints, Eric. We have his body. His fingerprints are on his fingers, which are part of his body."

"Oh. I didn't think about that."

EIGHT

"This is the best thing I've ever found for insect bites, provided you're not allergic and you're just looking for something to take away the sting."

"Yeah. I think I've used it before." Kurt Robinson stuck his hands in his pockets and leaned against the front of his desk, watching Randy Bogart pack supplies into the camp's first aid kit. "I do appreciate your help with this."

"Hey, man. Anything I can do, I'm glad to do it."

"Well, we thank you."

Randy closed the box and set it back on its shelf, and for a long moment the two men lingered in a not-entirely-comfortable silence. It was the morning after the police search and Robinson's office had been put back in order, but the empty space where a computer should sit and the presence of a new, cheap cell phone showed that his life was still far from normal.

"So, I understand you've had a pretty weird last year or so," Robinson said finally.

"Yeah." Randy scrubbed his palms on his jeans. "Ha. Yeah, you could say that."

"You doing okay?" Robinson went around behind the desk and sat down, and Randy accepted the implied invitation to drop into the chair across from him. "I'm thinking the kind of thing you went through could leave some marks."

"Oh, I'm fine," the younger man said dismissively. "No, really," he said when Robinson made a short, disbelieving sound. "I don't even really remember it mostly. I spent most of the time in a kind of drugged stupor. It's like, did you ever get really, really tired? And you'd fall asleep and when you woke up you didn't know what time it was or what day it was or anything? It's pretty much like that. I remember going into the fire, and then I remember finding myself in this big fancy house and not knowing who I was or how I got there. And that was only about a week or so before Death found me."

"I see. And how about Death? How's he doing?"

"What do you mean?"

"You know what I mean. Listen, man, I deal with a lot of vets. I can tell when somebody's having problems. You can see it in their eyes and the way they hold themselves, wary and tense and always braced for an attack. Your brother saw combat, didn't he? Afghanistan?"

Randy sighed. "Yeah. He went down. We almost lost him. He doesn't like to admit it, but he's disabled. His lung capacity is shot."

"I see. And how's he doing otherwise?"

The young paramedic scrubbed a hand through his short dark hair and shook his head. "Man, I don't know. Can you tell me?"

"You're his brother. You're the one who knows him, probably better than anyone in the world. How does he seem to you?"

"Different." Randy sighed and drummed his fingers on the desk. "This thing with his lungs has slowed him down a lot. People, I think, people who didn't know him before probably don't realize how much it's affected him. But it has. He used to be all action and motion. Now just taking the stairs up to his office wipes him out. And he has nightmares. Don't tell him I told you that. I think he likes to imagine that no one knows, but I do. I'm pretty sure his girlfriend does too." Randy laughed a little. "His taste in women has improved, I'll give him that. But he's going slow there, too. I suppose there's no reason to rush it, it's just..."

"You think he should?"

"I just wonder why he doesn't. I can tell he's head over heels for her, and it's obvious she feels the same way. When they get in a room together, they both just light up. But he acts like he isn't sure. He's always been decisive. I just wonder why he's so uncertain now."

Robinson started to answer, then stopped and turned his attention to the window behind Randy, in the wall overlooking the parking lot. Randy tipped his head in that direction then and heard running footsteps himself, pounding across the gravel toward them at a breakneck pace.

They waited, and the door burst open to admit Robin Keystone.

"Hey! I'm looking for Randy Bogart! Oh, Randy! There you are."

"Yeah, I'm right here, kid. What's wrong?"

"Can you come up to the old house real quick? Grandpa Roy just crashed his truck into the ravine."

———

With his long legs eating up the distance, Randy easily outraced Robin. He ran up through the old pasture, jumped an ancient, sagging fence, and wove his way between the trees.

He heard the shouting long before the wreck came into view.

"Oh, for the love of Pete, woman! I am fine!"

82

"You are not fine! You weren't fine to begin with, you crazy old fool! Now you're gonna sit right there and not move until Randy gets here and checks to see if you've rattled any of your tiny little handful of tiny little brain cells loose!"

"Sam—"

"You leave me out of this!" Sam Keystone told his twin. "I'm not getting in the middle of this argument. Anywho, what part of 'footbridge' did you not understand?"

Randy pulled up from his mad dash and worked his way into the crowd surrounding the ruined bridge. Roy still sat in his truck, wedged at a steep angle down into the ravine with his front fender mashed against the opposite wall and his front tires dangling about three feet above the creek.

"What happened?" he asked.

Leona turned on him. Her face was red and her eyes stormy. "This crazy old fool decided to drive his truck over the new footbridge to see if it would hold him. The damn thing gave way and dropped him into the ravine. I told him he had to stay where he is until you could check him over, even if he says he's fine."

She turned completely away from Roy, so he couldn't see her face, and fisted her left hand in the front of Randy's shirt. Her hands were soft and wrinkled but her grip was fierce. Her eyes glittered.

"Please tell me he's fine," she whispered.

Randy patted her shoulder and extricated himself from her grasp. "Well," he said, "his lungs are okay."

The truck was wedged in tight. Randy tested it gingerly for stability and concluded that it wasn't going anywhere without a lot of help. Satisfied that it was stable, he climbed down the bed, slid the back window open, and eased himself into the cab beside Roy.

"Good thing you're skinny," Roy observed. "Your brother couldn't do that."

"No, I don't reckon he could." Randy had noticed that Death and Wren were absent. "He and Wren off making out somewhere?"

Roy cackled. "They said they're at the library, but that's what that noisy old woman and I used to say when we were their age, too."

Randy grinned. He was making a visual assessment as he talked, and the older man looked good. He'd been wearing his seat belt when he crashed, so that was good. He was alert and active and so far he'd responded to everything anyone had said. Randy pulled out the penlight he always carried and shone it in Roy's eyes, fighting him as he tried to bat his hands away.

"Gah! Don't do that! Now I'm gonna see spots for the next hour!"

"I'm checking your pupils to see if you've cracked open your skull. Hold still."

Roy groused but complied.

"How fast were you going when you hit?"

"I wasn't going fast at all. I just wanted to test and see if we could safely drive across the bridge."

"Yeah? And what did you decide?"

"So it needs a little work. Smartass."

"I thought it was only supposed to be a footbridge anyway."

"Well, we're not exactly engineers. But we need a bridge that people can drive over. There are things in the auction that are going to have to be hauled away. I figured it was better for me to chance it first than for one of our customers to."

"Well, now you're gonna need a new bridge."

"Gee, thanks. How long did you have to go to school to get so smart?"

"I'm just sayin'. I suppose you could just leave your truck here and let people drive over that."

"I'd say 'everybody's a comedian' if you were even remotely funny."

"I think you're okay," Randy concluded.

"But I might be a little bit sore tonight and I should take it easy for the next couple of days," Roy prompted.

"Are you feeling sore?"

"No. I just want you to tell my wife that. The least I can get out of all this is a good back rub and a little bit of babying."

"I see. You're a grifter."

"You say that like it's a bad thing."

Randy helped Roy get his seat belt unfastened and climb through the back window and up out of the truck. While they'd been talking the Robinsons had come from the camp, driving around on the roads rather than walking, and a man in overalls was coming up the road with a tractor.

"Who built that bridge?" Nichelle asked.

"We did," one of the Keystone sons told her.

She tsked and shook her head.

"You know," Kurt said, "if you needed help building a bridge, you should have said something."

"Are you a good bridge builder?" Robin Keystone asked.

"I'm not," Kurt said. "I can barely build a sandwich. But it just so happens that my wife is an engineer."

———

"Penny for your thoughts," Wren whispered.

She and Death were sitting next to each other at an old wooden table in the reference room at the library. The Rives County Library was in a building that had been, back in the sixties, a car dealership. The circulation desk and adult fiction were in the main showroom, where a massive card catalogue still took up one wall. Nonfiction, the children's section, and a new computer room were in a low ell at the back that had once held the car repair shop. The reference room stood off to the side in a light, airy room that had been converted from a separate garage where the dealer had parked his own private car.

Death sighed and closed the book in front of him. It was a book of plat maps and aerial photos of Rives County, and he was looking for private tombs where someone might choose to be quietly buried in an antique uniform.

"I'm thinking about lies and murder and judgment, and how maybe mine isn't as good as I thought it was."

"What do you mean?"

"I can't see Tony Dozier as a killer, even under pressure, but maybe I'm wrong. He had the motive and he obviously had the opportunity. We can't prove he had the means, but he had a lot of chances to dispose of the murder weapon."

Wren folded her hands under her chin and leaned against him, just letting her shoulder press his. "What about the other people at the camp? They're all his friends, right? Maybe he's covering for one of them, if he feels like they did it for him. And his wife is dead, so he probably feels like his life is over anyway."

"Probably," Death said. His voice sounded tight and he cleared his throat. "The cops are thinking along those lines, too."

Wren slipped her hand into his and squeezed. He returned the pressure, and when he looked down and met her eyes, his own eyes were damp.

"You know," he said after a minute, "I think I'm going about this wrong."

"How so?"

"I'm sitting here trying to psychically sense what a bunch of people I barely know might or might not do under certain circumstances. I need to concentrate on the facts of the case, starting with the most basic fact."

"Which is?"

"August Jones was stabbed to death."

"Okay ... ?"

"Stabbing is a messy kind of murder. It's going to leave evidence. But so far no one's found a crime scene. That suggests it happened somewhere hidden. Somewhere people don't go often, and somewhere that hasn't been searched. He got a call from somewhere out around the vet camp before he died, and the police pinged his cellphone on their property before the battery went dead in it. So that suggests he was murdered somewhere in the general vicinity of the camp. Does this make sense so far?"

"Absolutely. But where?"

"I don't know. I need to think about this. Where would I arrange to meet someone if I wanted to get them alone so I could stab them to death?"

They sat for a few minutes in pensive silence.

"You know," Wren said, "we have the loveliest conversations."

Death snickered. "I'm sorry, sweetheart."

"Oh, don't be! I love being your sounding board."

There was a book of local history open on the table in front of Wren and she idly turned the page, then started and leaned in to look more closely at the picture in the middle of the page.

"Well, I'll be darned! Would you look at this? He wasn't always a gravedigger after all."

Death sat up as well and leaned in, his head close to hers. "What are we looking at?"

"It's a school picture from a one-room schoolhouse. Liberty School students in 1932. Aramis Defoe was the schoolmaster." She read through the children's names and smiled suddenly. "Look!" she said. "This little girl right here!" She put her finger beside a picture of a child of about ten, with a turned-up nose and long pigtails. "Do you know who that is?"

Death scanned the caption, matching names to their owners, and frowned. "Elvina Griffith? Am I supposed to know who that is?"

"You should know. She pinched your butt the first time you met her."

"Oh no. It can't be. Mother Weeks?"

"She married William Weeks, but her maiden name was Griffith. And the gravedigger was her schoolmaster. I wonder if she remembers him?"

———

"No, no, no," Nichelle said. She turned and nodded at Death and Wren, who'd just driven up and were walking over together hand in hand. "I'm going to show you how a flying buttress works. Come over here, Wren. I need another volunteer."

"What's going on?" Death asked, circling to where his brother and Kurt Robinson were standing a little to one side, watching the proceedings. "Is Roy okay?"

"Yeah. Nice of you two to finally show up," Randy said.

"We had our phones turned off. We were at the library."

"Sure you were."

"Shaddup," Death said, flicking his little brother in the head with his index finger.

"Nichelle is helping them design a bridge that won't collapse when you drive over it," Kurt said.

"Oh, right. Corps of Engineers. That's nice of her."

Kurt shrugged. "You're helping our friend, we're helping yours."

Nichelle had Leona and Doris Keystone standing side-by-side. She put Wren across from Leona, facing her, and grabbed Robin Keystone to stand next to Wren.

"Robin's standing with the girls!" seven-year-old Matthew Keystone crowed. "He's a girl!"

"You be quiet," Robin told his cousin. "I'll do anything the sexy lady pirate wants me to."

Nichelle raised an eyebrow at him. "Lady pirate?"

Robin turned red and started stammering helplessly.

"Because I have a peg leg?"

Roy's truck had been dragged from the ravine. It was parked off to the side and he sat on the tailgate watching. "We're sorry, ma'am," he called. "He's fifteen. His brain cells are drowning in hormones. I keep telling everyone we need to muzzle them at that age but nobody listens."

Nichelle snickered. "It's okay. I think that might be the nicest inappropriate thing anyone's ever said to me. No—" She grabbed Robin's shoulder. "You stay there, next to Wren. Now, Wren and Leona and Robin and Doris, I want you to take each other's hands and make a bridge, like you were playing 'London Bridge is Falling Down.'"

They did as she asked. She looked around and singled out Randy. "Now you, come here. I want you to get between them and try to pull their hands down."

"You say that like you think I can't," Randy said, joining the group. "You could have at least picked big guys for the bridge. You've got the four smallest adults here."

"That's the idea."

"I've seen this before," Kurt confided to Death. "It's pretty wild."

Randy squeezed between the two pairs and easily pulled their hands down.

"Right," Nichelle said. "Now, I need four more volunteers. "Size isn't important."

She selected four more of the Keystone teenagers and had one stand behind each of the four parts of the "bridge."

"Now, you four are the flying buttresses. I need each of you to put your hands on the shoulders of the person in front of you. You don't need to push or brace your weight or anything. Just stand there with your hands on their shoulders."

They did as she directed and she nodded at Randy. "Pull their hands down now."

He tried again and found that, this time, he couldn't do it. He pulled down harder and harder and finally wound up swinging from their hands with all his weight.

"Look," Matthew jeered. "Randy looks like a monkey!"

"Yeah," Death agreed. "And now he's acting like one too."

Randy stuck his tongue out at them both.

"So is this what we need for our bridge, then?" Sam asked. "A flying buttress?"

"No. Flying buttresses are used for vaulted ceilings. The vault pushes the wall out and the flying buttress redirects the lateral force to the ground. I just showed you because I thought you'd think it was neat. But we do need to consider the lines of force when we're designing anything."

While Nichelle lectured Randy and Wren and the Keystones, Death leaned back against a nearby tree and watched. "She seems like a remarkable lady," he told Kurt.

"You have no idea," he said. "After she got injured, we were at Landstuhl. You're probably familiar with the place?"

Death nodded. He'd spent some of the darkest days of his life at the US Military hospital in Germany.

"When she was released, we drove down to France before we flew home. There was this aqueduct she wanted to see in Nimes. Built by the Romans in the early first century AD and still standing to this day. The bridge that carries the aqueduct across the river is curved slightly, with the arch facing upstream. For centuries historians thought it was built that way on purpose, because the curve means that the force of the river itself strengthens the structure."

"But it wasn't?"

"Apparently not. Some kind of hi-tech scan they did of the bridge a few decades ago, I didn't understand all the technical details to be honest, but this scan showed that the stones had deformed over the centuries because of the way they expanded and contracted every day from the heat of the sun. They grew stronger together, the way couples and families and groups of friends do. Nichelle says the aqueduct is an analogy for people, especially people like us."

Death tipped his head to the side and gave Kurt his full attention, because the man, with a motion of his hand, had included Death in that "us."

"People like us?"

"Broken people."

The former Marine's lips thinned. He didn't like the label, but couldn't honestly deny it.

"See," Kurt said, "people always think that, when someone is broken, when they're badly injured, scarred"—he nodded in his wife's direction—"lose a limb, people think that, whatever they do, they can never be put back together as strong as they were before.

But that aqueduct, which has stood for right at two-thousand years now, you know what it was built with? Broken pieces."

Death considered. "I suppose you could say that."

"It's true. It's true of every bridge and building and structure that's ever been built of stone. They don't build them from complete stones. They break the stones into pieces and put them back together again. It's all a matter of how you shape the pieces, and how you fit them into a whole."

Death looked down and watched a bug crawling across a fallen leaf like it was scaling a mountain. "Even when all the pieces aren't there anymore?"

"That's when you have to find new pieces. Bits and braces and flying buttresses." Kurt touched Death's arm to get his attention and pointed at the logo on the side of Roy's truck. "You have to find your keystone, the one that holds all the others together."

"And you and Nichelle?"

"We're each other's keystones."

Death looked to Wren, now sitting cross-legged on the ground in the middle of the group. She'd come up with a notebook somewhere and was drawing careful diagrams under Nichelle's direction. Her face was intent and the tip of her tongue stuck out the corner of her mouth.

When they'd first met, Death had felt like a ragged collection of scraps, the broken remnants of the man he'd once been. In the space of a year he'd lost everything, even (he thought) his brother. Wren had taken those fragments and made him, somehow, whole again.

"I worry about hurting her," he admitted to Kurt abruptly. "She woke me from a nightmare once and I almost snapped her neck. She's promised not to wake me again, but the fear is still there. I can't sleep in the same room with her."

"Then sleep in separate rooms until you can. She loves you. She'll do what you need to make it work. Just don't fool around and put off living until it's too late." Kurt pinched the bridge of his nose, his face twisted in a bitter scowl. "Tony lost his keystone," he said. "He'll never be the same again."

"Kurt!"

They looked up to find Nichelle waving impatiently at them.

"Come here and tell me what you think of this."

"You're the engineer," he told her, but went obediently.

Death remained behind, thinking of bridges and broken stones. He thought of Wren and Randy and support systems. And he thought of Tony Dozier and the possibility that August Jones had been killed by falling masonry.

NINE

THE HADLEIGH HOUSE AUCTION was the largest one currently on the Keystone calendar, but it would still be several weeks before it was ready. In the meantime, there were other sales to prepare and conduct. For three days, Wren stuck with the rest of the company. With practiced efficiency, they packed up five households and sold off two more. On the fourth day, Roy took most of the sons and grandsons to conduct a livestock and farm equipment auction in the next town over while Sam went to bid on a job involving the estate of a local artist.

Wren was given Robin Keystone and sent back to the Hadleigh House to continue the work there.

While she'd been gone they'd gotten the electricity turned on, and she switched on lights against the darkness of an autumn thunder storm. There was no rain yet, but heavy clouds had turned mid-day to dusk. More than half of the upstairs rooms had been emptied now, and thunder rumbled and echoed through the cavernous old building. Robin was outside, cataloguing the garage and mooning over the old car parked there. Wren sat on a dusty loveseat in the first-floor conservatory and packed 1920s-era music books into boxes while the remaining strings in an ancient harp shivered and sang softly with the vibrations from the oncoming storm.

When an engine rumbled to life in the back garden, she thought at first that it was just another peal of thunder. It persisted, though, where storm sounds would have swelled and ebbed. Curious, she rose and crossed the faded rose carpet to peer out the window.

Robin Keystone was riding up through the back garden on a motorcycle, grinning maniacally as he crossed the lawn and came to a stop below her.

Wren wrestled the window up. "What...? Where did you get that?"

He shouted out something she couldn't hear over the engine's roar and pointed back the way he'd come.

"Turn it off!" Wren yelled, flapping her hand at him. "I can't hear you! Turn it off already!"

He turned it off and a momentary silence settled over the property just as the first fat raindrops fell. When he spoke, though, he was still shouting with excitement.

"Look what I found! There was a motorcycle! And it still runs, even!"

"Robin, that's ridiculous. That can't be part of the estate. Nothing here has been touched in decades."

"I know! And it still runs. Can you believe it?"

"No. The gas and oil would have broken down. The spark plugs would have rusted. Someone had to have left it here recently. Where did you find it?"

"Out there in one of those sheds that are falling over."

"The old slave quarters?"

"Is that what they are?"

"Yes. It was parked in one of those?"

"Yeah. Way back in the shadows. I only saw it because I was looking for something to lay out tools on to sort them. I was building a makeshift work bench with sawhorses and I needed a top. There was a sheet of tin in there I thought I could use, so I pulled it out and there was a motorcycle behind it."

Like the dining room, the conservatory had a French door leading to the terrace on the south end of the house. The lock on the conservatory door had rusted, though, and they hadn't managed to get it open yet. Rather than go around to exit through one of the other doors, Wren simply grabbed the top of the window and hoisted herself through it.

Dead grass crunched under her feet. Rain was falling faster now, cold and hard, and though there were still almost two months until November, the classic rock song flitted through her mind. Robin still straddled the bike and she circled it and him, studying it with a critical eye.

She wasn't, by any means, an expert on motorcycles. It was a smaller model by a manufacturer whose name she didn't recognize. The chrome was free of rust and the tires and seat upholstery were too new for the bike to have been abandoned for very long. There were screw holes in the front and back fender for license plates, but both plates were missing.

Wren sighed. "I understand you pulling it out to look at it. I probably would have done the same thing. But you really shouldn't have, you know." She fished her phone out of her pocket and dialed, bending over to shield it from the rain.

"Why not?" Robin demanded.

Wren, listening to her phone, held up one finger to signal him to wait.

"Hi, Cathy? This is Wren Morgan. I'm out at the old Hadleigh House. You want to send Jackson or whoever else is available out here? Robin Keystone has found an abandoned motorcycle in one of the outbuildings. It almost has to belong to the dead guy on the path."

She thanked the dispatcher and hung up. Robin was staring at her, eyes wide.

"We need to get inside before we're drenched," she told him.

Finally dismounting the motorcycle, Robin balanced it on its kickstand and followed her back to the house. He gave her a boost through the window and then climbed in after.

"Do you really think it belonged to the dead guy?" he asked, excited.

Wren slid the window down just as the sky opened up. Jagged shards of lightning slashed across the dark thunderheads and rain sheeted down the glass.

"Yes, maybe. Probably. That, or … "

"Or what?"

Heart heavy with dread, Wren turned from the storm to look at the younger man. "Death thinks August Jones was most likely murdered somewhere in this area. It's possible the bike belonged to him."

"You couldn't have left it somewhere dry?"

Orly Jackson stood at the music room window and stared forlornly out at the motorcycle sitting in the pouring rain.

"There wasn't really time to find a place to put it," Wren said. "He drove it up to the house just a couple of minutes before the downpour started."

"He could have left it where it was." As he spoke, the deputy tipped his head and gave Robin a dirty look.

"I didn't know it was evidence," the teenager defended himself. "I just thought it was part of the estate."

"You're a fifteen-year-old boy and you don't know enough about motorcycles to know that an engine wouldn't just start right up after thirty years?"

"Sure, it makes sense when you stop to think about it. But I didn't stop to think about it. I got excited! I found a motorcycle!"

"It's not like he's disturbed a crime scene," Wren said. "I don't see what harm he's done by driving it a couple hundred yards."

"Well, the rain has probably washed off any fingerprints, for one thing."

"But if it belonged to the dead guy on the path, you already have his fingerprints," Robin objected.

"Yeah. And we could have compared them to fingerprints from the motorcycle to see if it was really his."

"Oh."

"What did you do with the tin?" Wren asked Robin.

"What tin?" Jackson asked.

"The motorcycle was hidden behind a sheet of tin in the old slave quarters."

"It's still there in the building, I guess," Robin said. "I forgot about it when I saw what was behind it."

"So there's what you can fingerprint," she told the officer. "Whoever hid it had to have touched that sheet of tin."

"Okay, but you still didn't have to leave the motorcycle out in the rain."

Wren looked at him from beneath lowered lids. "You're planning on riding it down the path, aren't you? And you're mad because you're going to get your butt wet."

"I have to get it down to the road somehow. It's not like I can pull a bike trailer up a driveway that has a big ravine across it."

Nichelle's plans for the bridge involved using the top deck of an old car carrier for the frame. They'd located one at a junkyard a few towns over but had yet to arrange to get it transported and put into place.

Jackson sighed. "Well, all right. I guess you'd better come show me where you found it."

"You guys have fun," Wren told them. "I'll be in here if you need anything."

"You're not coming with us?"

"Why? I wasn't there when he found it. I don't see how I could help any."

"But aren't you curious?"

Thunder cracked and the downpour, already heavy, increased.

"Not that curious," Wren said.

The deputy sighed again. "I don't suppose there's any chance of a pot of hot coffee when we get back?"

"Sure, if you chop me some firewood and drive into town to get coffee." Wren laughed, not without sympathy, at his stricken expression. "I don't live here," she reminded him. "I'm only sorting out the contents for auction. The cookstove is a gas range and there's no gas in the tank. And if there's any coffee in the cupboards, it's been there since probably the mid-sixties."

"You're a heartless woman," Jackson told her.

"None of this is my fault."

"I know that. But you don't have to enjoy the situation quite this much."

"Yeah. Schadenfreude is a petty thing, but it's so very human."

"Shaden-who?" Robin asked.

Jackson sighed again and clapped the teenager on the shoulder. "C'mon, kid. Let's go drown ourselves in the name of duty."

"I'll see if I can dig you up some towels," Wren offered.

———

Randy parked his little blue Mustang on the town square and made a dash for the shelter of the awning that protected the front window of the Renbeau Bros. Department Store. It was one of the oldest buildings on the square, a massive brick structure with display windows on either side that ran parallel to the sidewalk before angling in toward a recessed entryway. The display window on the left was shorter than the one on the right to make room for a discreet wood-and-glass door.

A sign painted on the door's window read *Death Bogart. Private Investigations and Surety Recovery.*

Randy shook the rain off his raincoat before he went inside. He hung it on a peg in the tiny vestibule and climbed a steep, narrow set of stairs to his brother's combination office and apartment.

Death was at his desk, poring over a sheaf of oversized papers. He glanced up. "Bad?"

"Bad enough. Could have been worse." In spite of his rain gear, the younger Bogart was sopping wet. "We tell people and we tell people not to try to drive across flooded roads, and yet there's always somebody who thinks they can make it through."

"You get them out okay?"

Randy went through into the tiny apartment and started stripping off his clothes, but he left the door ajar so he could continue the conversation.

"Yeah. This time. Woman, two kids, and a dog. The driver's side tire got caught on the low railing leading up to the bridge. That's the only thing that kept them from being swept completely off the road and down into the creek."

He toweled off and pulled on dry clothes: a pair of sweatpants and a long-sleeved T-shirt.

"The cops are considering child endangerment charges. I swear, I think stupid should be against the law." He wandered back out into the office and helped himself to coffee from the coffeemaker that sat atop a bookcase under the front windows. "What are you up to?"

"Trying to figure out where to murder someone."

"Anybody I know?" Randy joked. "Hey! If it's Madeline, I'll help you get rid of the body."

"You'd help me get rid of the body anyway," Death said confidently.

"Yeah, probably." Randy dragged one of the visitor chairs close to the desk, turned it around, and propped one knee on it as he leaned in to study the papers his brother had spread out. It was a plat map, he realized. A large-scale map of the area around the Hadleigh House and the veterans' camp. "You thinking Jones was killed somewhere around there?"

"It would make sense. He got a call from someone in the area before he died. This is where the police pinged his cell phone and it's where Dozier was supposed to be headed when, he says, he found Jones wounded by the road."

"So what are we looking for?"

"If he got a call from the killer, chances are that it was to arrange a meeting. To commit a murder, it would have to be somewhere secluded. It would have to be somewhere that hasn't been searched yet, because no one's found a crime scene and there would have been a lot of blood. And it would have to be somewhere specific, probably. There's no reason to think Jones was familiar with the area, so you'd have to give him a landmark or map reference."

"But you wouldn't have to kill him at the same place where you met him," Randy pointed out. "You could say, 'Hey, let's go back in this really hidden part of the forest where we can talk without being seen.'"

Down in the foyer, the bell over the door jangled. The two men glanced up as heavy, slow footsteps began to climb the stairs, then returned to their conversation.

"You could, yeah," Death agreed. "But there's another angle to this that's bothering me. The same thing we're trying to figure out about the dead guy on the path. How did he get out there? It's about fifteen miles from town. These rural areas don't have any kind of public transportation, and there's only one taxi. The police already talked to the driver and he never saw Jones that day. If we're going on the assumption that he went out there to meet his killer, then how'd he get there? What happened to his transportation?"

"I can answer that."

The person climbing the stairs, it turned out, was Chief Reynolds. He dropped into the other visitor's chair, breathing heavily.

"Damn, son! You couldn't have gotten an office on the ground floor?"

"Good cardiovascular exercise." Death grinned before turning serious. "You know how Jones could have gotten out to the vets' camp?"

Reynolds tossed an oversized black-and-white photo on top of Death's maps.

"I'm not showing you this," he said. "I'm just putting it down on your desk while I catch my breath."

"Of course." Death and Randy leaned in, heads together, to study the picture. It was a still from a gas station security camera. Two heavily bearded men, looking uncomfortable in suits and ties, were standing beside a battered pickup truck. One leaned against the passenger door while the other pumped gas.

"That's Jones," Death said, indicating the passenger. "Where did this come from?"

"We've been studying security camera footage from area businesses for the day of the murder. This is that little mom-and-pop convenience store out on K highway."

"09:23," Randy said, pointing out the time stamp.

"Who's the other guy?" Death asked.

"You don't recognize him?"

"No. Should I?"

"Maybe not, but I thought you might have seen him around. His name is Dexter Wallace. He served with Dozier and Kurt Robinson. He was one of Zahra Dozier's pall bearers."

———

Jackson had covered the motorcycle with an old tarp they found and left for town to get a motorcycle trailer to haul it with. The rain moved on and a light breeze blew in, stringing tattered clouds across the sky. The storm gave way to a bright, pretty afternoon, with sunlight glistening on the wet grass and the first-fallen leaves of autumn.

Wren was working in the parlor, beside the music room, with Robin sticking close and staying out of trouble, when they heard voices outside.

"That must be Orly back for the bike," she said.

A loud, imperious knock sounded from the front door and she growled to herself.

"What does he need now?"

Brushing the dust from her jeans, she went down the hall to the entryway with Robin trailing along behind. Through the decorated glass of the front door she could see parts of two bodies, but not the faces attached. One was short and wore a blue shirt, the other tall and gaunt and dressed in a formal black suit. She opened the door.

"Yes?"

"We're here to search the place," Eric Farrington said. "Open up in the name of the law."

"You can't search this place," Wren told him, disbelief in her voice. "You're not a cop. You're just a jail guard. And even a cop would need a warrant."

"We have a warrant. Didn't you see us out here searching the other day?"

"Well, while I'll admit I'm not too clear on the legalities of re-searching a property on a single warrant, I do know that the warrant didn't cover this house, and that, even if it had, you wouldn't be authorized to execute it. So go away or I'll execute you."

The man with Eric drew himself up to his full height and deliberately stepped into her personal space. "Woman, we're coming in. Now step aside."

"No. You're not." She turned back to Farrington. "Who the hell is this anyway?"

"That's Tyler Jones." It was Robin who answered her. "The religious guy? The, uh, murdered guy's father? I've seen him on TV."

"Oh." Wren looked at the man again, with sympathy this time, expecting to see grief under his anger. "I'm sorry for your loss. I don't know what Eric has told you, but this is private property and there's nothing here that has anything to do with your son's death."

"We're looking for the victim's cell phone," Eric said.

"1 Corinthians 11:3!" Jones said. "Step aside!"

Wren blinked and frowned at him, confused. "What?"

"1 Corinthians 11:3!"

Robin looked it up on his phone. "He said because he's a man and you're a woman, that he's the boss of you."

Wren frowned. "That isn't the way it works around here. Goodbye." She tried to close the door, but he blocked it open with his foot. He thumbed through the Bible and found a page.

"Matthew 16:23!"

Robin sneered. "You had to look that up?"

"Even I know that one," Wren said. "And I am not Satan and I will not get behind you."

Jones leafed through the Bible once more. "Deuteronomy 22:5, you besom!"

"Besom?" Wren cocked an eyebrow at him. "Did you just call me a broom?"

Robin was searching the reference. "He said you're an abomination unto the Lord because you're wearing men's clothes."

Wren glanced down at herself. She was wearing one of Death's old USMC T-shirts over a pair of faded jeans. She snickered in spite of herself. "Yeah, I bet that's what Madeline thought when I ran into her this morning."

Jones had gone back to his holy book.

"Ezekiel 16:17!"

Robin Googled it. "He said you're a hooker and you're wearing his jewelry."

"Now, look," Wren said, "I sympathize with the loss of your son, and I'm cutting you a lot of slack because of that. But this property has already been searched by the authorities."

"They didn't search inside the house," Eric Farrington piped up.

"That's because they searched outside the house the morning the dead man was found on the trail and they were able to determine that no one had been inside for years. There is nothing in this building that either of you need to see. This is private property. You have no business here and you need to leave."

"Leviticus 15:19."

Robin looked it up and blushed. "He said that you're, erm, unclean because you're on your period."

Wren pointed a stern finger at Jones. "Mister, you're crossing lines that you do not want to cross."

Tyler Jones searched through his Bible again, finding his passage and marking it with his finger. "Defy me, a servant of the Lord, thou harlot, and thee shall be as Jezebel in 2 Kings 9:33-37."

Wren looked expectantly to Robin, who was already manipulating his phone. He looked back at her.

"He said he wants you to get thrown off a wall, trampled by horses, and eaten by dogs."

Wren gasped and glowered at him. "Well now. That's just not very nice!" She pulled out her own phone and selected a name from her contacts list. "You asked for this," she told Jones sternly. "Hello, Doris? Tyler Jones is here. He's trying to get in the house. I told him he can't come in and now he's scripturing at me. He called me an abomination and said he wanted me Jezebeled!"

She listened for a second and looked up with a glint in her eye. "She says Matthew 12:34."

Jones eyes widened. He scowled ferociously at Wren and consulted the Bible.

Robin was already searching it. "She said he and his people are a nest of vipers and evil and that they can't say anything good because their hearts are full of bad stuff."

"1 Timothy 2:11-12," Jones said.

"Doris? He said 1 Timothy 2—wait. What?"

"11-12," Jones repeated.

"11-12. 2:11-12."

"He told her to shut up and not argue with a man," Robin offered.

"Doris says Job 19:17-19."

Jones' complexion darkened and he rifled his pages with furious haste.

"She says he's got bad breath and no one can stand to be around him."

"Zephania 3:1." Jones was almost shouting now.

"Zephania 3:1," Wren echoed.

"Hey!" Robin, who was getting fast with the Google, snarled at Jones. "Don't you call my grandma filthy and polluted!"

"Doris says Judges 3:21."

Robin searched it and blinked. "I think she just threatened to stab him in the stomach and make him poop his pants!"

"Revelations 17:1-5!"

"He called her the Whore of Babylon."

"Deuteronomy 23:1." As quickly as Doris was shooting back the Bible verses, there was no way she wasn't doing this from memory. Even Wren, who'd known the older woman for years, was impressed.

Jones shook with rage. His dark eyes bored into Wren with an intensity that made her think of comic book villains shooting flames with the power of their minds. He turned back to his own book with a grim fury.

"She said he can't go to Heaven because he doesn't have any balls," Robin reported, a trace of awe in his voice.

"Revelation 14:11," Jones spat.

"He told her to go to hell."

Wren repeated Jones' verse, then relayed Doris' response. "Genesis 38:9."

"Grandma!" Robin yelped when he'd looked it up.

"What did she say?"

"I can't tell you! I'd get my mouth washed out."

"Revelation 21:8!"

"Doris? He says Revelation 21:8."

"He just told her to go to hell again," Robin said. "I think he's running out of stuff."

"Exodus 9:15. Doris says Exodus 9:15."

Jones consulted his Bible. "Ha," he said. "As if I fear that."

"She said that she's gonna smite him for his wickedness," Robin explained when he'd looked it up.

Wren waved her hand like a schoolchild seeking permission to speak.

Jones glared at her. "What?"

She pointed behind him. He and Eric Farrington turned around slowly.

Leona Keystone was standing on the porch behind them with a baseball bat.

She tapped the tip of the bat on the doorframe beside Eric's head, not hard, just a couple of light knocks, and his ruddy cheeks paled to the color of milk. He stumbled back, making a wide circle around her.

"You can't scare me," he said in a choked whisper. "I'm the law around here."

"Boo!" Leona said.

Eric turned, fell off the porch, picked himself up, and ran away. They stood for a minute, watching him climb the fence rather than take time to wrestle the gate open, tumble to the ground again, and hare off down the path between the lilacs.

Leona turned back to Jones. "You see that little man run away?" she asked. "He's not always as stupid as he looks."

Jones pulled himself up to his full height, a gaunt scarecrow of a man towering over her and glaring down balefully. "Get thee to a nunnery!"

"Hey, wait a minute!" Wren objected. "That's not from the Bible. That's Shakespeare. You can't switch from the Bible to Shakespeare just because you're losing."

"I'll see your Shakespeare and raise you Oppenheimer," Leona told him.

Jones blinked. "Who?"

She tapped the barrel of the bat on the palm of her left hand. "I am become Death," she said, "the Destroyer of Worlds."

The self-proclaimed prophet opened his mouth and closed it several times but nothing came out.

"I think the grandmas broke him," Robin whispered to Wren.

Tyler Jones pulled himself up with great dignity. "It does not do for the righteous to remain in the presence of the wicked and unholy," he announced. He turned and marched away. They watched him leave.

"I should start carrying my atlatl," Wren said drily. She turned back to the phone. "Doris? He's gone now. Thanks!" She listened for a minute. "Okay. I'll tell her. Bye!"

She turned the phone off and tucked it away. "Doris is going to call Chief Reynolds and talk to him about this. I have a feeling Eric's going to be in trouble. Oh, and she wants you to pick her up a sweet tea on your way back."

"I was going to anyway," Leona said. She smiled at the autumn yard, balanced the baseball bat across her shoulders like a slugger stretching before an at-bat, and leaned back against the wall. "We always have made a good team, me and Doris. She calls down Heaven and I raise Hell."

TEN

"HAVE YOU EVER RIDDEN a horse before?"

"I saw the Clydesdales in a parade once. Does that count?"

Kurt Robinson snickered. "Not exactly." Taking hold of the saddle horn, he swung his leg over Sugar's back and dismounted. "Here. Climb up here and I'll give you a riding lesson."

Death backed up a couple of steps. "Actually, I just need to talk to you."

Robinson sighed. "I know. We can talk while you ride."

"Why do you want me to sit on your horse? And have you asked the horse how he feels about it?"

"Sugar doesn't mind. He's a good guy. Riding is good therapy. It can help you with trust and confidence issues, develop muscles ... it's just a good thing." The Army vet ran one hand through his hair and blew out a breath. "Look, man. This is what I do. I don't know what else to do now."

And Death had been there, that point where you don't know what the hell to do, so you do the only thing you know. He reached out one hand and tentatively petted the big gray horse on its nose. It nuzzled him, turning its head to press its forehead against his palm.

He took a breath and stepped forward. "Okay, so how do I get on this thing?"

"You're on the left side, so that's okay. You always mount a horse from the left. Gather the reins in your left hand, grab the saddle horn, put your left foot in the stirrup, and swing yourself up."

Death gathered the reins and grabbed the saddle horn as instructed. He was a tall man, but even so the stirrup was knee-high and it was awkward getting his foot up. He got his foot in it and hopped around on his right foot, trying to find his balance and get into a good position to haul himself up.

Robinson steadied him with a hand on his back. "If you're having trouble, you can climb the fence and mount or we can get you something else to stand on. We deal with a lot of people with a lot of physical challenges. There are ways to work around them."

"I'm not physically challenged," Death huffed, out of breath.

"Sure you're not."

Death glowered at the other man, took as deep a breath as he was able, and hauled himself up. He paused, standing with his left foot in the stirrup and leaning over Sugar's back, until he caught his breath again, then shifted his body around and got his right leg over so that he was sitting up in the saddle.

"See?"

Robinson walked around the horse and put Death's right foot into the other stirrup.

"Good job," he said. "You can let up the death-grip on that saddle horn any time now."

"Ha, ha." Death relaxed his grip on the saddle horn and sat back in the saddle, feeling out his balance. When he felt marginally secure, he released the saddle horn and sat there holding the bunched reins and feeling vulnerable and stupid. "Now what do I do?"

"Just relax. Hold the reins loosely in your left hand. I'm going to walk him around a bit so you can get the feeling for motion."

Death tensed up, gripping the reins tighter and holding the horse with his knees. "I don't think he likes me sitting on him. I wouldn't like him sitting on me. Probably I should get down now and give him a break."

"Don't worry. If he didn't want you riding him, you'd be on your ass in the dust by now." Robinson smacked Death's leg with the back of his hand. "Relax."

He took hold of Sugar's bridle and got him moving slowly around the yard. The big animal made for a rocking platform, moving with a gentle rhythm that reminded Death of being on board a ship. He did begin to relax then, settling into the rhythm.

"See? I told you. That's not so bad now, is it?"

"Nobody likes someone who goes around saying 'I told you so.'"

"That doesn't make me wrong. It just makes me unpopular."

Death rode along in silence for a few yards. "I need you to tell me about Dexter Wallace," he said finally.

Robinson's shoulders tensed. "I don't know anything," he said.

"You gotta know something. He's one of your best friends, right? Driving around with a guy who's about to get murdered. That's the kind of thing that best friends tend to gossip about."

"Dex wouldn't kill anybody!"

"That's what you said about Tony."

"Neither of them would! Look, I know Dex looks like this big bad biker dude, but he's just a giant teddy bear. He has a family. He's got a three-year-old daughter who has him wrapped around her little pinky finger."

"Man, just stop, all right? Just stop walking for a minute and turn around and look at me."

Robinson stopped the horse and half turned to shoot Death a resentful glare.

"Where's Dex now?" Death asked.

"In police custody. They picked him up at home and took him in for questioning."

"When did you find out that he was the one who drove Jones out here on the morning of the murder?"

"When the police showed up again today, looking for him. I didn't know. I swear to you. What I think... I think he didn't even know who Jones was. Just some guy who asked him for a ride. Dex would do that. Give a ride to a stranger, I mean. It doesn't mean he had anything to do with the guy winding up dead."

Death sighed. "I'm on your side, okay? I'm trying to help you. But I can't do that if you're not going to level with me."

"I am levelling with you!"

"No, you're not. You're being honest when you say that you don't think he even knew who Jones was and that Dex would give a stranger a ride. But you're lying when you say that the first you heard of it is from the police today."

"I swear—"

"Don't. Okay? Just don't. Don't lie to me and swear you're telling the truth. There are tells. When someone is remembering something, they look to their left and down. When they're trying to remember something, they look to their left and up. When they're telling something from their imagination, a story or a lie, they look down and to the right."

Robinson sighed and deflated.

"I want to help you," Death said again. "I just need you to level with me. If you're really not involved and you really believe your friends are not involved, then tell me what you know so I can try to figure out what did happen."

Robinson turned away, shook the horse's bridle, and started leading him toward the trees. Death considered the questionable wisdom of calling someone a liar while they were controlling the large, unpredictable animal you were sitting on.

There was a picnic table under the trees at the edge of the woods and Robinson drew to a stop. He took the reins from Death and looped them loosely over a branch.

"Can you get down on your own or do you need help?"

"I can do it," Death said. He grabbed the saddle horn in both hands again, stood in the left stirrup, and awkwardly pulled his right leg up and over Sugar's back. He lowered himself until he was leaning against the horse's side with his right toes touching the ground and his left foot still stuck in the stirrup, and then faltered, trying to catch his balance and figure out how to get his foot loose.

Robinson came up behind him and caught him, supporting him and slipping the stirrup off.

"You know," he said conversationally, "falling actually isn't the most efficient way to dismount."

"You hush." Death went over to the picnic table and dropped gratefully into the inanimate seat. Robinson took the bench across from him and the two men regarded one another over the expanse of wood.

"So tell me about Dexter. What happened? Really?"

"What I said, mostly." Robinson put his elbows on the table and leaned his head in his hands. "Zahra was a Muslim. They lived up in the city and she belonged to a mosque there, but they spent a lot of time down here after Tony got out of the hospital, and when she died, this is where he wanted her buried. I don't know how much you know about Muslim funeral customs?"

"A little," Death said. "Burial is supposed to take place before the following sundown, right? And don't they take place outdoors?"

"Yeah. There are other details, but mostly it consists of prayer. Not really that different from Christian ceremonies, I think. You pray for the dead and you pray for the living. Anyway, the main thing is the time constraint. Zahra was killed at night. She was on her way home from some kind of candle party or something and she got broadsided by a drunk driver. Tony was falling apart. Dex and I got with her imam and contacted the local churches in this area and cobbled together a plan.

"The members of her mosque met up in the city that morning and prepared her body for burial, then we transported it down here, to the Episcopal Church because it's the closest to the city cemetery. We had a Christian memorial service there in the afternoon, then the pallbearers carried her up the street to the cemetery just before sundown and the funeral took place there."

"That sounds like a reasonable plan."

"That's what we thought. We weren't counting on Tyler Jones and his Church of the Army of Christ. And I'm using 'church' there ironically."

"They showed up to protest, right?"

"Yeah. We had no idea they were coming. I don't even know how they found out about it." Robinson laughed bitterly. "Except I do now, don't I? Augustus Jones had 'infiltrated' the mosque posing as a magazine reporter. He must have called and told them."

"What happened?"

"It was a madhouse. The Episcopal Church is on private property and they were able to keep them back, but the street and the cemetery are public. Normally when a group like that plans a protest at a funeral or such, volunteers show up to form a barricade. But this all happened so fast, with the accident and then having to plan the funeral immediately, we never even considered asking for help. We saw them outside the church. There were a lot of military personnel there, so we put the Muslims in the middle and the Army on the outside, but Tyler Jones and his people were right there. We're carrying this poor woman's body to the cemetery and they're waving signs in our faces and spitting and shouting that God hates us and that Zahra was burning in hell. We're soldiers, man. Soldiers fight. You know how it is. Things got heated and there were some clashes between the protesters and the mourners. I mean, what did they expect?"

"And that's when Tony hit Tyler Jones and threatened him? Walking between the church and the cemetery?"

"He didn't so much hit him. He shoved him away and Jones fell down. And he didn't exactly threaten him, either."

"What did he do?"

"He just asked him how he'd feel if it were someone he loved who was dead."

Death hooked his fingers in the space between the boards on the top of the picnic table and leaned back, looking up. The leaves were still mostly green, just a few yellow and brown among them, but there were fewer now than there had been just a week ago. The sky beyond them was a brilliant blue with a few fluffy, high-flying clouds. He sat up and drew his gaze back to Kurt Robinson.

"That's a perfectly normal thing to say, but you have to admit it sounds a bit ominous in retrospect, when you realize Jones' son wound up dead in Tony's car the next day."

"Yes, I know. And I know why they think Tony killed him. But I also know Tony and he's not a killer."

"You still haven't told me about Dexter and why he brought August Jones here in the first place."

"Man, it's like I said. Jones showed up at the mosque that morning and wanted a ride down for the funeral. He was posing as a magazine writer. We thought he *was* a magazine writer." Robinson laughed, but it wasn't a happy sound. "He said he wanted to do a human interest article on how members of the two different faiths came together during a time of grief."

Death considered. "So Dexter gave him a ride. But that gas station is between here and town. Did he bring him out here?"

"Yeah, a bunch of us met out here. Jones came along, said he wanted to do some interviews. Dex gave him a ride out and then he and I and the other pallbearers had to leave early to meet the body at the church. Jones said he'd catch a ride with someone else and honestly, I forgot all about him. I never thought a thing about him. Even after they found Tony with his body, I didn't know that's who it had been. Not until one of the news stories reported that he'd been posing as a reporter to infiltrate the mosque and they showed a picture of him with some of the members. Dex saw the same report and called me. That's when we decided it was probably best to just not say anything."

"Not the smartest decision you've ever made," Death said.

"We didn't have anything to do with him."

"But you knew where he was and what he was doing the day he got killed. Not speaking up makes it look like you're covering for someone."

"We're not!"

Death sighed and shook his head. "Okay, so just tell me this: when and where did you see him last?"

"I last saw him just before we left for the church, about three o'clock in the afternoon."

"Where?"

The picnic table they were sitting at was made of metal and weathered oak, with broad, thick gray planks forming the benches and the eating surface. Kurt Robinson reached out and rapped his knuckles on the wood.

"He was here," he said. "Right here at this table. He was sitting there, just where you're sitting, talking on his phone."

ELEVEN

WREN PULLED TO A stop next to a late-model burgundy sedan that sat canted at an awkward angle on the side of the county blacktop. A tall, imposing elderly lady stood leaning against the driver's door, her arms crossed and her mouth drawn down in a disapproving frown.

"Problems, Ms. Weeks?"

"Flat tire." Millie Weeks, the head of the Rives County Historical Society, shook her cell phone as if it had offended her. "Roadside assistance said it's going to take four hours to get someone out here to change it for me. Four hours!"

"Got a spare?"

"Of course. I don't suppose you know someone you could call to come help me?"

"Pfft!" Wren waved her hand. "Just hang tight. I'll have you back on the road before you know it."

She pulled in ahead of Ms. Weeks and, though the road was deserted but for the two of them, flipped her emergency flashers on.

She hopped out, reached in the back of her truck, and pulled out a tire iron and a hydraulic jack.

Ms. Weeks gave her a dubious look and Wren grinned back. "Don't worry. I know what I'm doing."

She got the jack situated and jacked it up just enough to hold it in place, then popped off the hub cap and went to work on the lug nuts.

"You know, I was thinking about you just the other day," she said. The nuts were on tight. She fitted the four-way, then got up and stood on the left arm and bounced a couple of times until it broke loose and slid her off. "I was wondering if it would be all right for me to come talk to your mother. I wanted to ask her some questions about a man she knew when she was a child."

"Oh, Wren. I'm not sure that's such a good idea. I mean, you're welcome to visit anytime, but Mother's memory isn't what it used to be. She's still in good health physically, praise the Lord, but her mind wanders. And then, of course, you're going to kill yourself changing this tire."

Wren just laughed and moved on to the next bolt.

"Who did you want to ask her about?"

"The man who lived in the house we're getting ready for auction. The old Hadleigh House. His name was Aramis Defoe. I found a school picture of a class he taught and your mother was one of the children."

"Oh, yes. The Gravedigger. Of course. My Aunt Delia had a terrible crush on him. I only knew him when he was old and I was young, but I understand he was very handsome, once upon a time. Such a tragedy."

Wren had all the nuts broken loose, and she was spinning them off and collecting them carefully into the upturned hub cap. "What do you mean? What was the tragedy?"

"Well, how he died, of course. There were parishioners who didn't want him buried in the cemetery, even after all the work he'd done there. He dug all the graves out by hand, you know, and never charged a penny. And if a family couldn't afford a stone, he'd carve them one, and not ask anything for doing that either."

Wren pushed herself up off the ground and stood to face the older woman, a sick feeling in her stomach. "Ms. Weeks, did Aramis Defoe kill himself?"

"You didn't know? The coroner ruled it an accident, as a favor to the pastor, but everyone knew what really happened. He overdosed on sleeping pills, right after he finished carving that angel statue for his grave."

———

"I rode that big gray horse today," Death said.

Randy closed the door to the stairwell and dropped into one of the visitor chairs beside Death's desk. "Wow. I wish I'd been there! I've never seen a horse with two asses before."

"Ha, ha, ha." Death turned the page in the newspaper he was studying. "Hit your head again?"

"Umm, no."

"I wasn't asking. I was offering."

"Oh. Ha, ha, ha." Randy leaned forward and propped his chin in his hands. "Whatcha doing?"

"I'm going over everything I can find that has pictures or video of Zahra Dozier's funeral. I'm trying to get a feel for who was where, when."

"Ah. Grasping at straws." Randy leaned back and propped his long legs up in the other chair. "I ran into Orly Jackson at a fender bender earlier."

"Yeah?"

"Yeah. He said he went up to the city yesterday and showed the horse thief picture around at the library and that research place. No one recognized the dead man."

Death grimaced. "Yeah, that might not have been the smartest suggestion we ever made."

"Why not?"

"I keep forgetting, and I think Jackson does too, that the dead man whose picture they have is not the person who actually bought the uniform. That was most likely the person who was buried in it, the one whose body the dead man stole it from. And that person, that's someone we don't know anything at all about."

"It's got to be connected to the church cemetery, don't you think?" Randy asked. "I mean, you've got clothes taken from a corpse and you've got a cemetery not half a mile away. There has to be a connection."

"It seems that way to me too, but Jackson swears it's not. He searched the whole cemetery and found no sign of any of the graves being disturbed. He also talked to the guy who operates the backhoe to dig new graves, and he said he hasn't buried anyone out there since late last winter."

Death stilled suddenly, his hands hovering over the paper, his breath caught in his throat.

"I'll be a son of a bitch," he breathed.

Randy leaned forward. "What is it? What did you find?"

Death turned the paper toward him and pointed out a picture in the middle of a page.

"It's the Doziers' wedding picture," Randy said.

"Yeah. Tony had one taped to the wall in his room at the mental hospital."

"Okay. And?"

"And I know where he was when he found August Jones dying by the side of the road."

———

"I found a notebook full of studies for the angel," Wren said. She pulled the flat tire off the car and rolled it to the side, letting it fall into the grass. "She wasn't drawn as an angel, though. She was just a woman in a scene from a war, offering soldiers water from a well. I just wondered who she was."

"I know he called her Agathe," Ms. Weeks said.

Wren got the spare that she'd earlier taken out of the wheel well in the trunk and rolled it into place. The car wasn't quite high enough to put it on, and she pumped the jack a few more times to raise it.

"Well, Mr. Defoe fought in the First World War. As I understand it, he was a brilliant man. And, of course, he was a wonderful artist. But they said he was never the same after the war. He was obsessed with death. Spent hours wandering around the cemetery, talking to the people buried there. And I remember one night, when I was very young, a pair of teenage brothers had been killed in a car accident. Their father propped the hood of their car up against a tree, to warn everyone that the road there was dangerous. It's still there, to this day, though so rusted and overgrown you can hardly see it. Anyway, Mr. Defoe spent all night digging their graves, side by side. When the preacher went out to the cemetery to check on him in the morning, he found him cowering in one of the graves. Sometime during the night he'd gotten confused and he thought he was back in the war, digging foxholes."

Wren fitted the spare tire on and began replacing the nuts. "Sounds like post-traumatic stress."

"Back then they called it battle fatigue. Now see here. Am I going to be safe driving on that thing?"

"Absolutely." Wren tightened the lug nuts, going around the wheel in a star pattern until she'd tightened them all, then lowered the car to the ground and tightened them again. "You still need to get your tire repaired and put back on as soon as you can, though. This isn't a full-size spare. It's only a donut. You'll need to drive carefully and don't go over fifty."

The sound of an approaching vehicle reached them and they both looked to their left expectantly. After a few seconds, a sheriff's department cruiser came around the bend and Orly Jackson pulled in behind Millie Weeks' car, flipped on his bubble lights, and got out.

"You ladies need any help?"

"Sure," Wren said "Put Ms. Weeks' flat tire in her trunk for her, would you?"

"Why do I gotta do the heavy lifting?"

"Because you didn't get here in time to call dibs on the easy part."

Grumbling, he did as she asked while Wren retrieved her jack and tire iron and tossed them into the back of her truck.

"Have you heard from your boyfriend?" he asked.

"No?" Wren got her phone off the truck seat and looked at it. "Oh, he texted me. It just says, 'call me when you get a chance.' Why?"

"Because I'm on my way to meet him. He says he knows how to find where Jones was stabbed."

Death and Randy were waiting in Death's jeep when Wren, with Jackson following her, pulled up at the entrance to the veterans' camp. Death leaned across his brother to shout at her between their vehicles.

"Park and hop in."

Wren did as he asked, climbing in behind him as Jackson walked up next to the driver's door. Wren looped her arms around Death from behind, wrapping him in a hug while being careful not to actually touch him with her hands.

"Greasy girl," he teased. "You have car trouble?"

"Not me. Ms. Weeks. I just changed her tire for her."

"Grease monkey looks good on you."

Randy rolled his eyes. "If you're going to get mushy, I'm getting out."

Wren dragged one finger down Randy's cheek, leaving a black smear, before sliding back and clicking her seat belt.

"You said you found me a crime scene?" Jackson prompted.

"Not yet. I was waiting for you. I know where to look now. Follow me."

Death waited for the deputy to return to his own vehicle, then led the way down the gravel road, past the cemetery to the church driveway, where he pulled in and turned around. Jackson gave him a confused, annoyed look but followed suit. Death drove back until he was next to the cemetery again and stopped and they all got out.

"Remember what Tony said in his statement? Why he said he stopped where he did when he found Jones wounded beside the road?"

"Yeah. He said he saw his wife's ghost."

"He did see his wife's ghost. Or rather, he saw something that it makes perfect sense for him to have mistaken for her ghost. Look at this." He proffered a paper, folded open to a picture of a couple standing close together. The man was in an Army dress uniform and had one arm around the woman. She wore a long dress and a light hijab. A strong wind blew her skirts to the side and she had one hand up by her mouth, holding her veil in place. In her left hand she was clutching a bouquet of flowers.

"It's the Doziers' wedding picture," Jackson said.

Wren took it and looked closely at it. "They looked so happy," she said. Zahra's smiling eyes looked back at her. She turned the paper a bit and her breath caught in her throat. "You know what she reminds me of, in that long dress and veil, standing in that pose?"

"Yeah," Death grinned. "Yeah, I do."

Jackson followed their gaze to the gravedigger's angel standing beyond the weed-filled ditch, gazing out toward the east. "So you think he thought the statue was his wife's ghost?"

"It makes sense," Wren argued. "He'd just buried her. It's night, he's driving down this dark road, and his headlights catch the statue. She's standing in the same pose his wife was standing in, in her wedding picture. I mean, the statue is holding her hair out of her eyes and Zahra was holding her veil, and the statue has a ladle instead of flowers, but it's close enough."

"He got out of the car and tried to run to her," Death said, "but he fell down in the ditch and found August Jones, bleeding. That on top of everything else triggered a flashback, and he thought he was back in the war. You know the rest."

He paced along the edge of the road until he came to a point where the underbrush was flattened and crushed. Jackson and Randy crouched on either side of him and Wren leaned over his shoulder as he pointed out the swarm of flies and other insects buzzing around the foliage.

"There's blood here. That's what's drawing the insects. See? The trail of crushed grass leads off into the cemetery. If we follow it, it should lead us to the place where Jones was attacked."

Rather than trample the weeds further and destroy possible evidence, they circled around through the churchyard and found the spot from inside the cemetery. The cemetery grass had been cut since the murder and the trail wasn't nearly so obvious. The weeds at the top of the ditch were barely disturbed, but Death's Jeep, still parked on the road, served as a marker. Looking closely at the low fence around the graveyard, they could see bloodstained fingerprints on the weathered wood.

"He was badly injured, staggering along. He made it over the fence and then collapsed just short of the road. If Dozier hadn't seen the statue and thought it was Zahra's ghost, he'd have probably died where he fell."

"We'll never be able to backtrack through this cut grass, though," Jackson said. "The blood will have soaked in by now."

"But we don't have to." Death was walking around looking at tombstones. "Here."

"What?"

"More blood. He had blood on his hands from trying to stop the bleeding and he was weak from blood loss, so he'd have grabbed onto anything that offered support. He left bloody handprints on the tombstones he passed. The traces are faint, so it's not obvious unless you're looking. Here's another one. He came from this way."

They followed an erratic path weaving along the edge of the cemetery until they came to the point where the ground dropped away above the creek. Here at the east end, opposite the broken tombstone stairway, there was a more gradual slope. Whoever had mowed the lawn had skipped this part and a flattened trail led up through the weeds.

"He must have crawled up on his hands and knees," Wren said.

"You know where this is headed?" Jackson asked. "It's headed right back toward that camp."

"It couldn't be," Death countered. "The dogs searched all the property that belongs to the camp. They would have found it."

"But there's nothing else down there."

"What about the tombs?" Randy asked.

"Tombs?" Jackson frowned at him. "What tombs?"

"There are tombs cut into the side of the hill. I thought you searched this cemetery when you were looking for an open grave."

"I did, but I didn't go down by the creek. I stood at the edge and looked over, but I didn't see anything but a stretch of empty grass and the cemetery fence. What kind of tombs?"

"Dead hobbit houses," Wren offered unhelpfully.

"Hobbits aren't real."

"Then it's probably not really hobbits buried there," Death said. "The stairs are over this way."

Down below the cemetery, they walked slowly from tomb to tomb, looking for some signs of Jones' passage. Death was the first to reach the third tomb from the east. He stopped and stood looking down.

The tomb was built of dark red sandstone that nearly hid the bloodstains on the door and down the front. There was a circular patio of the same stones in front of the door and blood pooled there, the stain extending under the door and into the tomb. The door was a heavy iron affair, bolted and locked with a heavy padlock. There was a decorative wrought-iron grill in it, and from within came the stench of decay and a buzzing of flies.

"Oh, this is lovely," Wren said, dismayed.

"We're looking for a murder scene," Randy said, nudging her with his elbow. "What were you expecting?"

Jackson had a flashlight on his belt. He stepped up, avoiding the blood, and shone his light through the grill. Wren and the brothers Bogart crowded close to peer over his shoulder.

Beyond the door was a small, dark cavern. A coffin had been pulled from its niche in the wall, and a rotting corpse, clad only in tattered long johns, dangled out at an awkward angle. There was a pile of clothes in the back of the tomb and a beer can lay on its side against the wall, below the defiled corpse.

There were blood spatters everywhere.

TWELVE

"The tomb belonged to a man named Gilbert O'Hearne," Wren said.

"Gilbert?" Leona said. "Really? Damn. I didn't even know he'd passed."

"You knew him?"

"Not really, but he was a regular years ago. Any auction that had a lot of antiques, he'd be there. I haven't seen him in a long time, now you come to mention it. I can well understand him being the one who bought that uniform, though. Do we have any idea who stole it from him?"

"Not that I've heard. After we looked in the tomb, Jackson chased us out of the cemetery and called in the crime lab."

Leona gave her a look. "Rives County has a crime lab? Really?"

Wren laughed, then held her thought while Leona assigned a number to a late arrival. Outside the cash tent, an auction was well underway. It was a glorious autumn morning, with a light breeze dropping red and gold leaves into the green grass.

"I think the city sent down a team. This is still their homicide investigation, even though it's all tied up with Orly's accidental death case now too. Dozier's lawyer told Death that if they could find where the murder happened, it would change the jurisdiction, but apparently it's not that cut and dried. To be honest, I'm confused by the whole thing. But she and Death are working at cross purposes anyway. She wants to convince a jury that Dozier was crazy when he killed Jones, and Death doesn't think Dozier's the killer at all."

"What do you think?"

"I think I trust Death. If he's that sure about it, then I'm sure he's right."

Another customer arrived, a Mennonite woman with two little girls. They wore long homemade dresses and bonnets and the girls had braids. The woman carried a purse over her arm and a smartphone in her hand. Wren waited while Leona issued her a number, then waved at the girls as they left the tent.

"Death asked me something last night," she said, broaching the subject tentatively.

"Oh?"

"You know how he can't sleep in the same room with me, because he's afraid he'll have a nightmare or flashback and hurt me accidentally?"

Leona nodded. The older woman was one of Wren's closest confidants. The Keystones were family to her and she knew Leona would never gossip about a friend.

"Well, I guess he's been talking to Kurt Robinson. This whole thing with Dozier, falling in love with Zahra and then losing her the way he did, it's really affected Death. Robinson told him that you can't wait for everything to be perfect. You have to move ahead with your life. Do what you need to go forward, any way that you can. So

131

last night he asked me if I'd be willing to let him move in with me and sleep on my couch until and unless he gets to the point where he's able to share a bed."

"And what did you say?"

"I asked him to let me think about it." Wren frowned down at her hands, unhappy. "I think I hurt his feelings. But it's not that I don't want him to move in with me. I'd love for him to move in with me. But my house is so tiny. Just one bedroom and nowhere to add on. I mean, it's a nice quiet neighborhood when no one's shooting at me, but the houses are all so close. And I'm just not happy with the idea of him sleeping on the couch. It can't possibly be as comfortable as a real bed. And the living room is a public space, sort of. I don't want him to live somewhere where he feels like an outsider, just camping out because he doesn't have a place of his own. I want him to belong."

"And did you explain this to him?"

"Not really. I didn't quite know how to put it."

"Words are a good place to start."

Wren sighed. "I know, but—"

"You have to communicate! Neither one of you is psychic. Listen, I've been married for over thirty years, but when I want Roy to change his socks, I don't go around dropping hints and hoping he'll pick up on them. I say, 'Old man, go change those stinky socks!'"

Wren laughed. "I do kind of have an idea," she said, "but it's pretty big and I don't want him to feel like I'm pushing him."

"That's why you have to talk. Good Lord, Wren! You're an auctioneer. Talking is something you shouldn't have a problem with."

Matthew Keystone poked his head in the tent. "Hey, Wren. They're getting close to those antique toys. Gramps wants to know if you want to come sell them."

She hopped up. "Yeah. I'll be right there."

He ducked back out and she turned to Leona. "I guess I'll talk to him when I see him tonight. Thanks for the advice."

"Don't mention it. Telling people what to do is my specialty."

———

"O'Hearne lived in Independence." Death refilled his coffee, offered the carafe to Randy, who waved it away, and returned to his seat behind his desk. "He died in a nursing home in Lee's Summit a week before Zahra's accident and his body was shipped down here for burial. His family had settled down here before the Civil War and they had a plot in the church cemetery. That crypt was originally built for an umpteen-times-great uncle, but he was never buried there. During the Civil War, guerrillas robbed a Union munitions train and the uncle was caught trying to smuggle guns and ammunition to rebel troops in southern Missouri. He was sent to a Union prison, died of smallpox, and was buried there."

"So how come Jackson didn't find any of this when he was asking about recent burials?"

"Because no one contacted the local cemetery board about it. The family already owned the crypt and, because it *was* a crypt, they didn't have any need for a grave dug. And there was no funeral service. There was a memorial service up in the city, then the funeral parlor brought the body down and put it in the crypt. No one from the family even accompanied it down."

"That's cold."

Death shrugged and scrubbed a hand through his hair. "It's not what we would do," he allowed. He and his brother had had too much experience burying loved ones. "I talked to O'Hearne's grandson. They weren't close. The grandson is mixed-race and I gather

O'Hearne was an ass about it. Anyway, he had no idea who the dead guy on the path was."

"So how are we going to find out?"

"I'm working on that. This is what we know so far: According to the funeral parlor, the dead guy on the path attended O'Hearne's memorial service. He didn't sign the guest book. He did stay after to talk to the funeral director and ask about burial. He told the funeral director a story about an illicit love affair between his dead sister and O'Hearne and convinced the funeral director to leave the crypt open so he could, he said, slip in and put her picture in the casket without the family finding out and being distressed by an old scandal."

"He just said, 'Hey, leave the crypt open so I can sneak in' and the funeral director said, 'Sure'? Just like that?"

Death laughed. "Oh, I'm sure that money changed hands. Not that the funeral director is admitting it."

"You talked to him?"

"No, the police did. I just got the scoop from Chief Reynolds. The funeral director left the padlock inside the crypt, on the ledge with the casket. He thought that, if he left it hanging on the hasp, someone might come along and close it. The agreement was that the guy sneaking in would put it on before he left."

"Ah." Randy leaned back and kicked his feet up on the desk.

Death allowed himself a moment to savor the sight. For the worst part of a year he'd thought his brother was dead, and now he had him back again.

"So how do you figure the whole thing played out, with O'Hearne and the murder and everything?" Randy asked. "Was the dead guy on the path involved in the murder of August Jones?"

"No, I don't think so. This is the way I figure it. The dead guy on the path wanted O'Hearne's Civil War uniform and arranged for the crypt to be left open so he could get in to steal it. The day of Zahra's funeral, August Jones hitched a ride down to the veterans' camp with Dexter Wallace because he'd gotten a phone call to meet someone down there."

"He got a call from someone in the vicinity of the camp, right?"

"Right, so possibly one of the vets, even though I hate to think that. Anyway, he got a call and they arranged a meeting in the church cemetery. He met the killer, either by chance or design, near the open crypt, and the killer stabbed him and left him for dead. The killer closed him in the crypt, but couldn't lock him in because they didn't know where the lock was."

"You know," Randy said, "whoever stabbed him would have gotten covered in blood. Stabbings are messy. Trust me. I know."

"I know. The killer could have washed the blood off their skin in the creek, but they'd have needed clean clothes and a place to change."

"There are cabins at the camp."

"But there were also a lot of people there, moving around. I have to think that, with that much blood, someone would have noticed. If they didn't see it—they'd covered it up, say—they still would have smelled it. And the killer would have had to leave traces in the cabin where they'd changed clothes, and if they did, the dogs should have alerted on that."

"But the dogs were just pups and not fully trained yet."

"Yeah." Death sighed. "For every argument, there's a counter-argument. For everything I think I should be able to deduce, there are a dozen alternatives."

"Okay, so anyway, the killer leaves August Jones for dead," Randy prompted.

"The killer leaves him for dead. But Jones manages to get out of the crypt and goes off in search of help. He makes it to the edge of the road below the angel, where Dozier finds him, like we talked about earlier."

"Right."

"That same night, the, um, other dead guy—or soon to be dead guy—gets drunk and comes down to steal the uniform. He drove down on the motorcycle that Robin Keystone found hidden in the falling-down building behind the Hadleigh House. He made his way to the cemetery, went into the crypt, and stole the uniform and put it on. In the dark he didn't see the bloodstains from the murder so he didn't know anyone else had been in there."

"Here's a question," Randy said thoughtfully. "How did he find his way through the woods to the cemetery in the dark? And wasn't there a storm brewing that night too?"

"Yeah. That's why Kurt had the horses in the barn, where the dead guy was able to get to them and steal Sugar. It was a dark and stormy night."

"Ha ha."

"But you know, that's a good question." Death sat back and thought about it, drumming his fingers on the surface of his desk. He sat up abruptly and reached for his phone.

"Hello, Jackson? Hey! I've got an idea for you."

He put the phone on speaker and set it on the desk, and the deputy's voice came across the line. "Of course you do. You're full of ideas. And then, after I spend eight hours in the library squinting at microfilm or waste an entire day and two tanks of gas driving up to Independence and back you're all, 'Oh, I guess that wasn't such a clever idea after all.' I'm not buying any more of your ideas, Bogart."

"It took you two tanks of gas to make it to Independence and back? You should get a tune-up."

"Don't change the subject. What's your stupid idea this time?"

"Actually, it's more Randy's idea."

"I had an idea?"

"Trying to shift the blame already?" Jackson asked.

"Shaddup and listen. Your John Doe parked his motorcycle at the Hadleigh House and made his way from there to the cemetery through the dark woods at night. Drunk, even."

"He probably wasn't that drunk on his way in. He took plenty of liquid courage with him. When we got into the tomb there were four more beer cans with the plastic holder that a six-pack comes with and an empty bottle of Jack."

"Okay, but he still found his way through the woods and to the cemetery at night."

"So?"

"So the chances are that he'd scouted it out ahead of time. How much gas was in the gas tank on that motorcycle?"

"It was over three-quarters full. You're thinking he filled the tank when he was scouting out the location of the crypt?"

"Yeah, and if it was that full, he had to have gassed up somewhere in this general vicinity. So if you ask around at all the local gas stations and maybe watch their security video for the time between O'Hearne's memorial service and the night that John Doe fell off his horse, maybe you can find where and when he stopped. If he paid with a credit card, boom! You've got his identity. And even if he didn't, maybe he wouldn't have taken the tags off his bike yet and you could get his license plate and run it."

"Huh." Jackson hummed thoughtfully over the phone line. "That's actually not a bad idea. And it would only take me, what? A week to interview gas station attendants between here and the city and study hundreds of hours worth of security video?"

"I never said it would be easy."

"No, you didn't, did you." The deputy laughed abruptly. "His name was Jack Harriman."

"He … wait. What? You know who he was?"

"Yeah. He left his wallet in the pants he took off to put on that uniform. He lived alone in a one-bedroom apartment in the city. No family. No friends. No pets. Huge collection of Civil War crap. Apparently he and O'Hearne were rival collectors. O'Hearne was buried in that uniform specifically to keep Harriman from getting it. Harriman thought he'd have the last laugh. Would have been really funny if he hadn't ended up dead. He was running around the countryside in a dead man's clothes with all his stuff locked into the vault with the corpse. I guess it never occurred to him to take his clothes."

———

Randy had gone back to the apartment to change, and Death was hunched over his desk studying photographs taken at Warriors' Rest the morning of the funeral when his phone rang. He had it set to vibrate, and it shuddered and skittered on the edge of the blotter. He caught it up and looked at the readout before answering

It was Wren, and his heart stuttered a bit with a dread that he was unaccustomed to feeling where she was concerned.

"Hello?"

"Hi, sweetheart. What are you doing?"

He sighed. "Going around in circles mostly. You?"

"I came back out to the Hadleigh House after the auction to get a little more work done." Her voice took on a dry, wry tone. "Tyler Jones came back. He's still looking for his son's phone. I can understand him wanting to find it, and I kind of feel bad that I don't feel sorrier for him, but he is *such* an ass."

"What did he do this time?"

"Oh, just the usual. I told him Proverbs 3:15 and he gave me a hateful look and went away."

"What's that? The Proverbs thing, I mean."

"It's what Doris told me to say if he bothered me again. Something like 'God's watching you,' I think."

"Ah. Good for Doris. I'm glad she's on our side."

"Yeah. Me too."

They lapsed into an uncomfortable silence. For probably the first time since they'd met, the conversation felt awkward and constrained between them. Death kicked himself for causing this and determined to make it right.

"Listen, I shouldn't have asked you that. I know we've only known each other a few months and I understand if you're—"

She cut him off. "Death! No! I want to live with you. And I understand you needing your own space to sleep in to feel secure. The only thing I have a problem with is you sleeping on the couch. Couches aren't for people who live there to sleep on. Not as a regular thing, I mean. They're for dogs and drunk cousins and friends who forgot their wife's birthday again."

Death laughed, lighthearted again. "I understand that. But honey, you only have one bedroom. Unless you want to build me a kennel in the back yard?"

She giggled at him, her voice warm and soothing over the phone. "I've got another idea, but I don't want you to feel like I'm trying to push you into anything before you're ready."

"Just tell me."

"Okay." She took a deep breath, the rush of air coming across the phone line. "I think we should sell my house and find one that's big enough for both of us."

Death sat back and blinked, because that wasn't at all what he'd thought she was going to say. "You want to buy a house together?"

"I know it's a big commitment! That's why I was afraid to say anything. I don't want you to feel like I'm rushing you. And we don't have to buy one if you don't want to. We could always just rent for the time being."

"Sweetheart … didn't your godmother leave you that house?"

"Oh, honey. Nana would understand." The warmth of her reply reached him across the phone line. "People are always more important than things. And to me, you're more important than anyone."

THIRTEEN

WREN WAS IN THE parlor, in the center of Hadleigh House, when she heard a knock on the door. None of the Keystones would knock, and neither would either of the Bogart brothers, so she steeled herself for another visit from Jones and stormed into the entryway with a chip on her shoulder.

It was not the religious zealot standing on the other side of the door, though. It was a massive man in a tan Sheriff's Department uniform. His shoulders filled the window and her eyes only came up to the middle of his chest. Wren relaxed and opened the door with a grin.

Sheriff Casey Salvadore ducked his head below the top of the doorframe and beamed at her. "Got any chips?"

"I just might have." She pulled the door all the way open and waved an invitation for him to enter. Salvy was a huge black man, a giant teddy bear with a perpetual, infectious smile and a spirit so great that even his six foot five frame seemed too small to contain it. The potato chips were an old joke between them.

Salvy, then a deputy, had been the first officer to ever pull her over. She'd been sixteen. It was only a week after she got her license and she was on her way home after a high school drama club picnic. Driving down Third Street, where there were no streetlights or lane markings and the parking lots came down to the road on both sides, she'd gotten onto the wrong side of the road.

When she saw the police lights behind her, she'd been terrified. Salvy had asked her a few questions about where she'd been and where she was going (and why she was on the wrong side of the road), and then he'd wanted to know what was in the paper bag on the back seat.

"Potato chips!" she'd shrieked, grabbing the bag and shoving it in his face. "Do you wanna see?"

Because she was so young, and because they were potato chips and not, say, cheap booze, the kindhearted officer had let her off with a warning. Now, years later, he still teased her about it.

"Did you really want potato chips?" she asked.

"Do you really have any?"

She had a stash of snacks and a small cooler of soda pop sitting beside the stairs, and she fetched him a little bag of chips. He took it but then hesitated.

"I'm not eating your lunch?"

Wren waved away his concern. "Those are left over from yesterday. Help yourself."

"How does anyone have leftover potato chips?" he asked rhetorically, tearing open the bag and digging in.

She let him eat a couple of handfuls before she spoke again. "You didn't really come all the way out here just to bum day-old potato chips?"

"Mmm. No." He sighed. "Tyler Jones has been making himself unpleasant. I understand his concerns, but he's meddling in an unsolved murder case. He's demanding to know what's going on with his son's missing cell phone, and he wants the police to make you let him search here for it. The detective up in the city asked me to see if I could get him out of his hair."

"I don't want him in here!" Wren objected. "He called me a broom!"

Salvy blinked and thought about it. "Okay, I'm not going to ask. Anyway, you don't need to worry. I've already explained to him that him searching anything isn't going to happen and that, if he doesn't stop pestering you, there will be consequences."

"Consequences?"

"Consequences. Like trespassing charges and restraining orders. I did tell him that I would see if you would allow me to look around. I don't have a warrant, but would you mind?"

"Of course not. I think you're wasting your time, but go ahead and look all you like."

Salvy finished his potato chips and Wren added the empty package to her collection of trash. He brushed his greasy fingers off against his uniform pants and looked around.

"This place is huge. Want to give me the tour?"

She shrugged. "The house is mostly just a big two-story rectangle with a one-story kitchen added onto the back, but there's a little, not a wing exactly, but a bit of an extension on the south end. See, the entry hall with the main staircase is right in the middle. It divides the north and south ends of the house and there's also a hallway running down the middle, north and south, that divides the east and west sides." She led him to the back of the entry hall. There was a door in the middle of the back wall and long hallways opening both left and right.

"This door is the downstairs bathroom. There are three more upstairs. If you take this hall, to the north, there's a morning room and then a game room on the left and a study and then a smoking room on the right. The smoking room has another door leading into the parlor and you can go through there into the kitchen, but we haven't gone through that yet."

"Did it look like anyone else had gone through there?"

"No. You can look if you want to. No one's been in there in decades and the whole room is coated with thick, greasy gray dust. Leona said to leave it for now. If Matthew gets into trouble, she'll make him clean it."

"Is she expecting Matthew to get into trouble?"

"Well … he's Matthew."

"True. What about that door at the end of the hallway? I understand this place was still closed up the night of the murder. Could someone have gotten in there?"

She shook her head. "That was the door out into the carport, but the carport roof has collapsed and the door isn't just locked, it's actually nailed shut."

"What about the other end of the house?"

They went across the room and stood at the entrance to the other hallway.

"On the right, at the front of the house, there's a parlor and a sewing room. The left side just has one big room, the dining room. You can get to it from the kitchen. There's also a music room in the extension that you can only get to by going through the dining room. It's beside the kitchen, but there's no door between them. The upstairs is all bedrooms and dressing rooms, except for three bathrooms and a library. We've pretty much cleared out the upstairs except for a few pieces of heavy furniture and the library. I'm going to be working in there today."

"And I'm guessing you haven't found a cell phone anywhere?"

"We'd tell you if we did," she said. "You know we would."

"Yeah, I know."

Salvy walked through the house with Wren trailing after, asking questions about the house and contents and about the sale and making observations about the architecture. When they were back at the front hall, he turned to her.

"Is there anywhere I haven't seen yet?"

"There's a storm cellar, but you have to go outside to get to it."

"Show me?"

"Sure."

They went out the back door, into the garden, and she led him to a mound of earth in the corner beyond the clotheslines. It had a metal pipe coming out of the top of it and a slanting door set in concrete on the side nearest the house. It wasn't locked and Salvy leaned down and easily dragged it open, with the *screee* of old hinges. It revealed a set of stone steps leading down to another door.

The space between the doors was completely filled with cobwebs.

Wren poked Salvy in the shoulder. "Well? What are you waiting for? Go search the cellar."

"Yeah, I don't think anyone's been down here."

"They could have dropped the phone down the vent pipe."

He gave her a baleful glare. "You had to think of that." He straightened up, took a flashlight from his belt, and climbed up on the mound.

"Salvy? What are you doing? Are you sure that's safe? That cellar's really old. It could collapse with you. I don't want you to get hurt."

Ignoring her, he lay down on the mound, shone his light through the vent pipe, and peered down into the cellar.

"Oh my God!"

"What?" she demanded. "What? What is it? What do you see?"

Salvy looked up and pierced her with a dark stare. Then, he grinned.

"I think I just found Waldo!"

———

"Dag *nabbit*, Roy! I swear!"

Wren was back at the Hadleigh House, working in the library, on the second floor at the opposite end of the hall from the room where she'd found the sketch pad. It was a glorious fall morning, and she had the window open to a warm breeze that tossed the curtains. Raised voices reached her again, a discordant babble, and she went over to look out and see if she could see what was going on.

The Keystone men, with the Robinsons' help, were attempting to put a new bridge over the ravine. Leaves had begun to drop and she could just make out a blur of activity beyond the thinning foliage. They'd gotten their hands on the top deck of an old automobile carrier and were trying to maneuver it into place across the gully with the help of Sam Keystone's brother-in-law's tractor and a block-and-tackle that Nichelle Robinson had rigged up.

Sam's voice reached her again. "I swear! There was a reason Mom said I was the smart one."

"Oh yeah?" Roy shot back. "Well, you might be smart, but I'm pretty. So there!"

Wren laughed, shook her head, and returned to her work. She was packing the books into boxes, but she was being more careful than usual about labelling them and she was reading the titles, publishing information, and condition for each book off into the recorder on her phone. Some of these were going to be rare volumes, and it would be a shame to let them go to someone who didn't know what they were. It would also be bad business.

There was no order that she could find to the library. It hadn't just been for show, she could tell that. These books had been read; some of them had been well-read, with dog-eared pages and broken spines. The sun coming in the window made her drowsy, and she breathed in the heady scent of old paper and printer's ink and daydreamed.

This would be a nice place to live, if it wasn't so ridiculously huge. It had a nice feeling to it. She and Death could have adjoining rooms and they could put a door between them. She could fill these shelves with her own books and have room for as many more as she wanted. Death could have the study for an office, and she could use the music room for her sewing and crafts.

She took another stack of books off the shelf, set them on the desk beside her, and read off the names as she put them, one by one, into the next crate.

Little Benji could stay over with them sometimes, and when he did he could sleep in the nursery. There'd even be enough room that they could just let Randy have the other end of the house to live in.

"*Shepherd of the Hills* by Harold Bell Wright," she read. "Fifties edition, excellent condition. *Stranger in a Strange Land* by Heinlein, paperback, poor condition."

For that matter, they could let just about anyone they knew live there, as big as the Hadleigh House was. Wren smiled to herself.

Madeline and Eric could stay in the cellar. If they could get the cellar door open. If not, they could have the crawlspace.

She considered the idea a bit more and shuddered. "Getting a little creepy there," she admonished herself.

"*A Tear and a Smile* by Kahlil Gibran." This book had a slip of paper just peeking from between its pages and she stopped and carefully opened it to see what was there. It was a letter, written on tissue-thin paper and stamped with a 1920s international airmail stamp that was valuable in its own right.

As Wren drew the paper out, she glanced at the pages it was between. It was a poem titled "The Beauty of Death," and the name rang a distant bell. She stopped and thought about it and eventually retrieved a faded memory of a long-ago ghost story. There'd been a young woman, a tragic young woman with a romantic temperament and an interest in Spiritualism and reincarnation. After she'd killed herself, her brother remembered that she'd been obsessed with this poem.

Wren's thoughts went to Aramis Defoe and the pill bottle on his nightstand. She set the book down and opened the letter gently and was not surprised to see his name in the salutation.

> Douaumont sur Meuse
> 24 April 1923

Aramis, my dear, dear friend,

I am so very sorry to report that I have found no trace of the young woman you told me about. I have checked with the authorities in Verdun and all of the local churches in the belief that a displaced refugee would go to one of those establishments in search of aid. Indeed, there have been thousands upon thousands of civilians in distress, but records are rare and, even when they exist, incomplete. No one remembers her, but that does not necessarily signify anything.

I would tell you, in hopes of cheering you, that I also have not found a grave nor any record of her death, but I know that you know as well as I that this does not mean much. We both remember, I am sure, how brutally the war tore through this once lovely land. Montfaucon is completely destroyed and they have no plans to try to rebuild it. Indeed, even the hill upon which it stood has been rent asunder. Agathe's farm, which you directed me to, is gone without a trace. It is cratered with shell holes. The buildings, the trees, even the well have disappeared. Only the grass and the wildflowers have made so bold as to return.

I will continue to make inquiries of anyone I meet who may, by even the slightest chance, have knowledge of her whereabouts. I think, though, my dear friend, that it would be well to prepare yourself for the probability that you and she are not destined to meet again this side of the veil. I have no doubt that, hopefully many years in the future, when the time has come for you to shed your mortal coil, you shall find her awaiting you in that more beautiful and peaceful countryside beyond.

Forever your friend,
Henri

Wren turned the letter over. On the back, penciled in lightly, was a very rough sketch of a woman standing beside a well holding out a ladle.

"A Mexican restaurant? Really?"

Death gave his brother a sideways glance. "You act like you think I made this up."

Randy shrugged. "Part of me thinks you did."

"I didn't." He held the door and let the younger man enter before him.

A large young man in a blue T-shirt and white apron met them holding two menus. He was dark-haired and dark-complected, but when he spoke his accent was Middle Eastern rather than Hispanic. "Two?"

Death started to say that they weren't there to eat, but Randy had gotten a whiff of what was cooking and spoke before he could. "Yeah! I'm starving!"

"Two," Death agreed. He followed the server to a booth near a window. "How can you be starving? You just ate!"

"This is lunch."

"It isn't even eleven yet."

"Then it's brunch."

"You've already eaten twice today."

"That was breakfast and second breakfast. What are you? The food police?"

"Your metabolism is insane." Death glanced at the menu, then looked up as the server returned with water and chips and salsa.

"My name is Sammy and I'll be your server today. Can I start you off with something to drink?"

"I'd like a coffee, please," Death said. "Hey, I was hoping to talk to Ali. Is he here?"

"Yes, sir. That's my cousin. He's back in the office. I'll get him for you."

"Thanks."

Randy asked for a soda and Sammy returned a minute later with their drinks. He was accompanied by a slender, dark-complected man in his mid-thirties.

"Hi, I'm Ali. Sammy said you wanted to speak with me?"

Death rose to meet him. "Hi. I'm Death Bogart. I'm a private investigator. I'm investigating the murder of August Jones. I understand he spent some time at your mosque and I was hoping you could tell me about him."

"Oh. Yeah, that whole situation was just terrible." Ali pulled a chair around from a neighboring table and sat down with them. Unlike his younger cousin, he had only the faintest accent. "I don't know what happened, but I swear to Allah, Tony Dozier is not a man who'd kill anyone."

"What do you know about August Jones?" Death asked. "What was he like? I'm trying to get some sense of him. Did you have any inkling that he wasn't what he said he was?"

Ali was shaking his head before Death finished speaking. "No. No, absolutely not. Gus introduced himself as a journalist, said he was doing a story about religion in America. When he first showed up, I think we all knew he was coming in with a bias against us. But by the time Zahra died, he'd really seemed to warm up to us. He was—or he seemed—honestly friendly. He went to a baseball game with some of us. He came to a birthday party for one of the kids. I thought he was a nice guy. I mean it. I really thought he was a nice guy."

"What did you think when you found out who he really was and why he was there?"

"That the world is a really screwed-up place. And it sucks that he got killed the way he did. Partly because of Tony being a suspect, but also because we never had a chance to talk to Gus about it."

"Was there anything about Gus that stands out in your memory? Did he ever seem nervous or afraid? Was there anyone he spent more time with? Anyone he avoided? Did you ever see him fight with anyone? Did you see him the morning of the funeral? I'm told that he was at your mosque that morning, and that's where he hitched a ride down to East Bledsoe Ferry."

"Man, I don't know. That morning was just horrible. My wife had been at that same candle party that Zahra was at. She was on her way home, you know. We just couldn't believe she was dead." Ali thought about it. "Yes, Gus was there. I remember seeing him at the mosque that morning. I think I saw him telling Tony how sorry he was about what had happened. And I know I saw him later, interviewing people. I didn't notice him at the funeral, but I didn't notice him not being there, either."

"He was interviewing people?"

"Yeah. You know? He said he was a journalist. He used to record everything on his phone. He even carried around extra SD cards so he'd have enough storage. That was just something you knew about him. If you were talking to Gus, chances were that he was recording you. Usually he'd tell people, but I think sometimes he'd forget. He'd just turn the phone on and drop it in his pocket."

They sat for a few minutes in pensive silence broken only by the sound of Randy crunching his way through the chips and salsa. By and by he dusted his fingers on the front of his shirt, took a long swig of soda, and said to Ali, "can I ask you something?"

"Sure. Shoot."

"You're not Mexican."

"Wow. You really are a detective," Ali teased. "That's not a question."

"No, that was an observation. My question is, why a Mexican restaurant?"

Ali laughed and shrugged. "Life happens? I don't really know. I came here to study business. I thought a degree from an American university would help me land a high-dollar job with some international tech firm or something. Somewhere along the line, Kansas City became home. I worked here, started as a busboy, when I was in college. When the former owner wanted to retire, I was able to get the financing and take over the business."

"That's cool," Randy said. "You speak excellent English."

"Thank you. So do you."

Death snickered into his coffee.

"Ha ha. English is your second language though, isn't it?"

"Third, actually. Sammy and I are from Tunisia. We speak French and Arabic."

"French? Really?" Randy lit up. "I've always wanted to learn French. It seems like a really romantic language. I bet the ladies love to hear it."

"Oh, they do," Ali agreed. "Hey, you want me to teach you how to say something in French?"

"Really?"

"Sure. I can teach you how to say 'Hi, do you want to be my friend?'"

"Cool!"

"Okay," Ali said, "repeat after me. *Voulez-vouz couchez avec moi ce soir.*"

Death stuffed his mouth with chips and studied the table, careful not to meet his brother's eye. Randy repeated the phrase several times until he was sure he had it memorized.

"Here," Ali said, "Sammy will be out in a minute with your food. Say it to him."

"Okay. Cool!" Randy jumped up and went over to wait beside the door to the kitchen.

Ali grinned at Death. "You speak French?"

"No, but I was a Marine. I can get my face slapped in seventeen different languages."

"But you didn't give me away?"

"Are you kidding? That's my kid brother. This is hilarious."

"Watch Sammy's face. He gets so embarrassed. That's why I do it."

The door swung open and Sammy came out with a loaded serving tray. Randy popped up beside him. "Hey, Sammy, *voulez-vouz*—"

Sammy turned bright red. He set the tray down on the nearest table and waved his hands in front of Randy's face. "No. No! It doesn't mean that! Don't listen to Ali! Ali *lies*!"

Randy spun around to glare back at the older men, and Death laughed until he was in danger of passing out.

Later, when they were back out in Death's Jeep, Randy decided to give him grief. "I know you knew that wasn't what he said it was. You could have warned me."

"Where would be the fun in that?" Death paused, his hand on the key in the ignition, and just sat there smiling at his brother.

"What are you doing?" Randy asked nervously. "You know, that's a little creepy. You just sitting there smiling at me like that."

Death shrugged. He started the engine but made no move to drive away. "I just ... it's just that I keep finding myself thinking. Remembering. How everything was a year ago. I never dreamed my life could ever be this good again."

They sat there in silence for a few seconds. "It's good, then?" Randy asked. "Really good?"

"Yeah. Really good."

"Good … are we having a moment? Do you need a hug?"

"Idiot," Death said affectionately.

"You know, I was thinking," Randy said. "If August Jones recorded everything—"

"There's a chance he recorded his own murder. Yeah. That occurred to me too."

"If I killed someone who recorded stuff on their phone," Randy said, "I'd want to be sure to take the phone with me when I left."

"Well, they didn't find it in the tomb, or in the ditch below the angel, or anywhere in between."

"So that would suggest that the murderer took it."

"That's certainly possible," Death agreed reluctantly.

"But the last place the phone pinged before it died was out at the vets' camp."

"Yeah, I know. Believe me, that's occurred to me."

"So what do you want to do now?"

"I want to go shopping." Death put the Jeep in gear and headed for the exit. "Do you want to come shopping with me?"

Randy gave him a wide-eyed, disbelieving look. "Okay. Should we get our nails done while we're at it? Hey! Maybe we can find a good shoe sale or get matching purses."

Death laughed. "That's not what I'm shopping for."

FOURTEEN

"But seriously," Randy said. "How many people do you think are in that car?"

"You know, if you're that curious, you could always go look," Wren told him.

"The windows are fogged up."

"If you tap on the door," Death said, "they'll probably open it."

"And invite you to join them," Wren added with a wicked grin.

Randy frowned at the other two. "Man, you guys aren't right, you know that?"

The three of them were sitting in the back seat of Death's Jeep, Death on the driver's side with Wren cuddled up close beside him, and Randy angled against the passenger door. They were parked in a sea of cars, on the old, cracked, and rutted parking lot of the Feed-n-Seed Emporium. On the last Friday of the month, the Rives County Volunteer Fire Department, the East Bledsoe Ferry Fire Department, and the MedEvac Helicopter Rescue Service staged Drive-In Movie Night as a joint fundraiser for their various charities.

There was no actual drive-in theater in the area, and there hadn't been for decades, but the whitewashed wall of the feed store served as the screen for a projection TV and they broadcast the sound as a podcast. Tonight, in honor of the onset of autumn and the approach of Halloween, the showing was a double-feature of classic horror movies. With no news on either of the police cases they'd become entangled in, they'd decided to take a night off and just enjoy themselves.

They could only hope that the movies would be scarier than being parked next to Farrington, Madeline, and whoever else they were sharing a vehicle with. There were at least three people in the car and they'd started a heavy makeout session early. Already the windows were fogged up and the car was rocking in a manner that suggested it needed new shocks.

"You know what they're doing, don't you?" Wren asked. "This is just like when they showed up in St. Louis. They're trying to make Death jealous. Madeline's trying to make Death jealous by letting him see her with another, um, something that passes for a man if you have a wild enough imagination. And Eric's trying to make Death jealous by letting him see him with his ex-wife."

"If they're wasting their time trying to make me jealous," Death said, "then I pity them. There's nothing either of them has that I want." He considered. "Well, I'd take Benji, but as long as I get to see him sometimes, I'm happy."

"Where does the third person in their car come in?" Randy asked.

"That I don't know. And I don't want to know, either!"

"Hey," Death said, "the movie's starting! Turn on the podcast."

Wren pulled up the podcast on her phone and they settled in to watch the film. "Man, these movies make me crazy," she said. "How come the people in them are all so stupid? You know, if one of these demon-possessed, undead serial killers ever had to take out a cabin full of smart coeds, they'd never make it out of the film alive."

"They don't make it out of the film alive," Randy said. "They make it out undead, the same way they went in."

"Smartass."

After half an hour of yelling at the screen, Wren took a deep breath, looked around at Death and Randy, and realized they were laughing at her.

"Oh, crap," she said. "I'm sorry! I just can't seem to keep my mouth shut. Am I ruining the movie for you?"

The brothers reassured her that she wasn't.

"Are you kidding?" Death asked. "You're way more fun than this movie. You do realize that the characters can't hear you though, right?"

She stuck her tongue out at him.

"Hey, look!" Randy said. "I think the blonde chick is going to put on her high heels and run through the muddy garden in search of help."

"What?" Wren turned back to the movie. "What are you doing?" she shouted. "Don't do that! If you can't find real shoes, go barefoot! And don't go out in the garden. There's nothing in the garden. Find your friends! Build a barricade! Arm yourself, for God's sake!"

"Oh, maybe she heard you. She's going to look in the pantry for running shoes."

"Is that what she's doing? Do you think that's what she's doing?" There was no dialogue at the moment and they were having to figure out the characters' thoughts and motivation from their actions.

"I think so. See, she's looking at her feet, and then her shoes, and looking from the pantry to the back door and biting her lip, like she's having trouble deciding what to do. Okay, now she's headed for the pantry—"

"Because everyone keeps their spare shoes in the pantry," Wren scoffed.

"I sense you're having difficulties with your suspension of disbelief," Death observed sagely.

"You're an observational genius."

"This has been said." Death cocked an eyebrow at the screen. "Hey, wait a minute. Didn't the short guy hide in the pantry a little while ago? Ten bucks says she finds his body."

"Ha. No bet," Randy said.

They watched as the blonde chick, as Randy had dubbed her, crept nervously across the kitchen and reached for the pantry door. The house, in the movie, was dark. The premise, as far as they could tell, was that a group of college kids had gone to an isolated vacation cabin for a weekend of debauchery, only to come across the path of an undead demonic serial killer who was now stalking them and leaving their gory corpses for their friends to find.

The blonde eased open the door. Her body stiffened. She put her hands to her mouth and let out a horrified, terrified wail. The camera lingered on her back as she stood in a convenient moonbeam, screaming into the pantry. Then it showed them a close-up of her screaming, and finally switched to the cause of her distress.

As Death had guessed, the body of the short guy dangled from the pantry ceiling, a piece of bloody metal protruding from his chest.

"Is that a meat hook?" Wren demanded. "Why is there a meat hook? Who keeps a meat hook hanging from the ceiling on a chain in a vacation cabin? You don't keep meat hooks in vacation cabins. You keep paper plates and, if you can remember to bring one, a can opener. Did the killer bring it? Is he walking around with a pocket full of meat hooks, just in case he comes across some drunk college kids?"

"You know," Randy said, "I do think you're being a little harsh with the college kids. After all, they're drunk and their friends keep getting killed and it's dark and all."

"It doesn't have to be dark. All they have to do is turn a light on."

"But the killer cut the power. Didn't you see?"

"He turned off the main breaker. All you have to do is turn it back on. Do none of them understand how a breaker box works? It's not that hard!"

"So what would you do?" Randy asked. "If you were there, in that cabin, just like that, being stalked by an undead demonic serial killer"

"Well, for starters, I'd turn the power back on."

"But wouldn't he just turn it back off again?"

"Then I'd turn it back on."

"So you'd spend the whole film flipping a switch at each other? You know, this could get to be an awfully boring movie."

"Oh, but he wouldn't turn it back off if he didn't know I'd turned it on."

"Wait, what?" Randy asked. Death was just sitting back in his corner of the backseat, holding Wren and laughing too hard to talk.

"I wouldn't let him know I'd turned it on. I'd make sure all the lights were out, then I'd turn the main breaker back on so there'd be power in the lines. Then I'd take that big lamp there and break the bulb, but leave it in the socket, and when the killer came looking for me, I'd stab him with it."

"So, what? You think that'd electrocute him?"

"Wouldn't it?" Wren asked. "Like sticking a fork in a light socket, is what I thought. You'd probably have to make sure the lamp was turned on."

"I don't know. Maybe. But he's undead and demonic. Can you electrocute undead demonic serial killers?"

"It's worth a try."

"What if it didn't work? Then what would you do?"

"I'd hit him with the lamp!"

Behind Randy, the car with Eric and Madeline, et al., finally stopped rocking and bouncing. Wren saw a hand wipe clear an area of the rear window and Madeline peeked out at the Jeep. Her face, in the reflected glow of the movie, looked wistful.

The front door opened and Eric stumbled out. He was shirtless. His belt hung loose, his pants were undone, and his hair was a mess. He gave the Jeep a drunken, lopsided grin and a thumbs-up, closed the front car door, opened the rear car door, and climbed inside. A woman's hand came out and caught the handle and pulled it closed.

"Now that," Wren said, "that over there? That's scary!"

———

"Man! Why you gotta do this to me?"

When Death picked Randy up after work, he already had a passenger in the back seat of his Jeep. A sullen, handcuffed, complaining passenger.

"You wouldn't have to do this if you'd made your court date," he told the man.

"I forgot, all right? I just got the days mixed up. You couldn't cut me some slack, man?"

"You shouldn't have tried to run."

"What did he do?" Randy asked.

"Attempted theft." Death tilted the rearview mirror so he could look back at his prisoner. "Grandy here thought he could run with the big boys, but Salvy caught him in the act at that place over on Second."

The East Bledsoe Ferry police station was on the town square, sitting kitty-corner to Death's office. The street was made up of two lanes separated by a line of parking spaces, with the inner lane travelling clockwise around the courthouse and the outer lane going widdershins. On a normal day, it was crowded but not packed.

Today was not normal. The entire inner lane was blocked off and half the central parking places were taken up by equipment vans and food trucks. Workers were busy building booths and a stage on the courthouse lawn, while a carnival set up rides and games in the street.

Randy looked around at the chaos. "What in the Sam Hill is going on here?" he asked.

"It's, ah, some kind of harvest festival," Death said. "Heritage Days or something. There's stuff going up all over town, but it seems to be centered here. Wren was telling me about it. I guess it's an annual thing."

"Huh."

Death maneuvered into a parking place in front of the police station and they went in to deliver his prisoner. When Grandy had been checked in and taken back to the cells, Death and Randy lingered to talk.

"What are you doing playing bounty hunter again?" Chief Reynolds asked. "I thought that was just a fallback if the private eye gig dried up."

"Favor for a friend," Death replied. "Hagarson's out of town and one of his clients skipped, so he called me. So, ah, have you heard anything new on the Dozier case?"

"I don't know anything you don't," Reynolds said. "I'm assuming, because of the way they're acting, that there's no hard evidence connecting Dozier to the murder scene in the crypt. No fingerprints or anything. The KC cops haven't come right out and said as much, but they haven't announced that they've got it wrapped up, either."

"We need that cell phone," Death said. "There's a good chance Jones recorded his own murder."

"I agree, but how are you going to find it? The last place it pinged before the battery died was out at Warriors' Rest. We've been over that ground with a fine-tooth comb. Tried dogs and metal detectors. Nothing."

"Have you considered a psychic?" Randy joked.

"Do you know one?" Reynolds countered.

"Well, uh . . . "

"That's what I thought."

"Now, I did date this girl once who always knew who was on the phone before she looked at caller ID. Sometimes she'd know before it even rang. Couldn't ever come up with lottery numbers or anything like that, though, so probably that wouldn't be very helpful."

The back door to the room swung open and Eric Farrington strutted in. He saw Death and Randy and his eyes lit up.

"Hey, Bogart! I was just thinking. Did you ever see that show about wife swapping? Well, I thought—"

"No."

"But—"

"No. And pray I don't tell Wren about this conversation."

"What the hell are you doing here?" Reynolds asked Farrington. "I thought I gave you a job to do."

"I did it. It's done. I did a helluva job, too."

"He did, Chief." Officer Grigsby had come in behind the jailor. "Those cells are practically sparkling. Of course, there were only two he could clean. The others are occupied."

"Well, good. Now he can go move the prisoners out of two of the other cells and clean them. And keep doing that until he's got them all."

Farrington's face fell. "But if I put prisoners in the clean cells they'll just get them dirty again. And if they see me having to clean them all, the prisoners I haven't gotten to yet will mess up the ones they're in."

"Yeah." Reynolds smiled. "It's gonna be a helluva job. Maybe while you're doing it, you can think about all the reasons you shouldn't be running around with a civilian trying to 'execute a search warrant.'"

———

"And-a-fifteen-and-a-fifteen-got-a-fifteen-and-a-sixteen-and-a-sevente—" Wren broke off in mid call. "Just a second here. Do you two know that you're bidding against each other?"

It wasn't her responsibility to point it out and a lot of auctioneers wouldn't have, but not doing so would have felt dishonest. Integrity was one of the cornerstones of Keystone and Sons.

The two women bidding from opposite sides of the crowd craned their necks to see one another.

"Mother?"

"Darlene! What are you doing? I said I was going to buy it."

"I didn't see you and I thought you were losing out, so I was bidding for you."

Wren tapped the top of the little wooden jewelry chest she was selling. "Okay, let's go back to the last bid we had from a third party." She pointed to a gentleman in the crowd. "You bid eleven, right?"

He nodded.

"Okay, then, starting with eleven…"

Later, after she'd handed the stepladder and microphone off to Roy's son Tim, Wren wandered around the kitchen of the house where the auction was being held. They weren't selling the house; the owners had opted to go through a realtor in the hopes of getting a higher price. It was a split-level ranch style home from the seventies, with an open floor plan and a lot of blond paneling.

"Whatcha doin'?"

She turned at the voice to find that Felix Knotty had come in behind her. Like Death, Felix was a Marine combat vet, but his war had been Vietnam. He'd been friends with the twins since they'd gone to school together and he worked now as an odd-job man for the auction company.

"Just looking around. You know, I've never really looked at any of the places we've sold from the perspective of a home buyer before."

"Are you thinking you might like to live here?"

"No, I can't see it. It feels sterile and mildly depressing and there aren't any trees in the yard." Wren shrugged and turned in a circle. "Anyway, we need to get our financing in order and figure out what we're looking for. It's kind of scary. How do you know you're choosing the right place? What if you make a mistake?"

"Are you talking about the house or about Death?"

"What? Why, the house of course!"

"I'm just saying. You're uprooting your whole life for a man you've known for less than a year. And a damaged man at that. That doesn't scare you?"

"No! Not at all!"

"How do you know you're doing the right thing?"

"I just do. It just…" She searched for an explanation. "It just feels right. It feels like the most right thing I've ever done."

Felix smiled. "Well then, I wouldn't worry about the house. That's just a detail. Finding the right person is the main point. Once you've done that, the details will work themselves out."

———

"Come to do some more horseback riding?"

Death's "no" was drowned out by Randy's "yeah, he did!"

"No, I didn't. You know I didn't."

"But you could, as long as you're here."

"It couldn't hurt." Robinson joined the argument. "It's good exercise and relieves stress. Helps rebuild confidence. And Sugar likes you. He's not going to dump you off and you're not quite clumsy enough to fall off on your own. And it's not like your brother would think less of you if you did fall off."

"Right," Randy agreed. "You're my big brother. I've thought you were an idiot all my life."

"Ha ha. Listen, I came out here because I wanted to talk to you about that missing cell phone."

"Man, I don't *know* where it is. I don't know anything about it beyond what I told you. Jones was talking on it the last time I saw him and that's the last time I saw it, too."

"I know. But it pinged on this property a week after he was killed. There's at least a chance that it's still here somewhere, only hidden well enough that no one could find it."

"I don't see how that could be. You know the cops searched for two whole days. They pulled up the floorboards in the cabins, looked in the attics, brought in the dogs and metal detectors, and crawled through the woods on their hands and knees. They even went through my wife's underwear drawer. I don't even go through her underwear drawer! And you know what they found? Nothing! A whole hell of a lot of nothing!"

Death sighed. "I understand that. Look, I'm just trying to do what you asked me to do. I'm trying to clear Tony Dozier. The best way to do that is to figure out who killed August Jones. Now the cops, they have all kinds of fancy forensics to fall back on. Maybe they'll find something at the murder scene that points to the killer. But all I've got is my eyes and my gut. I just think if I could get a better idea of the layout, I could maybe come up with some idea of what, exactly, happened that day."

Kurt Robinson frowned and thought about it. "So would you like a guided tour of the property?"

"It might help, yeah. Could you do that?"

"Oh, sure. Absolutely. On horseback."

———

"You know, I'm glad you suggested this," Death said. "I think I could get to enjoy horseback riding."

"Shut up," Randy growled. Like his brother, he was mounted. His horse was a big chestnut stallion. Randy was clinging to the saddle horn every bit as desperately as Death had on his first ride. Death could swear the horses looked amused.

He certainly was.

"If you look off to the right, that's south, you can still see remnants of an old barbed-wire fence. That's the property line between our land and the Hadleigh House." Robinson drew his own mare to a halt and pointed toward a line of trees. "The gully that Roy put his truck in runs down along the other side of that fence, crosses over onto our property just past this rise, then turns south again and crosses under the road through a culvert. The cops went through the gully with dogs and metal detectors and had a guy crawl through the culvert, but they didn't find squat."

Death looked back up at the Hadleigh House, high overhead and nearly hidden behind the trees. A trail of pin oaks, younger than the surrounding woods, wound its way up the hill.

"Your driveway used to be connected to the Hadleigh House drive," he observed.

"Yeah. This was all part of the plantation back in the day." Robinson led the way over a low rise and stopped beside a small bridge that carried the camp's driveway over the creek. The gully wasn't as deep here, but it was wider. The water was shallow and danced and sang over the rocks.

"If the creek leaves the property here," Randy asked, "what's the creek that runs between your land and the cemetery?"

"That's a little tributary to this creek. We're ringed on three sides by water."

"How much does it restrict access on foot?"

"It doesn't, really," Robinson said. "This is the only place you can drive across the creek, but there are a lot of places where you can get a horse down and back up the other side if you want to ride across, and you can climb down and cross it on foot almost anywhere."

Death grimaced. "You know that doesn't help me a hell of a lot?"

"Yeah. I know." Robinson nodded across the bridge. "Our property this way is a little, rough quarter-circle—or quarter-oval, really—between the creek, the road, and the fence line. Do you want to look at it or head on toward the north and the cemetery?"

"Let's go look at the cemetery and the woods between here and there."

Kurt Robinson turned his horse to the north and led the way through a low meadow that ran between the creek and the rise. Trees were beginning to lose their leaves now and here and there the gray-white gravel road was visible between the branches.

"I'm trying to get the timeline nailed down," Death said. "Jones was murdered on the 7th. That is, he was attacked on the 7th and then died in Dozier's car sometime during the night of the 7th to 8th. Because he had an arrest record—"

"Who had an arrest record?" Randy interrupted.

"Jones. Pretty much all the members of the CAC have been arrested at some time or other. Trespassing, disturbing the peace, etc."

"Okay."

"Okay, so because he had an arrest record, they were able to identify his body immediately. But they didn't find out he carried a cell phone until several days later, because it wasn't registered in his name. They started pinging it on the 13th and it showed as being somewhere on this property. That was a Tuesday, the Tuesday after the funeral. Who was here then, do you remember?"

Robinson sighed. "That was almost a week after the funeral. You've gotta understand that we only started this place up a couple of years ago. We've been putting it together on a shoestring. During the summer we have stuff going on pretty much all the time. Like a summer camp only for vets instead of kids. But aside from the one Nichelle and I live in, none of the cabins are insulated or set up for winter weather. So, after Labor Day, things start slowing down. We still do programs at the weekends, but weekdays are pretty slow."

"Just you and Nichelle, then?" Death asked.

Robinson hesitated, then sighed again. "Us and Dexter. He spent a couple of days here that week." He pulled up his horse and turned to look at Death directly. "He wouldn't kill anyone. I swear to you. On my grandmother's grave, I swear to you. Dexter wouldn't kill anyone."

FIFTEEN

"I HAD A POSSESSED rabbit once."

"I'm not even surprised."

On the square in downtown East Bledsoe Ferry, the Heritage Days festival was in full swing. On the northeast corner a Ferris wheel towered majestically over the courthouse. A merry-go-round spun gaily to the south and the air was filled with calliope music and the scent of peanuts and cotton candy. The easy joy around them reminded Death perversely of the Doziers and all that they had lost. The police were at a standstill, waiting for the results of tests on things they'd found at the crime scene, and Death resolved to enjoy the company of his own loved ones and cherish this time with them.

He and Wren were standing in front of a game booth. His Marine Corps marksmanship had won her a stuffed animal and the carny was trying to get him to wager it in another round for a chance to win the largest prize, a giant stuffed teddy bear.

"He was three feet tall and green and his name was Chauncey," Wren was saying. "I won him in a drawing when I was, like, nine."

"Someone had a drawing for a possessed rabbit?"

"Oh, I don't think it was possessed when I won it. I think that happened later, the night of the Ouija board."

Death grinned. "That sounds like the name of another horror movie. What happened The Night of the Ouija Board?"

Wren leaned one hip against the game booth counter and turned so she could look up at him. "Well, I had this Ouija board. I got it—"

"At an auction?"

"Of course. I was ten or eleven, something like that, and my cousin Jenny was spending the night. We opened it on the floor between us and we both crossed our hearts and swore not to push the pointer. And you know how, in the movies, there's always flickering lights and curtains that move with no wind and then the pointer slides across the board and says it's going to kill you and you hear voices and so on and so forth?"

"Yeah. So what happened?"

"Nothing. Neither one of us pushed it, so it didn't move. It was terribly anti-climactic."

"This is the most unbelievable ghost story I've ever heard."

"Why? Because nothing happened?"

"Because neither of you cheated and pushed the pointer."

Wren stuck her tongue out at him.

"So what made you think your rabbit got possessed?" the carny asked.

"Okay, so, the house I grew up in was really old. It's gone now. But the upstairs was just one room, under the eaves, with slanty walls on two sides and a stairwell in the corner. That was my room. There was a railing by the stairway, but it was the same height as my bed so my dad wouldn't let me push the bed against it because he didn't want me to roll out of bed and wake up dead."

"I approve of his logic." Death grinned.

Wren smiled up at him and went on with her story. "So I had Chauncey at the foot of the bed, between the bed and the stair rail, facing away from me like he was looking out the window. That night Jenny and I both had the same nightmare that he was possessed, and when we woke up he was at the head of the bed facing me."

"You don't think Jenny might have moved him?"

"I think I'd have woke up. Besides, how would she know about my dream?"

"I still don't see how that necessarily equals a possessed rabbit."

She considered. "'Possessed' might be too strong a word. He was definitely uncanny, though. After that, he moved around a lot on his own. And he seemed to have an extra-beady glint in his little plastic eyes."

"What ever happened to him?"

"He got stolen. I have a shirttail relative who's really light-fingered, and he came in my house when I was gone one day and stole Chauncey to give him to a girl he was seeing. She turned out to be a total psycho. I've always wondered if she was always that way or if the rabbit was responsible."

They stood there in silence for a couple of minutes thinking about it.

"Was there a point to this?" the carny asked.

"I think the point is that giant stuffed animals freak her out," Death explained.

Wren beamed and hugged his left arm, leaning her head against his biceps. "I love it that you understand me."

"But this bear is totally cool," the carny argued, "and I guarantee that it is 100 percent not possessed."

"Thanks," Death said, "but I think we'll stick with the smaller one. Which one do you want, honey? The blue one?"

Wren nodded. Death accepted the stuffed animal and handed it to her as they turned away.

The square was jammed with people and it never ceased to amaze Death, who'd grown up in St. Louis, how many of these people he recognized, even with half of them being in eighteenth-century costumes. He remembered how his life had been a year earlier. He had been fresh out of the military and fresh out of a VA hospital, abandoned by his wife and bereft of his supposedly dead brother. He had been broke and homeless, living in his car with pain and depression as his constant companions.

And now he was here, surrounded by friends, with Wren on his arm and his brother somewhere in the crowd.

"Penny for your thoughts," Wren said.

He smiled down at her. "I was just thinking we should ride the merry-go-round. You want to?"

"Okay! But we have to make it to the stage on the other side of the courthouse in time to get good seats for the talent show. Both of the elder Keystone couples are in it."

"Can do."

———

Robin Keystone was smiling broadly at the girl he'd had a crush on for the past two months. It was a frozen sort of smile, with clenched teeth and a manic gleam in his eye, and the pretty fifteen-year-old in the long dress and poke bonnet looked terrified.

Randy Bogart mentally face-palmed and inserted himself into the encounter before it could get worse. He walked over and dropped an arm over Robin's shoulder and addressed the girl.

"Hi there! Sarabeth, right?"

She nodded warily.

"Sarabeth, you're going to have to forgive Robin here. He doesn't mean to come off all creepy and stalkerish. The thing is, he wants to tell you that he thinks you look very pretty in that costume, but he's shy."

Robin turned bright red and for a minute Randy was afraid he was going to faint or throw up. Sarabeth was blushing too, now, and she ran a hand down her skirt hesitantly.

"Do you like it?" she asked. "I made it myself."

"Yeah. Yeah, it's awesome," Robin stammered. "I saw you earlier, in the parade. That stagecoach you were riding in is really cool. Your uncle builds those, doesn't he?"

"Yes, he does! My sisters and I help him do the research so they're totally authentic. Would you like to see it?"

"Yeah, I'd love to!"

Randy clapped Robin on the shoulder and stepped back to watch them leave. "Yeah, I rock," he said to himself and went to find his brother.

He met Death and Wren getting off the merry-go-round, and Wren waved a blue teddy bear at him. "Randy! Come with us. We're going to go see the Keystones in the talent show."

He fell in beside her and the three of them made their way around the courthouse. They were passing the bandstand, a large white gazebo across from Death's office that was currently occupied by a barbershop quartet, when Randy's eye fell on a group huddled around the street sign on the corner. He reached over and smacked the back of his hand against Death's shoulder.

"I didn't know there was going to be a freak show here, too."

"I see them," Death agreed with a wry grimace.

"See who? What? Where?" Wren stood on tiptoe, trying to see over the crowd.

"Over by the street sign. It's the CAC. What they're protesting here, I can't imagine."

"Oh yeah," Wren said. "I'd heard they might. They've been saying we're damned because we let a Muslim be buried in the city cemetery and that we should dig up her body and burn her as a witch to appease an angry god."

Randy shook his head in disgust. "His own son is murdered and this is how he honors his memory? By being hateful to strangers? The only reason you can even call them human," he said, "is because there's no animal that deserves such a vile comparison."

"I don't think their protest is having the impact that they were going for," Death observed.

The CAC protest was made up of half a dozen people holding signs that said things like *Jesus hates you* and *God damns you all*. The only festival-goers who were paying them any attention were a trio of drunken young women who were giggling insanely and using the CAC as a backdrop for selfies.

"I wish I was good with photo editing software," Wren said. "I'd take pictures of them and then change what their signs say."

"What would you make them say?" Death asked.

"Well, see that tall guy? I'd put one of those aviator caps with the big goggles on him and make his sign say 'I like the tinman.'"

The Bogart brothers both stopped and stared down at her.

"I don't get it?" Randy said.

"*A Christmas Story*? The movie? Remember? The weird little kid in line to see Santa? Never mind..."

Death laughed and gave her a one-armed hug as they turned away toward the stage on the west lawn. As he looked back, though,

Tyler Jones turned as if he sensed Death's scrutiny and their eyes met over the crowd. Jones glared and shook his sign at Death. It said *James 4:9*. When they'd reached the stage and found good seats for the talent show, Death took out his phone and looked up the reference.

"'Be afflicted and mourn and weep; let your laughter be turned to mourning and your joy into heaviness.'"

———

The stage, set up in the municipal parking lot on the west side of the courthouse, was actually a flatbed trailer donated for the evening by a local transportation company and decked out with bunting and makeshift curtains. The local radio station had set up a sound system, with giant speakers on both sides of the stage and a DJ in front of it playing music. They also had a roving reporter who was providing live commentary on the festival in between songs.

Death and Wren had listened to him in the car on the way over. Now Death was keeping an eye out for him, because if they saw him he'd need to be protected from Wren. His commentary consisted of a lot of "who is that? Is that who I think it is? That over there? It looks like…no, maybe not. Oh! Hey! What's going on over here? Well! Isn't this something."

Wren was planning to find him, smack him, and shout, "We can't see what you're looking at! There's no picture! You're on the *radio*, you moron!"

"When do the Keystones appear?" Death asked.

"Probably not for a while," Wren said. "They usually start with the little kids and work their way up to the grownups."

"Okay, so level with me. Are we going to be sitting here watching sickeningly cute children in elaborate costumes struggle through 'I'm A Little Teapot'?"

Wren whistled and looked away.

Death sighed. "That's what I was afraid of."

Randy made a popcorn run and got back just in time for the opening of the Forty-Fifth Annual Heritage Days Talent Show. "What did I miss?"

"Not a thing."

"Damn."

All in all, the children weren't as bad as Death was expecting. The first one on stage was a toddler in a dinosaur costume. The DJ put on a children's song, the baby's mother handed him a microphone, and he marched to the middle of the stage, put the mike up to his mouth, and announced, "I can go pee all by myself."

Then he proceeded to demonstrate.

By the time the audience settled down again there were a bunch of fifth-grade girls singing Motown and the roving reporter was standing beside Death's chair saying, into his own microphone, "Now, who is that little girl? The one in the red? I should know who that is. Do you recognize her?"

Death slipped his arm around Wren, pulled her close, and covered her mouth with his own, drawing the kiss out until the reporter had moved away. He released her and she sat up, blushing and gasping for air.

"You can't save him," she said when she could speak again. "I know where he lives. But please feel free to keep trying."

They sat through a surprisingly good clarinetist and a really bad juggler and finally the announcer stepped up and introduced "The Dancing Keystones!"

The crowd (many of them Keystones) roared, Death and Wren and Randy cheering along with them, as Sam and Doris Keystone danced their way onstage. Sam was dressed as a gangster, in a pin-striped suit, a narrow tie, spats, and a fedora. Doris was a flapper, in a bright blue, sleeveless dress that came just to her knees, and flat-heeled, black patent leather shoes. She had her hair done in finger waves and a wealth of long beaded necklaces.

The DJ put on some swing music that Death thought his grandparents would have probably recognized, and Sam and Doris danced and spun across the stage. They'd reached the other side when Roy's voice, sounding cranky, came from off-stage.

"Wait! Wait! You started too soon! What in tarnation are you doing, starting without us?"

"Well, you shoulda been on time!"

"Well you shoulda waited!"

"Well"—Sam waved his hand—"what in the world were you doing that took so long, anyway?"

"I hadda put my costume on and make myself pretty."

Sam rolled his eyes. "Brother, there ain't a costume in the world that can make you look pretty."

"You say that," Roy retorted, "but don't forget we're identical twins!"

He came onstage, finally, leading Leona by the hand, and the crowd went wild. Roy and Leona were dressed for disco.

Leona was wearing short-short blue jean cut-offs and a midriff-baring peasant blouse, and she had her hair done up in a huge cloud around her head. Roy wore a form-fitting polyester jumpsuit. It was brown on the bottom and a pale tangerine on top, with wide bell bottoms and a zipper down the front. He had the zipper open almost to his navel, and a welter of heavy gold chains and medallions nested among his gray chest hairs. He was sporting an honest-to-God afro.

Sam waited for the furor to die down before he turned to his brother and spoke again.

"I thought you were going to wear a costume."

Roy puffed out his thin chest and thumped his breastbone. "You're just jealous because you don't look snazzy like me."

"I remember when you wore that to prom."

"At least I got to go to prom."

"Hey! I coulda gone to prom," Sam protested. "I just didn't because I wanted to protect my best girl!" He put one arm around Doris and hugged her.

"Protect her?" Roy demanded "Protect her from what?"

"From having to see you in that getup."

Roy pushed his sleeves up and strutted up to his brother like he was going to fight him. Sam met him in the middle of the stage, belligerently, and their wives caught at their arms and dragged them apart.

"Now, come on, fellas," Leona said. "Are we going to fight or are we going to dance?"

"Yeah," Doris said. "We want to dance."

Roy pulled himself up, very proper, and sniffed at his brother. "The ladies," he said, "want to dance."

"I'll show you dancing," Sam retorted. He took Doris in his arms and they resumed their Jitterbug while Roy looked on, pantomiming annoyance.

Roy went to the edge of the stage and engaged in an elaborate, silent argument with the DJ that ended when he pretended to slip him a folded bill. The swing music cut off and was replaced with

180

the Bee Gees. A spotlight came on and found Roy, who strutted and pranced across the stage, pointing at the sky and wiggling his hips.

Leona stepped back and crossed her arms. "Yeah, I'm not gonna do that."

"Hey!" Sam protested. "Wait a minute! We were here first! What happened to our music?" He shouted and waved his arms at the DJ.

"He can't hear you," Roy said. "He's got a twenty in his ear."

"That's not dancing!" Sam ranted.

"This," Roy said, discoing and wiggling, "is just as much dancing as this"—he mocked a jitterbug—"is!"

"It is not! This"—Sam jitterbugged—"is dancing, and this"—he pretended to disco badly—"is not!"

"It's all moving in time to the music! It doesn't make any never mind whether you move like this"—Roy swung his hips side to side—"or this"—he wiggled them back and forth.

Sam disagreed. They danced a carefully choreographed argument around each other, swinging and jiving and bickering in time to the music until they both wound up stooped in awkward positions moaning about their backs.

Doris and Leona dragged a wheelbarrow in from offstage, piled their husbands into it, curtsied to the crowd, and wheeled them away to the sound of laughter and applause.

———

Wren was still giggling as she and Death made their way through the dwindling crowd, headed back toward where they'd left his Jeep. Randy had excused himself to go check on something and they walked close together with their arms around one another. It was getting late and the food and game stalls were beginning to close down, but the rides were still up and running. Death paused as they came abreast of the Ferris wheel and nodded toward it.

"It's a nice night. Shall we go for a ride?"

"Okay." Wren looked around. "We'll have to see if we can find a ticket booth still open."

Death held up two cardstock rectangles. "Got it covered."

"Well, look at you being all prepared!"

"I keep telling you, Boy Scouts got nothing on the Marines."

The line was practically nonexistent. They wound their way through the cattle rails, handed off their tickets at the entrance to the fenced area below the ride, and in just a couple of minutes were coming up under the wheel. They waited while the couple ahead of them boarded, then that gondola swung up and away, an empty one came down to a gentle stop, and it was their turn.

Death climbed on first and turned back to help her step from the solid deck onto the rocking car. When they were seated he put his arm around her shoulder and she snuggled up against him. The ride attendant latched the bar across in front of them and the wheel turned, gliding them back and up.

Death clenched his hand around her shoulder and took a breath, but waited until they were near the top of the wheel to speak.

"So, I've been thinking about us moving in together…"

"Oh." Wren turned a bit so she could see his face and steeled herself for disappointment. "Are you having second thoughts?"

"No. No, just the opposite, actually."

The fist-sized yellow bulbs that outlined the wheel cast a faint golden glow across the car without really illuminating anything. The merry-go-round was still playing in the distance, but the bright melody did more to accentuate the silence around them than to break it. Their gondola crested the wheel and a light breeze lifted

Wren's hair from her forehead. The town and the countryside and the entire Earth spread out below them, but here there were only the two of them.

They might have been the only people in the world.

"I love you Wren. And I want to spend the rest of my life with you. I'm more sure of that than I ever have been of anything. So I was thinking, instead of just moving in together, maybe we should go all the way."

Surprised, she made a little noise and gave him a weird look. He caught her eye, read her mind, and laughed.

"Silly! I'm not talking about sex."

"But then...?"

He reached his other hand over, took her chin, and turned her face up toward his.

"Wren Morgan, will you marry me?"

"Oh!" Surprise stole her breath away. Tears filled her eyes and her throat. Unable to speak, she simply nodded.

"You will?"

She nodded.

"Really?"

She nodded.

"Are you ever going to be able to talk again?"

"Maybe?" she said. It came out as a squeak. Death laughed and held her close.

"I have a ring for you," he said, "but I'm afraid to take it out up here. I think my hands are shaking. I'm afraid I might drop it."

"I know my hands are shaking," she agreed. "No! Don't drop the ring! That would be a bad omen. I can put it on when we're on the ground."

"And wear it and be mine. Always and forever."

The wheel had come around while they talked and risen again to the top of the world. It was a light night, with constellations worked in silver sequins against an old-denim sky. A crescent moon pendant dangled in the east. The stars above seemed closer than the lights of the midway below.

Wren put her head on Death's chest.

She could hear his heart beat.

SIXTEEN

"Mom? It's Wren. Call me when you get this, okay? I have something to tell you."

Wren hesitated. She didn't want to share this news in a voicemail, but she was going to be telling it over the phone anyway and she knew that her mother would worry and imagine terrible things if she couldn't get hold of her right away.

Wren's mom had been a medications technician. Her dad had been with the Department of Conservation. They were calm, dependable people who'd lived in the same place for almost forty years, working and raising their family. The last thing she'd expected them to do when they retired was sell their house and become nomads. With a pop-up camper hitched behind her dad's truck, they'd set out to see everything within driving range.

Her mom made stuffed animals and dolls and exhibited them at craft shows across the country. Her dad had won horseshoe tournaments in twenty-three states and counting. Neither of them had ever gotten the hang of technology. They weren't even interested. They had a cell phone for emergencies, but tended to leave it off and buried in the glove box for days at a time. Wren was more likely to get a postcard or a box of random souvenirs in the mail than a phone call. She didn't even know what state they were in. Last she'd heard, they were wandering around lost in the Appalachians.

She sighed.

"It's Death," she said into the phone. "He's asked me to marry him. We're getting married. Call me when you can and I'll tell you all about it."

She hung up and set the phone on the mantle in the Hadleigh House game room, noting that the battery was getting low and making a mental note to plug it in. The beautiful night had given way to a dreary, drizzly gray day. Nothing could put a damper on her spirits, though.

The game room was on the first floor at the northeast corner of the house. It featured a full-size pool table, two card tables with comfortable chairs, end tables, club chairs, a liquor cabinet that was still stocked with bottles she knew nothing about—she'd have to ask the twins what they were going to do with those, since they didn't have a liquor license—and a bookcase full of vintage board games.

Wren set an open box on the pool table and started dealing out a fancy old deck of cards beside it, sorting it into suits to see if they were all there. She stopped on the king of hearts to admire her new ring again.

Death had bypassed the standard diamond solitaire in favor of something more personal. It was a low-profile, so it wouldn't snag while she was working: a gold band inset with a design of linked hearts worked in sapphire, diamond, and opal. It fit perfectly and she was waiting for someone to notice it. Now that she'd told her parents, sort of, she felt that she could share the news.

So far, the only person she'd seen was Robin Keystone. He was walking around in a happy fog because he'd *talked* to Sarabeth Hensley the night before. Wren doubted he'd notice if a 747 came in for a landing on the lawn.

As if thinking about him had summoned him, the teenager appeared in the doorway.

"Wren? Do you mind if I go ahead and leave a bit early? Sarabeth's meeting me at the library tonight, to study for our history test."

She glanced out the window. The dark was gathering in early today and there were hints of lightning low on the horizon.

"Do you need a ride?"

"Nah. My dad's over at Great Uncle Bub's. I can walk over and ride back with him."

"All right, then. Be careful. The wind's picking up. Watch out for falling branches on the Vengeance Trail."

He rolled his eyes and smirked and was gone.

Wren put in another hour, packing up board games and daydreaming about marrying Death, before she looked outside again and noticed the way the storm had darkened the afternoon into an early evening. She didn't like driving on dark, wet roads, especially in the autumn when the deer were out in force, so rather than flipping on the lights she decided to call it a day.

Gathering her phone and her car keys, she locked the mansion behind her and paused on the porch, waiting for a break in the rain to make a run for her truck. After about five minutes she decided there wasn't going to be one, so she made a dash for it and climbed into the cab, soaked and out of breath.

At least, she reflected, she had her truck up here close. She'd have to remember to thank Nichelle again for helping the men put up the bridge.

She shook the rain out of her eyes, tucked a strand of wet hair behind one ear, and turned the key in the ignition.

Ruhr ruhr ruhr ruhr.

"You have got to be kidding me!"

She tried it a couple more times, just in case it was, she didn't know, a glitch in the matrix, maybe, rather than an actual problem. With the rain pouring down, she decided to call Death to come pick her up and worry about the truck in the morning. But when she pulled out her phone, it was dead and she couldn't get it to turn on.

"The battery. I forgot to plug it in to charge."

Cursing under her breath, she dug in the console. She'd left her big flashlight at home that morning, but she had a small but bright LED light on a headband that cast light on things while leaving her hands free. Putting it on, she popped the hood, steeled herself to a cold shower, and jumped down.

The ground squelched underfoot and the metal of the hood was cold and slick under her hands. She found the hood release, raised the hood, and leaned in under it, seeking some scant shelter as she peered at the motor, trying to see if she could see what was wrong.

The motor had turned over but wouldn't catch. Since the truck had run fine that morning, her first thought was that corrosion had built up on the battery posts and was keeping it from getting a full charge. The posts gleamed in the bright blue glow from the LED, though. The battery could be dead, but it was practically new and she hadn't left the lights on or anything.

Electricity, fuel, spark. The three elements of starting a vehicle. If it wouldn't start, you eliminated them one by one until you discovered what was missing. The battery should be okay, and she'd gassed up only that morning, so unless someone had siphoned her tank she should have fuel.

That left spark. It should have started, or at least tried to start, with one or even two loose spark plug wires. She had no other ideas, though, so she moved over and refocused her light to check them.

They were gone.

The spark plug wires were gone.

The only way they could be gone was if someone had taken them. The only other person she knew had been on the property that day was Robin Keystone, but the missing spark plugs meant that she was alone and stranded twenty miles from town. That wasn't a prank any of her friends would play on her.

With a sick feeling, Wren closed the hood, got her keys and her dead phone, and ran back to the house to lock herself in. Just inside the door, with her back to the wall, she closed her eyes and took a deep breath. The sound of the rain on the windows intensified, and she wondered who else was here and what they wanted with her.

———

Death, in his office on the square, was deep in financial paperwork, figuring his quarterly tax payment. His phone, lying on the blotter next to his left hand, buzzed and vibrated.

"Hello?"

"Do you own your home? Let me tell you what vinyl windows and doors can do for you!"

"I'm not interested," he said. "I'm on the do-not-call list. Don't call back."

He hung up, got up, and went to the mini-fridge in the other room for a can of soda. He'd just gotten back to his desk when he heard the door down at the street open and close and a set of familiar footsteps climbed the stairs. He kept his head down and kept working.

Randy crossed the office, came to a stop in front of him, and leaned down to put his face a couple of inches from Death's. Death looked up finally, grinning hugely.

"She said yes?"

"She said yes. Well, she nodded. Same thing."

"And the ring? Did she like the ring? Did it fit and everything? You didn't drop it off the Ferris wheel, did you?"

"No, I didn't drop it! I didn't put it on her until we were back on the ground. And yeah, it fit and yeah, she likes it."

Randy clapped him on the shoulder, beaming. "Man! That is so awesome!" He pulled up a chair and dropped into it. "Have you set a date yet? I better be your best man! Does Madeline know yet?"

"No, of course you are, and no, why would Madeline know?"

"You didn't tell her? I'd have called and told her first thing."

"What, like 'nanny-nanny-boo-boo! I'm engaged and you're not'?"

"Well, yeah!"

"Well, no." Death laughed and pushed the paperwork aside. "What happened between Madeline and me is in the past. I have more important things to do than gloat over my ex-wife."

"That's a very mature and healthy attitude. So can I?"

"What? Gloat over my ex-wife?"

"Yeah. I want to tell her that you're marrying Wren."

Death took a drink from his soda. "Why?"

"Because she's a bitch. And when you and she got married she was all smug and pleased with herself. And she told Wren, when you all thought I was dead, that it was karma because she didn't like me so I deserved to die."

"She said that? Really?"

"That's what your fiancée told me."

Death's phone buzzed again.

"Bogart Investigations."

"Do you own your home? You would be wise to listen to what I have to say!"

Death growled and hung up and tossed the phone in a drawer.

Randy frowned at him. "What was all that about?"

"Telemarketer. Keeps calling and trying to sell me vinyl windows."

"Oh. Yeah, telemarketers are a pain in the butt. Kind of like Madeline."

"Okay, fine! You can tell her Wren and I are engaged."

"Awesome!" Randy grinned ear to ear. "I know. I'll ask her if she's interested in a job in show business. When she asks why, I'll tell her I'm planning your bachelor party and I need a cheap stripper to jump out of the cake."

Death dropped his head into his hands. "Oh god. Knowing Madeline, she'd probably do it. Congratulations, Randy. I think you broke my brain."

"Well, it was never very sound to begin with."

"Just don't say anything to her until after Wren tells her parents. She wanted to tell them first, before we announce it or anything." Death drained his soda, set the empty can down, and leaned back, kicking his feet up on the desk.

"Where are her parents? I've never met them."

"Neither have I."

"Oh!" Randy grinned. "Nervous much?"

"A little, yeah. They're retired. They have a pop-up camper trailer they pull behind their truck and they just travel all over the US doing whatever they feel like doing."

"Sounds awesome."

On the desk between them, Death's empty soda can started to jitter and vibrate. It rattled and shook and danced across the wooden surface. Death and his brother both sat up and stared at it as it moved, by fits and starts, toward the edge of the desk.

Death yanked open the drawer. His phone lay there, vibrating with an incoming call. He snatched it up with a curse and ran for the door.

———

For the first time since she'd started working there, the Hadleigh House's long, echoing corridors and warren of empty rooms frightened Wren. Leaning against the wall, just inside the door, she half expected the pretty, engraved-glass window light to come crashing in and a hand to reach in and grab her. Or a claw. Or a meat hook.

Trying to shake off the horror movie imagery, she held her breath and willed her pounding heartbeat to still so she could listen for any sounds that might betray a presence. A sign that she was not alone. Only the sounds of the storm reached her, wind and thunder and rainwater gushing down the gutter spout off the verandah and dripping from the eaves.

Her best bet, she decided, was to get to somewhere she could secure, then plug her phone in and call for help. She ran over the house's blueprint in her mind. First floor would be better than second floor, she decided. If the person who took her spark plug wires was determined to kill her, the simplest thing to do would be to set the house on fire. While she really didn't see that happening, she didn't want to chance getting trapped on the upper floor if it did.

For that same reason, a room with at least one window she could escape from would be best. It would be a trade-off, though, because windows would render her vulnerable to an attack from outside. She needed a place with limited windows, a single door she could defend, and something she could use for a weapon.

She had a weapon in her truck, of course. As a hobby a couple of years earlier, she'd taken up using an atlatl that she'd gotten at an auction. The atlatl, a prehistoric spear chucker, was basically a short wooden stick that used the principles of leverage to add force and distance to a thrown spear.

Back in the spring, when she'd first met Death, she'd used the atlatl to help drive away an armed intruder. Ever since, she'd carried the weapon and a collection of six-foot-long spears in the back of her truck. It would have been simple to grab one, had she been thinking clearly, and she knew she would feel a lot better with a weapon in her hand. She was loathe to go back out into the dark now to fetch one, though.

That seemed like the sort of thing a character in a slasher flick would do, just before their friends started stumbling over their dismembered body parts.

"At least I don't have a group of friends with me. I'm the only character in this movie. That should work in my favor."

Perfectly aware that this reasoning made no sense, Wren forced herself away from the perceived safety of the front door and into the dark recesses of the old house. Ducking down to stay clear of the windowpane, she edged down the corridor, keeping near the wall on the left but careful not to touch it. She didn't want the sound of fabric moving against wallpaper to betray her presence.

Halfway back, she came to the corridor that ran north-south. She hadn't turned the lights on yet and she hesitated. The headlamp she wore gave her a bit of illumination, but it also might act as a beacon to someone stalking her. She had yet to hear anything other than the weather, though, so she decided to leave it on until she reached her destination.

Imagination running rampant with what might be waiting for her (and not all of the denizens of her imagination were living human beings), she ducked out quickly and looked down the corridor. The light on her forehead reflected back from the window in the nailed-shut door at the end of the hall, but the hall itself was empty. She had to pass three empty rooms—a morning room on her left and a study and a smoking room on her right—before she came back to the game room she'd been working in that day. At each doorway she paused and listened for movement or the sound of a breath, and then rushed past.

Finally, she was back where she'd started. Once she was inside with the door closed and certain that she was the only one there, she flipped on the light, turned off her headlamp, and took stock of her situation. The pool table was too heavy for her to move and the lighter furniture would make no barricade at all.

In addition to her atlatl, Wren was proficient with a slingshot. She had one that she'd disguised as a necklace, with throwing stones threaded on like beads, but she'd had to take it apart and use it when they'd rescued Randy in St. Louis and she hadn't put it back together yet. She did have her dead cell phone and a charging cord still gripped tightly in her hand.

She searched the room for an outlet, plugged the phone in, and waited impatiently for it to power up. It cycled through introductory screens and the opening music began to play, an odd lyrical counterpoint to the dark and the wind. She put her thumb on the volume button, hastily turning it down to mute, and finally the lock screen came up.

She unlocked it and hit 911, but nothing happened. In the upper right-hand corner, the icon for "no signal" flashed.

Wren cursed under her breath. With the weather the way it was, she should have expected this. Still, it didn't make her feel any better about being stranded, alone and cut off from civilization, at the mercy of whomever had sabotaged her truck.

It occurred to her that she could make a run for the veterans' camp, through the rain and the darkness. But what if someone at the camp was behind this? What if that was what they wanted, for her to come running to them? She didn't feel that the Robinsons were dangerous killers, but was that because they weren't, or because she liked them and didn't want them to be?

A brilliant flash lit up the windows and a deafening peal of thunder came simultaneously. Lightning had struck somewhere in the woods. Somewhere along the haunted Vengeance Trail. The light in the game room flickered and died, and Wren's phone glowed briefly, flashed a dead battery warning, and shut down.

She stood in the darkness, hardly daring to breathe.

The storm sounds seemed suddenly muted, as if the blast had stolen all the energy from the atmosphere. Rain still drummed down, but without the sheer fury; the sensation of standing beneath a waterfall. The wind whispered around the dark corners of the old house.

Somewhere off in the distance, from one of the lonely, empty rooms, came the sound of glass breaking.

SEVENTEEN

The wipers were at their highest setting but still they battled the rain sheeting down the Jeep's windshield. Death leaned forward, trying to see out. Randy, clutching the chicken grip, cracked his window and craned his neck. Their breaths were fogging up the inside of the glass, but with the window down, the rain driving into his eyes nearly blinded him as well.

"Man, can you see at all?" he asked.

"Hardly. Help me watch."

"I am. Okay, the road's coming up. You're almost there. Turn now."

Death eased a right turn onto the gravel. The road leading to the vet's camp was narrow and rough, but the trees lining both sides gave them a windbreak and the rain lessened enough that he could turn the wipers down a notch and still have improved visibility.

Lightning flashed almost continuously, painting fleeting, grotesque pictures of the sodden landscape. They climbed a hill, the ditches on both sides running like creeks, and passed the carcass of the abandoned church on their right. Another fifty yards and a long series of lightning bolts showed them the gravedigger's angel.

She—Agathe—looked almost alive in the dancing white light. She peered out at them, across the underbrush and across the decades, in windblown robes. She held her hair out of her eyes and offered them a ladle dripping with rainwater; victim of the War To End All Wars, reaching out to a soldier of the war that came a hundred years on.

The road dipped down again, crossed a culvert where the stream had risen nearly to the surface of the gravel, and they came at last to the driveway into the camp.

The driveway curved before it crossed the little bridge over the gully. Death eased the Jeep down and around it, through a shallow, puddle-filled dip in the road and out into the gravel parking area. The lights were on in the Robinsons' cabin and in the barn and he could see, in the stormlight, horses and humans running in the pasture beyond.

Death and Randy went through the barn and found Nichelle, dripping, in the paddock arguing with Kurt.

"It's okay," she shouted over the wind and the rain. "They'll be fine!"

"Just stay here while I get the others!"

Sugar and a little roan mare were in the paddock, still saddled. Three other horses ran in the pasture, wild with the lightning. To Death, they seemed more energized by the storm than frightened of it.

Kurt had run back out, calling to them. The Bogart brothers turned to Nichelle.

"What's going on?"

She shrugged helplessly, turning up her palms to the sky.

"We went out for a ride in the rain. It was peaceful, you know? We didn't realize a storm was coming up. We were clear over by the river when it got bad. Thunder and lightning, they freak Kurt out. He feels like we're under fire and he's not happy until everyone is safe under cover. We rode home as fast as we could, and now he's trying to get the rest of the horses in out of the weather."

"We can help," Randy said.

Robinson was coming back, leading two prancing mares. He walked between them, his hands tangled in their wet manes, and Randy hurried to open the barn door so he could take them inside.

Death went out into the pasture, where one horse remained. He recognized her as Leia, a paint filly he'd petted when they were out the day before. She wasn't saddle broke yet, and was too young for an adult to ride, in any case. A beautiful animal, she was going to be a show-stopper some day. Water dripped off her mane and tail and off Death's nose and the near-constant lightning created a disco effect.

"Come on, sweetheart," he coaxed. "Let's get inside, out of this storm."

She butted him playfully and pranced away. He had just gotten hold of her, her wet mane tough and wiry in his grip, when a massive bolt of lightning struck on the hill above and the thunder washed across the valley. Leia jumped and tried to run, her eyes rolling in terror, nearly pulling his arm out of the socket. And then Robinson was there on her other side, and between the two of them they were able to coax her back to the paddock and the safety of the old barn.

Nichelle followed them in, leading Sugar and his mate, still saddled. Death closed the door. Outside, the storm raged on, muted but hardly silenced by the thin barn walls.

Kurt Robinson was still on edge, bustling around trying to take care of everyone at once. To the right of the paddock door, opposite the stalls, there was a desk with a hanging light over it and a chest of drawers. He went to the chest and started pulling out towels and tossing them at the other three.

"Here. Get dried off. You're dripping wet. Randy, can you help me rub the horses down? Sit down, sweetheart, I know your leg's hurting. Death, you need to get out of those wet clothes. Go ahead and strip down and I'll get you a blanket to wrap up in until we can find you something else to wear."

Death blinked. "You want me to just take my clothes off? Right here?"

"Yeah, man. With your lungs the way they are, the last thing you need is to wind up with pneumonia. What? You're a Marine. You mean to tell me you're shy?"

"It's just a little rainwater. I'm fine. You're fine, Nichelle's fine, Randy's fine. The horses are fine. Just calm down and breathe for a minute."

Nichelle and Randy were putting the other horses in stalls, draping rough blankets over their backs and making sure they had food and water.

"Dry off yourself," Nichelle told her husband. "Randy can help me get these guys settled. Can't you, sweetie?"

"Glad to help," Randy agreed. "What else do we need to do? These other two horses need their saddles and stuff off?"

Sugar and the mare were still out in the common area. There were two empty stalls waiting for them, but one of those was the one from which Sugar had been taken by the drunk in the dead man's uniform. Both animals were staying well away from that part of the barn.

"Yeah. Here, we'll start with Sheila. I'll show you what to do."

"But—" Robinson protested.

"But nothing. Just sit down and take it easy now."

While Nichelle and Randy worked to rid the mare of her tack, Death went back to the other door, cracked it open, and peered out across the dark parking area and toward the road beyond.

"What are you looking for?" Kurt asked. "What's the matter?"

There was no one in sight, and no sign of headlights on the driveway or up on the road. Death held up a hand for silence and listened, but he couldn't hear anything but the sound of the rain beating on the barn's tin roof.

"I was looking to see if there was any sign of a police car," he said. "Deputy Jackson is supposed to be on his way out."

He turned back to find the Robinsons staring at him, wide-eyed and wary.

"I know where August Jones' cell phone is," he told them. "I know where it is and how it got there."

———

Wren toed off her left shoe, leaned down to pull her sock off, and then stuck her bare foot back into the wet sneaker. She was standing next to the pool table, and she reached down into the corner pocket, took out a pool ball, shoved it into her sock, and tied the top of the sock to make a cosh. It occurred to her that she was ruining a perfectly good sock, but that, at the moment, was the least of her worries.

The pool cues were in a holder on the wall and she crossed the floor carefully, avoiding the random boxes full of games and things that she had stacked there earlier, ready for auction. There had been no further sounds from within the dark house since she'd heard breaking glass. She wanted to think it was a coincidence, a windblown tree branch shattering an aged window pane. She didn't believe it for a minute, though.

Someone had taken her spark plug wires. Now they, whoever that person was, were here, inside the dark house with her, stalking her under cover of night.

She considered the room she was in, trying to remember the layout and examining and discarding her options for hiding places. There were no closets in this old house, none at all. It had been built at a time when closets were taxed, so people had relied on chests and wardrobes instead.

There was a trunk in the room. She'd been admiring it earlier. It was carved from cherry wood and served a dual purpose as a coffee table and a storage place for vintage jigsaw puzzles. It wasn't nearly big enough to hold a human, though. The liquor cabinet had a glass front and was, in any case, still filled with liquor.

It occurred to her that she could make Molotov cocktails, but she couldn't think of a single scenario, given her current situation, where that would be anything but a terrible idea.

Otherwise, there was nowhere to hide except for behind or beneath the pool table. Either place would be obvious to anyone coming in. Neither would offer more than minimal cover if the intruder was armed, and hiding under the table would hamper her own ability to maneuver.

From somewhere in the depths of the house there came a light thunk, as of a cabinet door closing.

A pair of sturdy side tables flanked the door of the game room and Wren turned her attention to them. Climbing on a table would put her at an unexpected level and perhaps give her an edge. Plus, being just inside the door would allow her to strike at someone as soon as they came in.

The door opened inward, so waiting on the hinge side meant she would be hidden behind it when it opened. The open door would keep her from striking immediately, though, and anyone with an ounce of sense would check behind the door first thing, weapon at the ready.

A door opened and closed nearby and she could hear someone moving through the morning room next door. They were searching, opening drawers and dumping out her carefully packed boxes. They weren't even trying to be quiet.

Wren pocketed her useless phone and the charger and climbed up on the table next to the door. She stood with her cosh in her left hand and the pool cue in her right. Her back was against the wall.

The footsteps left the morning room and crossed to the study. She could hear them searching in there, dumping things out and throwing things around. The intruder seemed angry. When they left the study, they slammed the door behind them. The vibrations travelled through the walls and shivered up her back. A heavy tread approached the game room. Yellow light showed under the crack in the door, casting a fleeting beam across the faded rose carpet.

They were so close, Wren could feel their presence. The doorknob jiggled and turned and a tall, gaunt man came in. He held a flashlight in his left hand and a gun in his right.

The light, after the darkness, made Wren's eyes water. From her odd, high angle, his features were a sharp silhouette against the glare. She didn't recognize him, though she felt she would if only she could see him properly. She was to his left, so his gun hand was on the other side. He'd have to turn and point it across his body to aim at her.

She leaned down and struck swiftly, before he had time to register that she was there. She swung the cosh at his right hand, as hard as she could, catching him in the meaty part of his palm and forcing his arm to fly out and hit the solid old door.

The gun went off as it flew out of his hand, skittering away among the confusion of boxes. A sound of breaking glass and a glugging, dripping noise suggested that the bullet had lodged somewhere in the liquor cabinet.

The cosh, on the rebound, caught the tip of the flashlight and broke the lens, plunging the room back into sudden darkness. The intruder was bent forward and hunched slightly by the force of Wren's attack, and before he could straighten up, she struck again. She swung the pool cue down with all her strength, aiming for his head, but she managed only a glancing blow that caused him to stagger but did not fell him.

She swung it a second time, holding it vertical this time and striking him between the shoulder blades with the butt of the cue. He fell forward and scrambled awkwardly away from her, into the room. She jumped down and bolted into the hall, still carrying her weapons and pulling the door closed behind her.

EIGHTEEN

Nichelle Robinson lowered herself into the chair beside the desk and her husband went over to stand next to her. He squeezed her shoulder and they turned to face Death and Randy.

"We didn't kill August Jones," she said, voice level. "We don't have his phone."

"I know you don't have it," Death said. "And I know you don't know where it is. But it's here."

The rain was beginning to ease up now and they could hear a car approaching along the road and up the driveway. Death went over and opened the door a crack, watching a Rives County Sheriff's Department cruiser roll up and stop beside his Jeep.

Orly Jackson got out, wearing a neon yellow slicker over his uniform. Death held the door open for him and waited while the officer ran up and dashed in dripping.

He pulled off his raincoat and dropped it over the door into Sugar's abandoned stall.

"You said you found August Jones' cell phone?"

"We haven't found it yet," Death said, "but I'm sure it's here and I know how it got here."

"So help me God, Bogart, if you've dragged me out here in the rain on another wild goose chase I'm going to kick your ass."

"I'll pretend like that scares me later."

"Tell us why you think it's here," Kurt demanded.

Sugar, still saddled in the common area, shook his head, rattling his bridle, and clomped over to stand beside Death. Death leaned against the nearest stall and scratched the horse's nose absently while he spoke.

"August Jones was stabbed outside the crypt, then dragged inside and left for dead. If he really had been dead, that would have been an excellent place to hide his body. No one was likely to go in there again for years, if ever. And even if someone could smell August's body decomposing, there was another fresh corpse there that was supposed to be there. They'd most likely just think it was a case of poor embalming and avoid the area until the smell went away."

"Okay," Jackson said, nodding along.

"So I've been wondering, why take his cell phone? If it really does have a recording of the murder, the killer would need to get rid of it. They already had it somewhere where it was never likely to be found. All they had to do was take the battery out so it couldn't be tracked."

"Maybe they wanted to destroy it?" Nichelle offered.

"But they didn't destroy it. They didn't even take the battery out. Because it was still turned on and working when the police tried to GPS it."

"So what's your stupid theory this time?" Jackson asked.

Death spared him a brief look. "I don't think the killer *did* take it out of the crypt."

"But it wasn't there!"

"I know. But the killer wasn't the only one in that crypt between the time August Jones crawled out of it and we found it again."

"Jack Harriman?" Jackson asked.

"Who?" Kurt demanded.

"Jack Harriman," Death explained. "He was the drunk who broke in and stole the uniform off of O'Hearne's body. He and O'Hearne were rival Civil War enthusiasts. O'Hearne had bought an authentic Confederate cavalry uniform at one of the Keystones' auctions, years ago, and decided to be buried in it. Harriman found out about it somehow. Apparently he wanted it for himself, and maybe he objected to a museum piece being used for grave clothes. Anyway, he made a deal with the funeral director to leave the crypt open."

"Right," Nichelle said. "I read that in the paper. He told them something about slipping a picture of an old sweetheart into the coffin or something."

"Yeah, that. Well, the night after Zahra's funeral, while Tony Dozier was driving around searching western Missouri for an allied military installation and August Jones was dying in his back seat, Jack Harriman took the license plates off his motorcycle and drove down here to steal the clothes off a dead body."

"It was stormy that night, like it is tonight."

"Not quite as bad a storm," Kurt Robinson said, "but stormy, yeah."

"Right. And Harriman was riding a motorcycle. There was no bridge over the ravine on the driveway up to the Hadleigh House yet. He must have ridden up the Vengeance Trail, past the point where he was going to die before morning."

Nichelle shivered. "Creepy."

"Yeah."

"Why didn't he just ride right up to the cemetery?" Randy asked. "It's not like anyone was apt to pay him any attention."

"The same reason he removed the license plates," Death said. "He was paranoid. He was also drunk and getting drunker by the minute. He had a six pack of beer and a bottle of whiskey. He hid his bike in the old slave quarters behind Hadleigh House and hiked from there, down here through your woods and out the other side to the cemetery. When he got inside the crypt, he finished off his beer and liquor, got the uniform off the body in the coffin, and stripped down and put it on himself."

"Gah!" Nichelle shuddered. "That's disgusting."

"Well, he had to be really drunk by then. He left his wallet and keys and everything in the pocket of the clothes he'd been wearing, but I'm guessing that he found August Jones' cell phone lying in the crypt and stuck that in his pocket just out of habit. Pick up cell phone. Stick it in your pocket."

"Oooooh!" Jackson said.

"Then he locked the gate behind himself and headed back for his bike, much drunker than he'd been when he arrived. On his way back, he stumbled across the stable and decided that, since he was dressed as a cavalry officer, he should go for a ride. The storm likely already had the horses on edge, and the stench of formaldehyde and body liquor would have put them in a full-blown panic. But they were shut in their stalls, so he was able to get on Sugar's back just the same, get the gate open, and ride away. How he managed to get as far as he did, drunk and bareback, I can't imagine."

"I can explain that," Jackson said. "Harriman came from Kentucky. He'd worked around horses his whole life. He was even a jockey for a while back in his twenties, though he never won any big races or anything like that."

"That makes a lot more sense then." Death nodded. "So, he gets on horseback and makes his way back up the hill, missing the shed where he hid his motorcycle. He got back on the Vengeance Trail, passed out, fell off, and died there."

"But by then, he didn't have the phone anymore."

"No. Because it fell out of his pocket here, in the barn, when he was trying to mount an uncooperative horse, and the horse kicked it back under the manger and against the wall."

"You think?"

"Yeah. I'm pretty sure. It was the moving beer can that tipped me off, though I only figured it out this afternoon. I had my phone, set on vibrate, in my desk drawer, and there was an empty soda can on my desk. The phone rang and the vibrations made the can slide across the desk. I remembered seeing the empty beer can do that when it was on that shelf, and that's when I realized what must have happened. August Jones' phone was set to vibrate. Someone was trying to call the phone, and the vibrations were travelling up the wall and making the beer can move."

"You didn't look yet?" Jackson demanded.

"We were waiting for you, because you're the police and we wouldn't like to be accused of tampering with evidence."

"That's uncharacteristically levelheaded of you."

"Also, the floor's dirty."

"Yeah, that's more like it."

Orly Jackson unhooked his flashlight from his belt, went into the empty stall, and lay down on the floor so he could look under the manger. There was only about two inches of clearance.

"See anything?"

He had his cheek pressed into the dirt and his left eye closed so he could see into the deep, narrow recess. "Yeah, there's something back there, I think. You know, I should probably leave it there and call the city police to come retrieve it."

"You know if you do they'll be jerks about it," Death said. "They'll announce to the press that they've found the missing cell phone and they won't even let you listen to it until it's been presented in court and everything's all over."

The deputy cursed and climbed back to his feet. "Hang on a minute. I've got to go to my car for my camera and gloves and an evidence bag."

"Why didn't you bring them in with you?"

"I thought you were just yanking my chain again."

———

Wren was still wearing her LED headband, but she didn't want to take the time to turn it on just there, with only a single door between her and a dangerous man. With the thought of barricades foremost in her mind, she crossed the hall and entered the smoking room.

It was a small, cozy room, furnished with deep armchairs and footrests and old-fashioned ashtray stands. There were Tiffany lamps and an antique gramophone, a small fireplace (too small to hide in) behind an iron grate, and a small, plain door in the back wall that led to the pantry off the kitchen.

The room still smelled faintly of cigarette smoke and pipe tobacco. Wren felt her way across it, staying as silent as she could. She hadn't done any work in here yet, and the scattering of furniture was unfamiliar to her. She bumped into dusty, upholstered beasts of armchairs crouching in the shadows and barked her shin on a low table. Across the hall, back in the game room, the intruder was throwing things around and muttering to himself.

He was looking for his gun, of course. It wouldn't be easy to find in the dark, but she supposed she'd best assume that he would. Hopefully, by the time he came out, he wouldn't have any idea where she'd gone.

She was remembering a conversation between the Keystone twins the day they'd gotten the electricity turned on in the old house. "Whoever buys this old mausoleum," Roy had said, "the first thing they need to do is get an electrician in here and get the place up to code."

"Is it that bad?" Sam had asked. "Are we going to be safe working here?"

Roy had shrugged laconically. "Hasn't burned down yet. Ah, it'll probably be okay. I wouldn't want to live here, though. This wiring is from the 1920s, and it's all tied to the one fuse box in the kitchen. I got a box of spare fuses, by the way. I'm gonna put 'em in a drawer in there, in case we need one."

If the lightning strike had caused a widespread outage, there was nothing Wren could do. But it was possible that it had simply blown a fuse, and if that was the case then replacing the fuse would turn the lights back on and allow her to plug in her phone and try, again, to call for help. For that matter, if it was a blown fuse, it was possible that the lights weren't out in the entire house.

She found a lamp on a table by the window. It took her several precious seconds to find the switch in the dark and when she flicked it, nothing happened.

She eased through the small door into the tiny, dark pantry and took time to switch on her LED headlamp. Floor-to-ceiling shelves lined three walls, leaving an upside down L-shaped path from the door into the smoking room to the door into the kitchen. Her light caught a bare bulb screwed into a ceramic receptacle in the ceiling with a chain dangling from it. She reached up and pulled the chain, but that light wasn't working either. She headed for the kitchen door, then stopped and took a second look at the contents of the shelves.

Under a half-inch coating of gray dust, blue in the light from her lamp, lay old Tupperware canisters, moldy, mouse-eaten boxes of crackers and cereal, and several dozen Mason jars.

They were ubiquitous. Quart jars with rusting brass lids, filled with the sludge of someone's prized tomatoes or a lump of rancid jelly. It seemed that any time she worked in an old house in the country, especially one that had sat vacant for any length of time, she'd find these reminders of the days when everyone canned their own food for the winter. Normally, they'd throw them out. The price they could get for the jars wasn't worth the time it would take to empty them and scrub them clean.

Now, though, she put them to another purpose, pulling them off the shelves as she passed and laying them on their sides on the floor behind her, to trip up her pursuer if he came this way.

The door into the kitchen was fashioned from a single sheet of thin plywood, painted white and fastened with a thumb latch. She opened it carefully, worried about knocking something down and betraying her location, and emerged into the long, wide kitchen.

There was a switch in the wall to her right and she flicked it as she had the others, just in case, but there was no power here either.

She was at the back of the house now; the windows in the gravedigger's room upstairs looked out over the kitchen roof. To her right and sitting at a ninety-degree angle to the wall she'd come out of, a second door identical to the pantry door sat at the top of two steps. It led to the landing of an enclosed back staircase that she had yet to explore. A long counter with a double-bowl stone sink in the middle of it ran along the back wall, to her left. The entire length of the counter was lined, underneath, with drawers and cabinet doors.

The wall above the counter was lined with windows. They showed the back garden, dark in between lightning flashes. Wren could see the yard light, high up on its pole, dark against the stormy sky. That might mean the damage was in the power lines and there was nothing she could do, but it also might mean that the lightning had been bright enough to fool the yard light into thinking it was daytime.

The only way to tell if she could fix it was to find the fuses and the fuse box and try.

She got a sturdy kitchen chair and braced it under the pantry door handle. It wouldn't hold the door closed for long, but it might slow the intruder down if he tried to come through it.

She started on the left side and started pulling drawers out and opening cabinets. She didn't bother to rifle through the contents. The box of fuses would be on top of anything else in a drawer, or sitting on the front edge of a shelf in a cabinet.

She was three-quarters of the way down the counter when she found them sitting in the top drawer to the right of the sink. It was a box of twenty, in assorted sizes.

Roy wasn't the first person to use this drawer to hold fuses, she saw when she picked up the box. There were maybe two dozen more lying loose in the bottom. The fuses, which served the same purpose that breakers serve in newer buildings, were heavy little disks, about as big around as a fifty-cent piece and maybe an inch and a half thick. They were made of ceramic and metal and glass and color-coded for amperage, with a little plug on the back like the base of a light bulb.

Wren's right pocket bulged with her cell phone and charger. She filled her left pocket with old fuses and took the new box with her as she moved on. Roy had said the fuse box was here in the kitchen, but it could be anywhere.

She forced herself to stop and think. Where would she put the fuse box, if she were going to wire this house?

The intruder was still throwing things around in the dark distance. He sounded closer now, and she suspected he was tearing up the smoking room. If he came through the pantry, she'd hear him falling over her mason jars, but if he went back down the hall and approached the kitchen from that direction, she'd have set the booby trap for herself.

Originally, the kitchen would have been in a completely separate building. That way, if it caught fire, it wouldn't burn the whole house down. And, too, on a less catastrophic note, the heat from baking wouldn't warm up the house on a hot summer day. She didn't know exactly when this room had been built, but the fact that it only shared one wall with the rest of the building meant that wall was the most likely place to locate the power junction.

That wall, opposite the back wall and its row of windows, held a custom cabinet built in under the slanting line of the stairwell, an antique gas stove from the nineteen thirties with a built-in water heater, the door into the dining room, and an ancient refrigerator.

She pulled open the cabinet doors in quick succession, noting cobweb-covered pots and pans and garish, flowered wallpaper on the back walls that didn't match the rest of the room. In the topmost cabinet she could just glimpse something metallic fastened to the wall. Wren dragged a second chair over to stand on and pushed aside a teapot and a coffee percolator.

It was a round metal plate painted with a thick coat of yellowing white paint. The paint was flaking off now, allowing the metal to catch Wren's light. Not the fuse box, then. At one time, there must have been a wood stove where the cabinet was. The plate was covering the hole where the stovepipe had been.

She almost overlooked the fuse box. It was above the stove, a bulging cover about the size of a small cake pan, hinged at the top and painted to blend into the cabbage rose wallpaper. She scooted the chair over and climbed up again, fitting her knee in between the burners and setting the box of spare fuses on the stovetop beside her.

None of the fuses looked blown. Normally the glass would be black and smoky. Most likely, either the problem was in the lines or one of the two cartridge fuses in the master cylinder was bad. She had no way to check those, and no spares in any case.

On the off chance that one of the fuses had blown without appearing to have blown, she began changing them as fast as she could, screwing out the old fuses and screwing new fuses in their place. She'd only gotten three changed when she heard the door from the smoking room to the pantry open and the sound of a body tripping and falling.

He was close enough now, with only the thin door between them, that she could hear him breathing heavily and cursing under his breath. His voice sounded familiar. She'd heard it before, she was sure of it, but at such a low volume, in the dark and the confusion, she couldn't place it.

Bangs and thumps and crashes came from the pantry. It sounded like a maddened wild beast was trapped there. And then the room grew suddenly silent. The storm sounds had begun to abate, though lightning still played across the sky. It was a pensive silence, as if the whole world was waiting with bated breath.

Wren had a sense of vacancy, a feeling that he was no longer there, just the other side of the door. It was so strong that a little voice in her head urged her to pull the door open and see.

"Uh, yeah," she said to herself. "Not that stupid, thanks."

She listened, straining with every fiber of her being to hear every noise within the old house. If she hadn't been so focused, she'd have missed it. It was just a faint thud, a slight scrape, as of a bumped chair sliding on hardwood before being caught.

It had come from the dining room.

The intruder—the armed intruder—had circled around. He was sneaking up on her from the dining room, and the path back through the pantry was a minefield of her own making.

NINETEEN

THE CAMERA FLASH COMPETED poorly with the lightning still playing across the sky, visible through small windows high up on the wall. Orly Jackson took several pictures of the manger, from different angles and distances, then lay back down on the floor and held the device against the dirt to get a shot of the cell phone lying in situ.

"I'm going to need something to fish it out with," he said. "My hand won't fit and it's clear back against the wall."

"How about a hay hook?" Kurt asked.

The deputy tried it. "No, it's not long enough and I can't get it under any further because the handle gets in the way."

"A coat hanger would probably work," Death suggested.

"You got one?"

"Got some in the house," Robinson said. "Hang on a second and I'll run and get one."

"Those poor dogs," Nichelle said when he'd left.

"Dogs? What dogs?" Jackson asked.

"Sherlock and Mycroft. The bloodhound pups, remember?"

"Yeah." Death gave her a rueful smile. "They probably found it. They tried to tell us, but we thought we knew better. We thought they were smelling the dead guy on the beer can, and I'm sure they were. But they were also smelling their target scent on this phone the whole time."

Kurt Robinson returned with a wire coat hanger. He took it in both hands and pulled it out of shape to make a long, skinny hook and handed it off to Jackson.

The deputy lowered himself back to the ground with a long, put-upon sigh.

"Oh, stop it," Death said. "You love this."

Orly, on his knees, paused to cock an eyebrow at the ex-Marine. "Oh really?"

"Ever since you got involved in this case the city cops have been treating you guys like a bunch of simple-minded, bumbling hicks. And now you're about to break their case for them. So stop acting like you're being abused."

"I'm going to enjoy handing them their case," he admitted. "The crawling around in the dirt in a horse stall not so much." He went down to all fours, paused, and rubbed a handful of dirt between his fingers. "Is this manure in here?"

"Probably," Robinson said. "You're in a horse stall."

"Ha, ha."

Jackson lay down on his stomach, stuck the coat hanger into the dark recess beneath the manger, and slowly drew the missing cell phone out into the light. It was a slender smartphone, caked with dirt but with the face intact. He took two more pictures of it lying there, next to the hook he'd used, before picking it up in gloved hands and dropping it into a clear plastic evidence bag.

"You're going to let us hear what's on it, aren't you?" Death prompted.

"Now why would I do that?"

"Because I was nice and I called you in on this. I could have just waited and gotten it out myself and then given it to you."

"That would have been tampering with evidence."

"Hard to prove that in court. After all, I wouldn't have *known* it was evidence until I listened to it. For that matter, we don't know now that it's evidence."

"Of course it's evidence! Don't be stupid."

"Are you sure it's evidence? I mean, we know there's a cell phone missing and we found a cell phone, but you don't actually know it's the same cell phone."

Jackson snorted. "Oh, please."

"There've been a lot of people through here. Any one of them could have lost a cell phone in this barn." Death caught at the officer's arm when he would have turned away and looked him in the eye. "Come on, man. This concerns all of us. I think we have a right to know what's on that phone."

"And you know what?" Jackson said. "I agree with you. And I would let you listen. But in case you haven't noticed, the phone is dead. No one can listen to it until I find a charger that will fit it."

"What kind of plug does it take?" Nichelle asked. "I probably have one in my old cell phone charger drawer."

"You have an old cell phone charger drawer?"

She shrugged. "Sure. Doesn't everybody?"

The deputy followed the Robinsons to their cabin through the rain. The storm had lessened so that it was no longer an onslaught, but it was still coming down steadily. Death and Randy brought up the rear, flanking him slightly.

Jackson glanced back at them. "Guarding me so I can't get away."

"We're protecting you," Death said.

"That's your story."

"And we're sticking to it."

The cabin the couple lived in was only slightly larger than the ones they maintained for visiting vets. It had a cozy living room decorated with Royals baseball memorabilia, an eat-in kitchen, and a single bedroom and bath on the ground floor. A narrow staircase led to a loft under the eaves.

Kurt nodded at the stairs as they went by. "Tony and Zahra used to sleep up there when they'd stay with us."

Death rested his hand on the other man's shoulder and didn't say anything. There was nothing he could say.

Nichelle pulled open a drawer in the kitchen and came over to the table with a Gordian knot of white and black chargers. "I'm not sure what's here, exactly. Most of these are from cell phones but there are other things too. I know some of them are interchangeable. We'll just have to see."

The men seated themselves at the table and started untangling cords. Nichelle pulled up a tall stool and perched on it to watch. In the brighter light in the kitchen, she looked tired and drawn.

"This one probably won't work," Death observed, holding up a sturdier cable with a round connection.

"Hey!" Robinson said. "That's to my cordless drill! I wondered where that went."

"I think this one will fit," Randy said, separating out a cord and charger.

Jackson took it, removed the phone from the evidence bag, and plugged it in. The dirty touchscreen lit up and went to a charging graphic. He held down the button on the side of the phone until it powered up, and then held it up to show them a lock screen with a pattern of nine dots.

"He's got it locked. Unless you geniuses have any suggestions for what his pattern is?"

"He's a Christian fundamentalist. Try a cross," Death suggested.

Jackson tried it. It took him several attempts because his gloves were interfering with his ability to use the touchscreen, but he finally got it to register his finger. He drew a cross on the phone face without lifting his hand, and the phone opened to a home screen. It was a landscape picture, probably the one that came with the phone, with a sprinkling of apps showing.

Jackson tapped *call log* and the record of the last calls on the phone came up. The last caller was identified simply as *Sir*. He showed the others.

"Any of you recognize this number? Be honest with me now."

The others all looked at it and shook their heads.

"The 816 area code is Kansas City," Nichelle offered. "That's no one that I know, though."

"Call it," Randy suggested, caught up in the excitement.

Death reached around and smacked him on the back of the head.

"Ow! What was that for?"

"Great idea, genius," his big brother teased. He pretended to be making a phone call. "Hi, is this the person who murdered August Jones? Yes, I just wanted to let you know that we found his phone. We know who you are now and we're coming for you, so if you want to go on the lam or take hostages or anything, now would be a really good time."

"Smartass," Randy said. "I didn't say call him from that phone. Call him from yours or mine or Nichelle's maybe. Find out who it is, and then pretend you've got a wrong number."

"A call from anyone even remotely connected with the case could tip off the killer, though," Death said. "If that happened, the city police would have our butts in a sling."

"Not ours. We're just bumbling civilians," Randy protested. "They'd have Orly's butt in a sling."

"Oh, you're right. Okay. Go ahead and call then."

"You guys would make lousy comedians," Jackson said, pulling the phone away. "Hang on a second while I find the recorder app."

He found the icon and tapped it, then scanned the list of recordings it brought up. "Jeez. He's got a ton of these."

"He recorded a lot," Robinson said. "That's what the members of Zahra's mosque said. He recorded everything."

"This is the most recent." Jackson hit play and set the phone down on the table. There was a slight buzz of sound, and a rustling noise.

"Fabric," Death said, "brushing against the phone. He had it in his pocket."

They sat in silence while thirty interminable seconds crawled by, broken only by the sound of cloth moving against the microphone. A clock ticked on the mantelpiece and the rain outside tapered off to a gentle patter. There was an indrawn breath and then a single word.

"Sir."

Jackson paused the recording. "Who is that? Is that Jones speaking?"

The other four looked around at one another and shrugged.

"We never met him," Robinson said.

"And he was already dead before Randy and I even heard of him," Death added. "But he made a phone call to someone listed on his phone as 'sir' and he's talking to someone he calls 'sir,' so if we're assuming this is Jones' phone, and I'm sure it is, then it makes sense that he's the one speaking. Turn it back on and see what happens."

Orly hit *play*. After a few seconds of silence, the first voice spoke again.

"Are you just going to stand there? Do you not have anything to say for once?"

"What serpent are you, that comes to me in this disguise? What devil has turned this Judas against me?"

Nichelle gasped. Jackson and Robinson both nodded.

"Who is it?" Death demanded. "Is that who I think it is?"

Jackson paused the recording again to answer. "Yeah, it is. Haven't you ever heard him speak before?"

"No, I've been lucky." Death turned to Randy, who still looked puzzled. "It's Tyler Jones, the head of the CAC. The day he died, August Jones sneaked off to a meeting with his father."

———

Carrying the box of fuses with her, Wren climbed the two steps to the back stairwell and tugged on the door. The wood was swollen with the damp and it stuck. For a minute she was afraid that it was painted closed, but she pulled hard and it opened suddenly, nearly knocking her back to the floor. She caught her balance and pulled herself through just as a gunshot rang out and a bullet buried itself in the door jamb by her head.

She glanced back and her light found the face of her assailant, shone in his eyes and made him shy away and cover his face, but not before she recognized him.

It was Tyler Jones.

And I thought he was bad when he was scripturing at me!

She pulled the door closed behind her but there was no lock. The staircase was steep and narrow; Death's shoulders would have brushed the walls. There was a wooden handrail on the right-hand side, nothing fancy, just a plain board painted gray. The steps were bare wood, red in the light of her headlamp, with a worn spot in the center of each tread where generations of feet had passed.

Everything was covered in a thick layer of dust and the scent of it filled her nose and clogged in her throat. Wren climbed swiftly, and as she went she scattered fuses on the steps. She waited until she was three-quarters of the way up to start. She wanted him to trip on them and fall far enough to get hurt. He'd found his gun, but his flashlight was broken so he was still running in the dark.

The door at the top was also stuck, but she put her weight into it and tumbled through just as Jones yanked open the bottom door and put another bullet into the fabric of the old house. She slammed that door behind her and took stock.

She was standing in the upstairs hall, with the end of the hall and the gravedigger's bedroom to her left and the main staircase to her right. There was a window at the end of the hall and she could see, through it, lights at the vets' camp down in the hollow.

Across the hall from where she'd emerged was another door, leading to a staircase to the attic. She yanked it open, then closed it most of the way in the hopes that it would misdirect Jones if he made it to the second floor. Then she ran down the hall to the gravedigger's room to the sound of Tyler Jones falling down the stairs.

———

"I'm not a demon. I'm your son. Your son who's done everything you ever asked of me."

"If you'd done everything I've ever asked of you, we wouldn't be here."

"You sent me to the mosque to learn about the people there."

"No! Beasts. Devils. Savages. Not people."

"People! You said they were doing horrible things. Having orgies and worshipping Satan and sacrificing babies and making bombs. You sent me to infiltrate, and get evidence, so we could drag their crimes out into the light. So I went in and I infiltrated. And you know what I found? They're just people."

"You've been seduced by the Father of Lies. God himself has spoken against them, striking down with his own hand their she-devil bitch."

"She wasn't a she-devil and she wasn't a bitch. She was a nice lady. She liked old American country music and she sang off-key and she pretended she liked burned sugar cookies so the little girl who made them wouldn't feel bad."

"And God in his wrath raised up his staff and struck down the harlot."

"She was killed by a drunk driver. People die every day. It's part of being alive. It doesn't mean that someone is evil. We're alive so we're going to die. Every one of us."

"You would betray God for those heathen swine!"

"They're people! They're just normal people! They talk about baseball and share cat videos on the Internet and they're kinder to their children than you ever were to us."

"You are no longer of my church." Tyler Jones voice was raising, in pitch and volume, with every word.

August's, in contrast, was growing quieter.

"No, I'm not," he said. "I realized weeks ago that I could no longer be a part of what you're teaching. But I am still your son, and as your son I'm asking you, this one time, to walk away. Cancel your protest at Mrs. Dozier's funeral. Leave my friends to mourn in peace."

There was a brief silence, and, when he spoke again, Tyler Jones' voice was quiet now too.

"You are my son," he said.

There was a sudden, pained gasp. August's voice was tight and shocked.

"Sir, what have you done?"

There was a dull thud, like the sound a body might make falling on a sandstone patio. Something creaked and groaned, low and dismal.

"That's the gate to the crypt," Death said.

They heard a dragging noise and a puffing sound; someone out of breath and panting from exertion. There was a low moan of pain.

Tyler Jones spoke again. "Deuteronomy 21:18-21," he said.

There was another long, rusty squeal from the gate and a clang as it closed.

"If he had his phone with him," Randy said, "why didn't he just call 911?"

"No signal, maybe?" Death offered. From the phone they could hear fumbling noises and labored breathing. The face of the phone was streaked with dark stains. "It sounds like he took it out of his pocket. He probably was trying to call for help. That's how it wound up being left in the crypt for Harriman to find."

"Reception is iffy around here at the best of times," Kurt said. "The nearest cell tower is the other side of the church. No way he's going to have any bars down under that hill."

Orly reached out and turned off the phone. "This recording goes on for hours. It must have continued until a timer went off or the file was full or something. I think we've heard the important part, though."

"What was that Bible verse Jones referred to?" Randy asked. "Deuteronomy something?"

"Deuteronomy 21:18-21," Death said.

"Yeah, that." He took out his own phone, turned it on, and sighed. "Case in point. No signal."

Nichelle went into the living room and came back with an old leather-bound Bible. "Deuteronomy, right?"

Death repeated the chapter and verse for her and she looked it up. She read it to herself, silently, and her eyes teared up.

"Here," she said, handing it off to her husband. "Here. You read it. I can't."

Robinson took the book and read aloud.

"'If a man have a stubborn and rebellious son, which will not obey the voice of his father, or the voice of his mother, and that, when they have chastened him, will not hearken unto them: Then shall his father and his mother lay hold on him . . . and all the men of his city shall stone him with stones that he die.'"

TWENTY

WREN CLOSED THE BEDROOM door behind her and tossed the empty cardboard box that the fuses had been in into a corner. She'd left her pool cue in the kitchen, but she still had her cosh gripped in her right hand and half a dozen fuses in her left pocket. She tried the light, as she'd been doing in every room, but it seemed as if the power was, indeed, out throughout the entire house.

They'd already nearly emptied this room. The bed had been disassembled and carted downstairs along with the bedside table, a couple of small dressers, a lounge chair, and all the boxes of smaller items that she'd packed up. All that remained was an empty wardrobe, taller than Wren and nearly four feet wide.

She listened for a long minute, but there was no sound coming from the hallway. She hadn't heard the door to the back staircase open, nor any sounds from it since Tyler Jones stumbled over her scattered fuses and fell back down. If she was lucky, he was lying unconscious, crumpled on the tiny landing.

It was equally possible, however, that he was circling around and coming up the main staircase, where she hadn't had an opportunity to set any traps for him.

There was no lock on the bedroom door. The wardrobe wouldn't keep him out entirely, but it would slow him down and buy her time to prepare if he tracked her to this room. On the other hand, if he didn't know where she was, the sound of her moving the heavy piece of furniture could very well betray her position.

Wren weighed the pros and cons in her mind and swiftly decided that she had to have some sort of barricade. While he was forcing his way in, if it came to that, she could be figuring out some means of defense or even, if necessary, climbing out the window to make an escape.

The eastern windows looked out over the roof of the kitchen ell. There was still a light rain falling. The steeply pitched roof, with its tiles glistening black under the strobes of lightning, looked anything but inviting. But necessity, she had found, made for a great motivator.

She ran her fingers over the ring on her left hand, tracing the cool, smooth gemstones in the darkness. She was *going* to come out of this encounter alive.

She sized up the wardrobe, gripped it by the upper edge, and tried to drag it across the floor. It was too heavy for her to move quickly against the friction it created. Changing tactics, she opened the doors, took hold of the top, and pulled it toward her. It tipped as if it were going to fall on her and she was able to lift one front corner and pull it out. She let that corner come back to the floor and tipped it again, lifting the other front corner, walking it across the room.

She got it in front of the door and pushed it up as close as she could get it. With the entry as secure as she could make it, she turned her attention to the window.

She'd had the windows up every day she worked in this room, even though it had been a struggle to get them to move in their frames. A couple of those days had been humid, but nothing like it was tonight. She wanted the east window open, in case she had to use it as an egress. The north window opened over a straight drop onto the remains of the carport. If she went out that side, she'd be lucky to walk away with only moderate injuries.

The window stuck, and she prised and shook it, trying to loosen it up. The right side came loose, but the left side was stubborn. She had to raise it an inch at a time, pushing one side up, then lowering it again to even them out and free up the other side.

It had just gotten up high enough for her to climb through when she heard footsteps in the hallway. The door opened two inches and hit the wardrobe.

There was a pause.

The door was drawn closed, then slammed open as far as it would go, striking the big antique with bruising force. There was a high-pitched squeal and the wardrobe slid across the hardwood for half an inch, leaving a scar in its wake.

Jones closed the door and slammed it open again, edging the barricade a little bit further into the room.

Her heart in her throat, Wren turned back to the window and took off her headlight.

———

"I've put a BOLO out on Tyler Jones," Jackson said. "Salvy says I have to call the city and explain what we learned. They're gonna want to know why I listened to the phone recording."

"Because the sooner you knew who the killer was, the sooner you could take steps to get them off the street and under lock and key," Death replied promptly.

The deputy snapped his fingers and pointed at the ex-Marine. "Exactly!"

"You know, Jones showed up at the Hadleigh House a couple of days ago looking for this phone. Eric Farrington brought him out. I guess we know now why he wanted it. I don't understand why he didn't destroy it when he had the chance, though. Considering what was on it."

"I can answer that," Jackson said. "He didn't know about it. There was a mention of it in the case notes I read. They asked him if he had any idea what had become of it and he said he didn't know what they were talking about. When they told him they had reason to believe that August had a cell phone with a recording of his murder on it, Jones became agitated and demanded to know what they were doing to find it.

"Yeah, I'll bet," Death said.

"He had to have known about it," Randy objected. "He called him on it."

"Yeah, he had to have known that August had a phone. But I'm betting he didn't know he recorded people on it, or that it was even possible for him to do so. My impression is that he's pretty clueless about technology in general. I've spoken with Tyler Jones several times since the funeral. Mostly because people complained about him and his group trespassing and disturbing the peace or because he called us to complain that people were interfering with his first amendment freedom of speech." Jackson rolled his eyes. "I've probably explained to that man fifty times that freedom of speech means you can say whatever you like. It doesn't mean that no one can call you an asshole for it."

"Did they tell him that they pinged it out here?" Nichelle asked.

"I doubt they'd get that specific with a civilian. The standard line is 'sir, we're doing everything we can and we just need you to trust us.'"

"Maybe Eric Farrington told him," Death suggested.

"Maybe. Self-important little twerp. That's the sort of thing he'd do. Jones is famous, never mind what he's famous for, and it'd be just like Farrington to try to ingratiate himself with him. Does the chief know about his little adventures?"

"Oh yeah. I understand the jail cell toilets are very clean now."

"What's going to happen with Tony now?" Robinson asked.

Jackson shrugged. "I can't really speak for another department, but this recording seems pretty cut-and-dried to me. I'd guess that they'll charge Jones and drop all the charges against Dozier. He'll probably be out tomorrow. I wouldn't worry about him. He should be fine now."

"He might not be in trouble with the law anymore," Robinson said, "but he'll never be fine. He's lost his keystone and I don't know how we're going to keep him from falling apart."

"He needs something to do," Death suggested. "A goal. A purpose." He remembered Aramis Defoe and how he'd killed himself, all those years later, when he'd finished carving the angel for his grave. "A project," he said, "that isn't ever going to be done."

"I need to call the city. They can get us a warrant for Jones' arrest," Jackson said, messing with his phone. "I don't suppose you have a landline I can use? 'Cause I got no bars."

"Sorry, afraid not. Why don't you try going out on the porch? It's usually better out there." Robinson dragged himself to his feet. "I need to go back out to the barn, too. I haven't unsaddled Sugar yet. Poor guy's still standing around in his wet tack."

"I'll go with you," Nichelle said, standing as well.

"No, sweetheart. I know you're tired. You wait here. Take a hot bath and try to relax."

She leaned against him and rested her head on his shoulder. "August Jones was killed by his own father because he was trying to be a decent human being and I just really don't want to be alone right now."

"Okay," her husband said gently, running his hand across her back. "Okay, it's all right. We'll stick together. We'll take care of the horses and get them settled and then fix some supper and watch a movie or something. How would that be?"

She sighed and nodded, and Death nudged Randy. "And I think that's our cue to leave."

———

The storm was moving away to the northeast now. Wren could see it, a still-fierce bulk of dark clouds dancing with near constant steaks of lightning. A thick bolt sizzled down, striking somewhere on the horizon, and she cringed away from its ferocity. It had left this corner of Rives County behind, though. Sparkling stars covered the freshly-laundered sky in its wake and a gibbous moon shone down on the sodden landscape.

The winds had deprived some of the trees of their autumn finery. She peered down the hill, past bare branches and dripping evergreens, at the lights shining in the yard at Warriors' Rest.

Tyler Jones was throwing himself at the door to the room in a frenzy, breathing hard and muttering imprecations. With every strike the barricade gave a little. Wren glanced behind herself. Moonlight cast the outline of the window in bright relief against the dark floor, her own silhouette a part of the pattern. The rest of the room was pitch-black by comparison.

Headlamp in hand, she leaned out the window into the cool, fresh night. She could see the yard light down at the camp, but that was at the top of a pole. There were other lights visible through the trees, but she couldn't see exactly what they were and she didn't know if anyone standing on the ground would be able to see her, even on the off chance that they were looking up the hill.

She tried to remember, from when she'd been down there the day they walked through the woods to the cemetery, if it was possible to see the Hadleigh House at all. This was, she realized, a long shot at best. She was determined to take every possible shot offered her, though.

Before she could begin to signal, the sound of a gunshot made her jump and cringe away. It was followed by two more. She turned to look.

The door was open wide enough now for Jones to get his hand and gun inside. He couldn't come anywhere close to pointing it at her yet, but that hadn't stopped him from putting three bullets into the plaster wall.

———

Death stopped at the edge of the porch steps and looked up. "What was that? Was that someone shooting?"

"Nah," Robinson said. "I think it was Old Man Pickering hammering. He builds weird things out in his shed and sells them to tourists at one of the flea markets."

"At this time of night?"

"Yeah. He's got insomnia. I think I heard him a couple of times earlier, during the storm."

"Are you sure? Because that really sounded like gunshots to me."

"I know." Robinson gave Death a rueful smile. "I think it's a military thing. We think we hear gunshots because we expect to hear gunshots. But we're not in a war zone now. It's only a hammer."

———

Wren put a hand on her heart and forced herself to breathe. If he were shooting an old fashioned six-shooter, she thought inanely, he'd only have one bullet left, assuming he hadn't had a chance to reload. Of course, she had no idea what kind of gun he was shooting and he'd had plenty of time to change cartridges, so she supposed that was a pointless line of thought.

In any case, it was going to be several more minutes before he was able to get far enough into the room to be a serious threat.

She leaned out the window again, wasting no more time, and pointed her light down the hill, at the other lights there. *Light speaking to light,* she thought.

Dash, dash, dash … dot, dot, dot … dash, dash, dash. Dash, dash, dash … dot, dot, dot … dash, dash, dash. Dash, dash, dash …

———

"OSO?" Nichelle said, puzzled.

"What?" Death turned to her. She was gazing up the hill with a perplexed look on her face.

Robinson had gotten as far as opening the barn door and Jackson was nearly to his car. They stopped and came back.

"There's a light coming from the Hadleigh House," she said.

The men turned and looked. The second floor of the old mansion was just visible above the trees. A tiny blue light flashed from one of the upper windows.

"It's Morse code, I think," Nichelle said. "But it spells out OSO."

Death felt a sick shock run through him and settle in his stomach. "Wren," he said. "It's Wren. Tyler must have come back looking for the cell phone. She's calling for help." He started down the steps, then turned back, imploring them to understand. "It's the only Morse code she knows. SOS. But she always gets the letters mixed up!"

———

Jones hit the door again and the wardrobe scooted a good four inches. He stuck his whole arm through the gap, firing wildly and taking out a window. Wren ducked away, turned off her light, and turned to face the door.

One more good push and it would be open enough to admit him. There was no time to climb out the window. He and his gun were going to be right here in the room with her any second.

TWENTY-ONE

"You wait here. I'm on it," Jackson shouted, jumping in his cruiser and peeling out of the parking lot in a spray of gravel.

"Like hell," Randy spat, heading for the Jeep. The Robinsons were right behind him. "How far is it by road?"

"Two and a half, maybe three miles?" Kurt Robinson shook his head. "The road curves so much ..."

They reached the vehicle, and it just then dawned on Randy that his brother wasn't with him. He turned back and Death was still standing on the porch steps, staring up at the dark bulk of the Hadleigh House.

"Death? Are you coming? Do you want to wait here? Death?"

Death glanced at him, then back up the hill. Three miles by road. Just a couple hundred yards on foot, but straight uphill and he knew his lungs would never take it. At worst, he'd pass out somewhere and they'd have to send someone to rescue him. At best, he'd arrive out of breath and useless to help his Wren.

Inside the barn, Sugar fidgeted. He was still saddled.

"Death," Randy said, voice low with worry. "Death, that's a really bad idea."

———

Wren pushed the window up one last inch, deliberately forcing it and making it shriek. She took the last of the fuses from her pocket and dumped them out, sending them rattling and tumbling down the steep slope of the kitchen roof. Then she ducked back, very quietly, into the corner behind the door and waited.

Tyler Jones, muttering and cursing, shoved the door. He had to have turned his back and put his legs into it, making one big final push. The wardrobe scraped and skidded over the wooden floor and he came in, a tall, gaunt shadow against the moonlight.

He crossed, limping, in front of her, casting a misshapen silhouette across the floor, and leaned to peer out the open window, leading with his gun. Wren rose silently from the deep black behind him, crept up close, and swung her makeshift cosh at him as hard as she could.

She was aiming for the back of his head, but he moved at the last minute. She still caught him in the head, but it struck him between the shoulder blades first and deflected some of the force. He toppled forward and lost his gun. It skittered and tumbled down the dark shingles and disappeared over the edge.

She stooped and caught at his legs, trying to pick him up and force him headfirst out the window, but he got one hand on the windowsill, and as she pushed his legs and lower body through he was reaching back to grab at her.

"Jezebel!" he spat. "Harlot! She-devil! Demon!"

He got hold of her hair and she swung her cosh wildly, cracking it into his elbow, bloodying his nose.

"Wow, you're nuts," she said, trying to pull away.

Seeking some form of leverage, trying desperately to keep from being forced out the window, he got one hand on the neckline of her blouse. Not even thinking, acting purely on reflex, Wren slapped his face hard enough to raise a welt.

He let go and she pressed her advantage, swinging her weapon at his face and his ribs and his fingers where he was gripping the window frame. He looked like some kind of mutant lizard, clinging to the side of the house.

"Give me the phone," he demanded. "I know you have it. Give it to me now."

Wren pulled her cell phone from her pocket. "This phone?"

Jones' eyes fastened on the phone and his face lit with manic avarice. "Yes!"

"If you want it, get it," she said. The window he had shot out earlier was six feet to her right and also looked out over the kitchen roof. She tossed the phone through it, hearing it hit and slide away. Jones startled and dived toward it.

Wren helped him out with a vicious shove. Without waiting to see if he fell or not, she turned and ran.

———

Death ran into the lighted barn and led Sugar out, holding his mane.

"Buddy, I need a ride up the hill," he said. "My girl's in trouble up there and I can't get there on my own. Do you think you could help me out?"

The big horse stamped and snorted and shook his mane. Death chose to take that as a yes.

"Come on, man," Randy said. "Don't do anything stupid. Listen, I'll run up the hill and find out what's going on. You can take the car around the road and be there in time to help me clean up."

In Death's ears that came out as "you sit here and wait while the two people you love most are in danger."

Mounting was still awkward for him, a time-consuming struggle. With no time to spare, he led the horse over to the gate to the field and climbed the gate until he could swing himself into the saddle. Sugar stood patiently, allowing him to get settled.

"It's dark. It's wet and slippery. There are probably limbs and branches down and places washed out." Randy ran one hand through his hair in frustration. "You're not that good a horseman, Death."

"I don't have to be," Death said. "Sugar's that good a horse. Catch up when you can."

He wound the reins in his right hand and, with his left, gripped the saddle horn. He clicked his tongue and tapped Sugar in the flank with his right heel, and Sugar turned and bore him into the night.

―――

Wren slipped and skidded, going around the wardrobe and through the door and then making a sharp left turn toward the stairs. The thought in her mind was to get out of the house and make a run through the woods to the vets' camp. They had power. Maybe there'd be a working phone down there. In any case, they'd have lights and vehicles and they'd know what to do when under attack.

Since this began, she'd been running in a state of controlled panic, and she didn't know how much longer she could continue, or how many more showdowns she could emerge from victorious. Her haste, though, was her undoing. As she came out of the bedroom at a dead run and tried to pivot, her foot slipped out from under her and she fell flat, knocking the wind out of herself. She lay there helpless, choking and struggling to draw in a breath, while a lack of oxygen set off a roaring in her ears.

She put her head down and concentrated on drawing air into her lungs. The first breath was a long, painful wheeze. She was trembling and her heart thudded against the old wooden floorboards beneath her. Her hearing returned with her breathing.

Within the bedroom behind her, a series of thumps and scrapes told her that Jones had not fallen off the roof and that he was, even now, fighting his way back in the window.

Wren took one more gulping, gasping breath and forced herself back to her feet. Her legs felt like jelly and she couldn't imagine how it was that her knees still held her. She heard one more loud bang and a vicious muttering, too low for her to make out any words, and she turned again and ran for the stairs.

———

The path between the fence and the edge of the trees was barely wide enough for Sugar at the best of times. The fence marked the property line and Robinson had never made any provisions for riding through there. Now, in the aftermath of the thunderstorm, wet branches drooped across the trail and saplings leaned in as if reaching out their spindly arms to catch at passers-by.

It had not escaped Death that he was riding the same trail, on the same horse, that Harriman had ridden to his death, but he didn't bother worrying about it. If Sugar was still traumatized by the experience, he didn't show it. As for Death, he had more important things to worry about.

They reached the point where the path angled off and headed uphill toward the Hadleigh House. This was the way he and Randy had come, the first day they accompanied Wren out to see the old, haunted plantation. Randy wasn't with him, and Death suspected that he had headed off at an angle, fighting his way on foot through the brush and head-high sumac in an attempt to get up the hill first.

The path was wider here, and as Sugar made the turn he gathered his legs under him and sped up. He was strong and fast and sleek and he seemed to understand both their destination and Death's urgency in reaching it. Death leaned forward, over Sugar's neck, and let the animal run.

They rose through the stand of pine trees and through the old apple orchard with the white moon casting a mystical glow over the countryside and painting the world in a kaleidoscope of silver light and absolute shadow. In the field beyond the orchard, with the Hadleigh House framed against the sky, there was a fog rising from the underbrush.

It had been less than twenty-four hours since he had proposed to Wren.

He heard Randy struggling along behind him, shouting at him to slow down and wait, but he ignored him and urged his steed on. The wrought-iron fence that circled the garden had three gates, including the one across the driveway, but chances were that all three were closed. It was too high for the horse to jump, but he calculated that if he came up beside it he could drop off on the other side. Then he would have to circle the house, going for either the front or the back door and hoping that the one he chose was open.

He was still two hundred feet away from the fence when a high-pitched shriek rent the night, sent a thrill of horror through him, and settled into his stomach with sick dread. It was a shrill wail of pain and terror that rose to a sharp peak and was abruptly silenced.

Wren ran down the hall to the main staircase with the knowledge that Jones was just a few steps behind her. At the stairs, rather than risk running down them, she turned and slid down the curving bannister. At the bottom she dropped off and crouched down in the dark beside the staircase.

Moonlight streaming through the window painted blue-white squares on the floor. She took stock of what she could see. There was an ottoman to her right, a stack of boxes tipped over and rifled, their contents spilling out, a tall floor lamp broken free of its base, and ...

Footsteps sounded overhead. She could hear doors being opened and closed. He was looking for her, but he didn't know where she was.

She picked up the floor lamp. It was a long, hollow iron bar that branched into three light sockets under a fringed shade. Wren turned it so the broken end of the bar was away from her, reached up, and slid it across the stairs as high as she could reach. Then she slammed her cosh down on the nearest step to draw Jones' attention.

There was an instant of breathless silence. A door slammed and then he was running full-out, headed for the stairs, determined to catch her. The house shivered with the rhythm of his feet along the hall. Now he was on the staircase, headed down. She waited until just before he got to the lamp base, then pulled down on the end of the lamp over her head. The near edge of the step it was on acted as a fulcrum. The rest of the metal rod rose up across Jones' path and caught his foot, and he fell with a terrified shriek, abruptly silenced.

For a long minute he lay crumpled and silent at the foot of the stairs. Wren hovered in the shadows, debating whether it would be wise to creep up and hit him a couple more times just to be safe. Then he groaned and dragged himself to his feet.

He staggered around and saw her and his face, pale in the shadows, blanched even further.

"What manner of she-devil are you," he breathed, "that does not relent and will not die?"

Wren blinked and tried her damndest to think of something witty to say. Nothing came to her. *The hell with it,* she thought. *When in doubt, attack!* She raised her sock-turned-weapon, swung it around her head, and yelled, "Yaaaarrrrgh!"

And that was too much for Jones. He turned and ran.

———

Sugar had halted with the sound of the scream coming from the Hadleigh House, horse and man alike stopped in their tracks. Death leaned forward in the saddle again and urged his mount on.

"H'ya! H'ya! Giddyup! Giddyup!"

The animal responded, driving forward and covering the ground between them and the mansion at a pace that sent the wind rushing past Death's face. Sodden brush caught at his legs and soaked through his jeans and his heart pounded in time with Sugar's hoof beats.

They were almost at the fence, where Death could drop off onto the lawn, when a second yell sounded from within the house. The front door opened and Tyler Jones ran out, limping and staggering.

He made a bizarre spectacle in the moonlight, a tall, gaunt figure like a scarecrow. He ran with an awkward, uneven gait, limbs flailing. His dark coat streamed out behind him and his hair stuck out around his head.

Wren's truck was still parked in the yard and Death was torn between pursuing Jones and going in search of her. Before he had to make a decision, she appeared. She was running after Jones, swinging some sort of weapon in circles over her head and screaming like a banshee.

Jones was headed for the front gate and the Vengeance Trail. Death turned Sugar, following the old path along the fence that Doris, as a child, had taken to church on Sundays. Wren saw them and broke off her pursuit, turning instead toward her truck.

Jones reached the gate and wrestled it open. He ran through and looked at Death, coming toward him on horseback. For a moment he froze, face a mask of horror.

"No!" he shouted. "Oh dear God in heaven! No!"

He dashed, in a blind panic, between the nearly bare branches of the lilac bushes, tripped going down the steps set into the path, and rolled to a stop at their foot.

Death had intended to stop at the top of the steps, not wanting to risk injury to his horse, but Sugar ignored his command, leaped the shallow flight of stairs, and came to a halt the other side of the fallen man. He turned to stand over him and reared up on his hind legs, pawing the air with his front hooves.

Death leaned forward and held on until the horse dropped back down to all four feet. Wren had appeared at the top of the path, holding one of the spears that went with her atlatl. Her other weapon was a weighted sweat sock. Her hair stood out around her head and her eyes glittered in the starlight.

She looked, to the man who loved her, like a medieval shield maiden.

"No!" Jones moaned, staring up into the darkness with a madness in his eyes. "God! No! Revelation 6:7-8! It has come to pass!"

"What?" Wren demanded.

Randy was panting and puffing along the trail behind her, and Jackson appeared running up the path from the road, his gun at the ready.

"What was that? What did he say?"

"Revelations," Death said drily. "Revelations 6:7-8."

"But what is it?" she demanded. "I don't have my phone. And it's dead anyway. Do you have your phone? Look it up! Google it! I want to know what he said."

Randy was making a choking sound that his brother recognized as breathless laughter. Death sighed and shook his head.

"I don't have to look that one up," he told Wren. "I know that one."

"Well, what is it?"

"'When the Lamb broke the fourth seal,'" he quoted, "'I heard the voice of the fourth living creature saying, 'Come.' I looked, and behold, an ashen horse.'"

Jackson had reached them. He flipped Jones over and cuffed his hands behind his back.

Death guided Sugar gingerly around them to the foot of the steps and Wren came halfway down so that she was within arm's reach. He reached out and brushed one strand of damp hair from her cheek, tucked it behind her ear, and finished the verse. "'And he who sat on it had the name Death,'" he said, "'and Hades was following with him.'"

EPILOGUE

"I wish I'd had a camera," Wren said. "You should have seen him on that rearing horse, standing over Tyler Jones while Jones babbled and gibbered for mercy."

The day after their confrontation with the killer, the day after the massive thunderstorm, had dawned clear and bright, but with a bite to the air that signaled summer was well and truly over. Wren had taken the day off, with the Keystones' blessing, and she and Death had slept in. It was mid-afternoon now and the twins and their wives had come over after the day's sale to check on her and hear the story firsthand.

Randy was there as well. They were waiting on pizza they'd ordered and her living room was crowded and homely. She thought, for a brief second, that she would miss this when she moved. But then again, she thought, she wouldn't. The building would be different, but it was the people who filled her life with such warmth, and they weren't going anywhere.

"My brother's a drama queen," Randy teased.

"Me?" Death squawked. "What makes you think I had anything to do with it? That was all the horse. Sugar's the drama queen. I was just along for the ride. Besides, Wren was the one chasing him with a nine-ball in her sock."

"Are you saying I'm a drama queen?" she challenged.

"I'm saying you're a warrior maiden," he clarified with a cheesy grin. "A really hot warrior maiden."

"Thank you. I like that better."

"Well, I for one am very disappointed in you," Roy said.

Wren gave him a hurt look.

"What was it Jones said to you again? What kind of demon are you that won't die? Something like that? And you couldn't think of a *single* smartass thing to say?"

"I know," she said. "I failed at banter. I'm disappointed in me too."

"So what do you suppose happens now?" Randy asked

"Well," Leona said, "Duncan stopped by the sale this morning and we spoke for a bit."

"Duncan?"

"Chief Reynolds," Death told his brother. "He and the Keystones went to school together."

"He'll always be Dunc to us," Doris said.

"Not me," Roy objected. "To me, he'll always be Slippery Reynolds."

"Do we want to know?" Death asked.

"It's a long story," Sam said, "and it involves a greased pig contest at a county fair, many years before any of you were born."

"I see." Death nodded. "So what did Slippery have to say when you talked to him?"

It was Leona who answered. "They've dropped the charges against Tony Dozier. The Robinsons have gone to pick him up. He's going to

247

stay with them for the time being. He's going to have a difficult time of it. I don't know that he'll ever be all right, but at least he isn't a murder suspect anymore."

"And they charged Jones, right? We didn't screw that up by listening to the cell phone, did we?" Death gave Wren a guilty glance. "I talked Orly into letting us hear it because I wanted to know, but it occurred to me later that we could have really messed up the state's case."

"I don't think you did any harm," Roy said. "And if you hadn't stuck around to listen, you might not have been standing out in the yard to see Wren's SOS, er, uh, OSO."

"You hush," she told him, then turned to Death. "He's right, you know. I don't know what I'd have done if you hadn't ridden up when you did."

Randy snorted. "You'd have chased Jones down and beat him up some more."

"They're charging him with armed assault and a whole bunch of other things because of last night, too," Roy told her. "Of course. I don't suppose you'll be surprised to hear that he's pleading insanity."

"Ha," Wren said. "I could make that case for him."

"Well, don't, okay?"

There was a break in the conversation as the pizza arrived and they got it paid for and distributed. Wren fetched everyone plates and silverware and Death and Randy passed around beer and soda pop.

"You have a lot of dishes," Randy observed.

"Yeah, do you need any?"

"No, I'm good. I was just thinking that it's going to be a pain to pack all this up and move."

"I know. I was thinking that I should go ahead and start packing now, even though we haven't found a house yet."

"Do you have any idea what you're looking for?" Sam asked.

Wren shrugged. "We haven't even had a chance to talk about it. We have a lot to talk about."

Death reached out and took her hand. "Did you tell them?"

"No. I've been waiting for someone to notice, but they're all shockingly unobservant."

The Keystones blinked and sat up, alert.

"Notice what?" Leona asked.

They were like family to her, but Wren felt suddenly shy and bashful as she held out her left hand. "It's an engagement ring. Death asked me to marry him. We're going to get married."

"Yes!" Roy cheered, his response so enthusiastic that Death and Wren were a little taken aback.

"I'm, uh, glad you approve," Death said.

Sam rolled his eyes. "Don't mind my idiot brother," he said. "He's just excited because he won the pool."

"The pool?" Death looked from one man to the other, eyebrows raised. "There was a betting pool on whether or not we were going to get married?"

"When," Roy clarified. "Not whether. When you were going to get engaged."

"It's a very small town," Doris said apologetically. "There's not a lot to do for entertainment."

"Well, now that the gamblers have had their say," Leona put in, "allow me to just say congratulations. You're a lovely couple and you're going to be very happy. After all, if Doris and I can put up with these two all these years…"

"Bah." Roy flapped a hand at his wife. "Don't let her fool you. Another week and she'd have won the bet."

"Have you set a date?" Sam asked.

"Not yet," Death said. "We really do have a lot to talk about." He turned to Wren. "Where are we going to have the wedding? Do you want to do it in a church or outdoors somewhere or what?"

"I know a really unique place you could have a wedding," Doris offered, "if you were willing to wait until spring."

"Oh? Where's that?"

"There's a group of Viking reenactors—did you know there were Viking reenactors? Here, in Missouri?"

"No. Seriously? What do they do, raid Kansas?"

Leona laughed. "I don't think they really do the raids so much. Mostly they're into the clothing and the lifestyle. A lot of Vikings were peaceful farmers and artists and such. They do have one of those longboats with the dragon head carved on the prow, though. I've seen them sailing on the lake a few times."

Doris nodded. "They have a Viking settlement built on the lake-shore a few miles north of here and they do encampments and things. I've seen pictures from a couple of weddings they did last year and they were beautiful, and really quite charming. I thought of them because Sam and I were up that way yesterday, looking over a possible sale."

"Anything interesting?" Wren asked.

Sam shrugged. "There's a little cove there. The only things on the cove are the Viking settlement and a private yacht club that went in when the dam was built back in the seventies and never really did very well. The club's gone out of business again and the trustees are trying to sell it. I gather there's a big resort firm interested, but they want the Viking settlement too and it's not for sale."

"Is there a mystery?" Randy asked.

"Why would there be a mystery?"

Randy shrugged. "I don't know. It's just starting to sound like the plot for a *Scooby Doo* cartoon, so I figured there must be a mystery."

"My brother's insane," Death observed.

"I know how you feel," Sam agreed.

"Actually," Roy said, "there is kind of a mystery. It's a very old one, and I don't know how you'd solve it, but ... "

"But what is it?" Randy asked.

"There's a reason the reenactment group built their settlement where they did. The leader of their group is a poet and historian who specializes in Viking history. Back in the late seventies, he was a member of the yacht club. He had a daughter named Ingrid who disappeared when she was about seventeen and was never seen again. She went missing from her home, in Columbia, but when her father's group wanted to build a Viking settlement, he persuaded them to build it next to his old yacht club."

"Why?" Wren asked.

"Because he said that was where he felt close to her. Because that's where he saw her ghost."

THE END

© About Faces Photography

ABOUT THE AUTHOR

Loretta Ross is a writer and historian who lives and works in rural Missouri. She is an alumna of Cottey College and holds a BA in archaeology from the University of Missouri–Columbia. She has loved mysteries since she first learned to read. *Death & the Gravedigger's Angel* is the third novel in her Auction Block Mystery series.